To Bobbi,

The Burden

Authored by Valorie Hein

Cover by Kyle Genther

I hope you like my book & that we can meet some day, since we are cousins :)

Hugs, Valorie

For my Husband, Brad

I love you

Acknowledgements

I began this book five years ago, and after four rewrites I am excited for my characters to finally come to life in your imagination. I would like to take this opportunity to thank my friends and family. First and foremost I thank my husband for his endless encouragement and the long nights of thoughtful fantasizing and discussion. My children for keeping me motivated. My Mother-in-law, Jan, for her edits and comments. My mother, Kathy, for her proofing of the story line. I also want to thank Kyle for helping me with the cover and graphics, and Emma for agreeing to be the face of my protagonist. I also owe a huge thank you to Maggie and Sue. I have so many friends that have encouraged me throughout this endeavor that I dare not try to recognize them by name for fear of skipping that special someone. Thus, I thank all those who have supported me, believed in me, and now can finally read what I have finally finished.

CHAPTER 1

"Here. I will get out here," Natasha told the driver handing him a crisp hundred. Not waiting for change she entered the madness on foot. Her taxi was stuck in bottleneck traffic due to an accident, a fatality according to the dispatcher. The last hour they crept forward half a block.

Glancing toward the sky she noticed the sun was dangerously low. Panic, a feeling she hadn't experienced in decades, crept through her veins like a drug as she realized she should have left the vehicle much sooner. Sirens screamed and emergency lights flashed in the distance. Drivers honked and argued as she quickly weaved through the metal maze.

Natasha made it to the sidewalk as the street lamps buzzed to life. She followed the cobblestone sidewalk a minute before slipping between two antebellum buildings. The alley was narrow and smelled of whisky. Holding her stomach to ease the pain in her back, she shuffled around a young man passed out next to a puddle of vomit. He wore the traditional festival colors of green, gold, and purple. A glittered top hat was his pillow on a bed of asphalt.

She emerged from the quiet alley into a completely different chaos. People dressed in homemade costumes mingled with those in regular clothes crowding the sidewalks and streets. It was Fat Tuesday and the Mardi Gras celebration was in full swing along the French Quarter. *If Ever I Cease to Love* flowed from a brass band in the balcony above.

Jackson Square was a few blocks away. Snaking her way through the crowd, she passed one. It looked exactly like the previous she'd spotted from the taxi, cloaked in black wearing a full face mask of gold glitter framed with purple ribbons. Natasha felt its crimson eyes hunting the crowd. Deep fried breads and spicy Cajun dishes saturated the humid air helping to mask her fading scent of humanity.

Stepping behind a large dark skinned woman, Natasha watched from the corner of her eye. The cloaked creature stopped for a moment before disappearing into the alley she just left, a predator hunting for prey. She hoped the man in the alley would not wake to the vicious death she knew was coming to him.

Her abdomen tightened, followed by intense pain deep inside her pelvis. Natasha grabbed her bulging belly as she doubled over falling to her knees.

"Watch it," the large woman snarled reeling around. "Lady, you need some help?" she asked much more concerned after seeing Natasha's condition.

Natasha shook her head biting the inside of her cheek to keep from crying out. A minute later the pain was gone, but she knew it would return.

"Holy cow. Sister. You need a hospital?" the large woman asked.

Without answering Natasha turned and headed toward Jackson Square. She'd seen two vile creatures within five minutes, but there were more, many more. It wouldn't take long before they realized what she was and tracked her down.

Natasha reached the gated entrance. It was dusk. She saw the three white towers of St. Louis Cathedral across Jackson Square penetrating the night sky. The cross perched atop the center steeple was barely visible. In the square, a bronzed Andrew Jackson in battle regalia upon a rearing stallion was an island in the sea of partiers. It looked as if the statue was trying to escape the madness.

A gush of fluid splashed to the patterned sidewalk from beneath Natasha's cotton dress. Then pain. Her stomach felt as hard as the iron post she leaned against for support. Holding her belly and breathing with focus, she stared at the cathedral. She might be able to cross Jackson Square in time to deliver her gift, but Natasha knew she would never make it without being detected. The putrid scent of evil, becoming more recognizable as her once surrendered senses returned, flooded the square.

The pain subsided. She turned and was able to single out a green van in a line of vehicles stopped at a red light. The driver sat in his seat waiting.

"Hey. What do you think you're doing?" the man yelled as Natasha slipped onto the passenger seat.

"Hospital," she groaned clutching her stomach.

"I don't think...," he began but stopped when Natasha flashed him a look of urgency, one no human could refuse. The light turned green. Vehicles behind them honked impatiently. "Okay. Hold on," the driver said hitting the gas.

"You are a doctor," Natasha groaned before they reached the arterial.

"Yeah. How'd you know that?" he asked.

"It is coming now," she said through clenched teeth avoiding his question. "You must help me."

Before the van fully stopped, Natasha moved to the back. A moment later the doctor was with her. Natasha lay with her back resting against the side panel, her small frame barely fitting between the bench and driver seats. She gripped her bent knees. The doctor grabbed a jacket from the rear of the van and took position against the van's sliding door.

"Wow. You weren't kidding, were you," he said. "Push with the next one."

The contractions came quickly. Natasha's entire body forced her to push. She focused on the doctor and her breathing to keep from screaming. Sweat streamed down her face into her eyes and mouth, her long brown hair was pasted to her body in artistic swirls.

"The baby is crowning," he said. "Next contraction, push hard."

Natasha focused as the pain began.

"Okay, alllmmmooost there. Now one big push," the doctor ordered, his years of experience showing in skill.

Natasha felt a relief of pressure from her pelvis as the doctor gently pulled the baby from her body. The van was filled with the wail of a newborn's cry.

After wrapping the baby in the jacket, the doctor leaned forward to hand the infant to Natasha.

"It's a...," he began but stopped as soon as he looked at her. "Y...y...your eyes," he stammered still holding the baby.

Natasha reached out and gently lifted her baby from the doctor's arms. The wailing quieted, replaced with a clumsy suckling noise after Natasha brought the baby to her breast.

"We should go," Natasha said softly. Nodding, the doctor slipped silently back to the driver seat.

Natasha felt her humanity die with that final push. She cried silently as she held her baby close for the short ride. The fragile future of her baby and the human race was now less certain.

"We're here," the doctor said over his shoulder as he pulled the van under the emergency awning. "Wait just a minute. I'll get some help."

The doctor ran as fast as his age would allow through the entrance. Before the automatic doors slid shut behind him, he was returning to the van followed by two female nurses in white.

Hearing the cries of a newborn, he slid the van door open. There, placed on the bench seat was an angry swaddled baby wailing for its mother, who was nowhere in sight.

CHAPTER 2

18 years later.

"Tall triple Caramel Macchiato," the fat man finally ordered taking his sweet time.

"Sure thing," I answered before sliding the window closed.

I felt his eyes burn through the window, watching my every move as I worked on his drink. Why couldn't I have found a job at Starbucks, where they had comfy polo tees? Instead I was stuck at Joe's Hot Shots. Tight tank tops and black bottoms happened to be the uniform. The color of the tank changed with the season, not the weather. I was wearing green for spring.

While mixing his drink, I glanced at the clock. My shift was over five minutes ago. Sarah was late. She was why I worked at Joe's. She was the one who told me how great it was, and she who hooked me up with a job. But she was also the reason I couldn't quit.

"That'll be three fifty," I said opening the window.

The man held out a ten next to his truck, forcing me to reach through the window. I bent through the window handing him his drink, then taking the money.

"Keep the change, Babe," he said with a wink, his pinched

face and upturned nose reminding me of Porky Pig.

"Thanks," I answered sliding the window closed.

No other vehicles were waiting to be served so I texted Sarah, WHERE R U?.

"Right here," she answered opening the door to the small drive thru coffee stand. "Sorry I'm late, Dimples." Sarah was the only one who could get away with calling me that.

"Whatever," I said rolling my eyes. She knew I had plans.

"Early morning rush is over," I said from the bathroom. Peeling off my leggings and sliding on a pair of old Levis, I felt like a contortionist changing in such a small space. I put on my old sneakers and black sweatshirt before pulling my long hair into a ponytail.

"Sorry, Dimples," Sarah said again. "Really." She stuck out her bottom lip, batting thick lashes over blue eyes. Her blond hair and copper tan contrasted to my dark hair, green eyes, and pale skin.

I didn't look at her as I left the stand, closing the door harder than I should.

"Call me later," she called from inside.

If I hadn't been in such a hurry, I might have been a little more understanding. On my way to my car I realized again that working with my best friend wasn't nearly as great as I thought it would be.

The voice of Lady Ga Ga singing *Born This Way* blared from my radio. I turned the music up and sang along, ignoring the vibration and static from the speakers. My 89 Ford Escort was old and plain, but dependable.

According to the morning forecast, the day was supposed to be clear and sunny with highs in the upper sixties. So far the morning sun had been alone in the blue sky, a good sign the meteorologist may have got it right.

Summer was on its way. I could feel it as I headed to Chewelah Peak, a mountain with a popular resort called 49 Degrees North set on top. I'd tried skiing there once, which was a disaster. Unable to turn and too scared to stop, I ran off course into the woods. It took all my energy and the help of the ski patrol to get out of the waist deep powdered snow. I flushed remembering the way I had to squirm and crawl to finally escape. I was so embarrassed.

Today I planned to hike a specific trail higher up the mountain called Viewpoint. Last month a customer told me about the trail. I found it online that same day. Reviews gave it five stars. The trail was easy going and supposed to have great panoramic views of the surrounding mountains and valleys.

After a couple hours of driving north from Spokane, I made it to the mountain. Once I turned off of US 395, I followed the signs that directed traffic up Flowery Trail Road to the resort. As I began ascending the curvy two-lane paved road, I noticed the peaks of the taller mountains still had snow on them and hoped I remembered to pack a jacket.

The forest was lush with sprouting flora along both sides of the road. I cracked my window, inhaling the crisp air. I'd pass a pullout or driveway every now and then, but mostly I drove between two tall walls of thick trees and brush, almost like a tunnel. On either side of the road a small stream trickled down the mountain. Broken trees and branches littered the ditches and deep ruts scarred the earth, evidence the stream had once been much larger and vigorous. After a few switchbacks, the road narrowed and soon the yellow center line disappeared altogether.

About three-quarters of the way up the mountain I had to slow due to orange cones and warning signs. I rounded the next curve and saw several men wearing orange vests and hard hats scrambling about with shovels. A backhoe and two dump trucks were in the middle of the road.

An older heavy set man wearing the same orange vest and hard hat as the other workers stopped me with his SLOW/STOP sign. He strolled to my car dragging the long sign beside him. I lowered my window halfway once he was close to my door.

"Sorry, Miss," he said in a husky voice, "but the road is closed."

"Seriously?" I whined. Not what I wanted to hear.

"Snow runoffs caused some damage that needed fixin'. It'll be closed for at least a couple hours. You can try back then," he said without sympathy. He tipped his head and walked back to his post next to a white pickup parked alongside the road. He looked way too big to fit in the small cab.

I watched a large yellow bulldozer disappear around the next bend wondering what next. I didn't want to turn around and go back to my dorm room. My roommate and I didn't really get along, plus she had a final that she was studying for and was totally stressing out. I finished my last final yesterday and got an early start to spring vacation, which I was going to spend at home with my parents.

I didn't want to go home yet, but I didn't want to just wait for the road to open either. There was a small town named Chewelah that I drove through at the base of the mountain. It seemed like a tourist town, with boutiques and cafés along the main street. I decided to backtrack there and grab something to eat then try Viewpoint again later.

I rolled up my window, silencing the construction noise, and began backing. The several full sized pickup trucks parked alongside the narrow road were making it difficult to find a place to turn around. I found a spot between two gray Chevies and headed back down the mountain.

Why couldn't there have been a warning sign sooner? It would've been nice not to have driven so far before being forced to turn around because the stupid road was closed. Gas was expensive. The morning was not turning out at all like I wanted.

After a few miles my spirits lifted when I thought I passed a national forest sign pointing to a park trail. While searching Washington State's website, there had been several hiking trails listed on this mountain, but I didn't pay attention to where specifically. I was too focused on finding Viewpoint.

I flipped a U-ie and sure enough, saw a sign for the Northern Woods trail. It was camouflaged between trees and brush growing up around it, easy to miss until right on it.

Maybe I'd get to do some late morning hiking after all. Mentally I crossed my fingers hoping for good luck as I followed the dirt road a mile or so.

I had my choice of spots in the designated parking area at the dead end. A quick glance around didn't reveal a sign or barrier stating the trail was closed. I was good to go.

I visited the outhouse, grateful it was open, and grabbed my gear out of the trunk of my car. I checked my pack's contents. I remembered my jacket but doubted I'd need it after all. The sun was bright and warm. I stopped briefly to read the Colville National Forest information sign at the trailhead.

The Northern Woods was a thirteen mile, easy-to-medium trail, with high traffic. I didn't think I'd run into anyone else on the trail though, since my car was the only one in the parking area.

According to the information sign, the trail didn't have any scenic spots, but it did have lots of wildflower and wildlife viewing. I was eager to get started and figured that if this trail sucked, I could always go back to Viewpoint after a couple hours.

The forest cover wasn't thick. I could see a long way into the woods. Blue paint on the trees meant the area had been logged. The forest floor was relatively clean of deadfalls and slash-piles. The sparse canopy above allowed the sun to beat down on the trail. The heat felt good. At certain angles, the sun's rays hit new blossoms making them glow and look as if they floated in mid-air. It was a whole different world from the city.

Following the trail, admiring whatever caught my eye, my

mind wandered. I was in the middle of my second semester at Gonzaga University, a private Jesuit school. So far my freshman year was okay. I was busy with studies and didn't really have much in the way of free time. Neither did Sarah. She went to a different university nearby. The only time we really saw each other lately was at work. We'd been best friends since the 5th grade, when my dad moved us to Spokane from Albuquerque, but we were growing apart.

I decided not to let the fact I was losing my best, and really my only, friend ruin my time hiking. I spotted a fresh flower, probably its first time blooming, and picked it. Thanks to a flyer I grabbed from the information sign, I was able to identify it as a Bluebell. The dainty bloom reminded me of a fairy's skirt. I tucked it behind my ear.

The farther I hiked the worse the trail became with obstacles and debris. I crossed over several deadfalls here and there, but didn't encounter anything I couldn't handle. The weather stayed warm and calm, barely a breeze to rustle new leaves. I paused once in a while to watch a chipmunk or squirrel as it would dart up a tree trunk disappearing behind branches. They'd chatter warnings to one another of my presence. It felt good to be alone, out of the city.

I made it to the seven mile marker and saw a bench next to the trail, a perfect spot to rest. The bench was made out of a log cut in half lengthwise placed atop two carved stumps, very stable.

I checked my watch which revealed it was close to five, time for me to turn around and head back. But as I sat there, my gaze found a smaller footpath that detoured off of the main trail heading down the slope of the mountain. The more I noticed, the more curious I became. After finishing my apple, I followed the small trail to take a quick look.

The narrow path cut into the mountain and soon I hit a spot of exposed bedrock, not the compacted earthen trail I'd been on. A little farther along, I came across a section covered in scree. It was as if the mountain had a puncture that bled black rock covering the trail completely.

I didn't see a way around the accumulation of fist sized loose rocks. To my left, the scree sloped steeply down maybe ten yards. To my right was a tall cut embankment of rock covered in brush. But farther along the footpath, on the other side of the maybe fifteen foot dangerous span, lay a nice dirt pathway that continued on a few yards before disappearing around a bend. As steep as it was right here and with what looked like a clearing ahead, I figured there was an awesome view of the surrounding mountains and valleys.

I began inching my way across. There was no trail, just a steep slope of rock. Each step I took was careful and deliberate. I used the brush that grew from the embankment to help keep balance. Past the halfway point, just a few feet from the other side, I felt the rocks shift under my weight.

I froze, still holding onto branches of a bush with both hands. I watched as several rocks tumbled down the embankment below me, but the ones beneath my feet settled. My chest began burning; I realized I was holding my breath. I inhaled long and deep, which was instant relief to my lungs but my heart raced.

I was stuck, too afraid to move. Sweat beaded my forehead and my hands began to cramp. Several minutes passed with nothing happening and it seemed like the rocks had stabilized. I changed my mind about going farther. My desire to stay alive overrode any curiosity.

Still holding the bush, its coarse bark and branches digging into my palms, I rotated my feet back the other way. I lifted my foot slightly to take a step when the rocks beneath my feet shifted, but with more force than before. The movement propelled a chain reaction. I held on as my legs were swept from under me in a wave of rock.

I felt the plant's roots starting to let loose as my feet scrambled to find purchase, only to be swept away by more rock. I could sense the plant was about to give, unable to bear my wiggling weight. Suddenly I fell hard onto my butt with the bush still in my grip. I tossed it aside bracing myself as I rode the small rockslide a few yards, stopping suddenly as rocks kept tumbling down the slope on either side of me. Several rocks hit me in the back, some sure to have left bruises, when it went eerily still and silent.

I sat there unable to move. I had to get off the rocks but how? Should I go down to where there was a thick wall of brush, or back up? I felt like I was on a slope of marbles, no matter where I went, it'd be the wrong way. I decided to go up, but take a diagonal approach.

I stood, steady and slow but before my legs were straight the rocks let loose again. I wind-milled my arms to keep balance, surfing the rockslide when I hit the wall of brush. The sudden stop flung me forward through branches. Then I was falling.

The drop was long enough I twisted in the air before landing onto a thick shrub that barely cushioned my fall. The left side of my body took the brunt of the impact. I was conscious and lucid, but in total disbelief. I took a moment to catch my breath before struggling to untangle myself from hundreds of branches.

I barely registered any pain as I freed myself. Once I as loose I began checking for injuries. My left wrist and hand hurt. My wrist was stiff but I could rotate it and move my fingers, a good sign. I had a deep cut along the heel of my palm that was bleeding. But after examining it, I doubted I'd need stitches. Another plus. I checked my left leg. It seemed okay, no bones sticking out anywhere. But I wasn't so sure about my ankle. I thought I moved a toe. Crap.

"Flippin great..." I said to myself. I knew better. I should never have tried to cross that spot.

The moisture seeping into my jeans from the damp ground brought me out of shock. I needed to get moving. I stood on my right leg and tested my left ankle, which was proving with every second the pain could get worse. I couldn't put any weight on it.

I scanned my surroundings. It appeared I'd fallen into an ovalish shaped hole, at least fifty feet long and thirty feet wide, give or take. Tall trees around the edge of the hole made it look much deeper than it actually was.

I was at the base of the boulder I fell from, maybe a fifteen foot drop. The boulder was only a few feet wide and either side had large shrubs tangled together. The branches were pretty much bare, their leaves just beginning to sprout. It felt like I was caught in Mother Nature's net. The ground was hard and uneven with sharp black rocks of different sizes. If I'd missed landing on the plant, my injuries would have been a lot worse, if not fatal.

I didn't see an easy way out. The thick brush ranging from knee high to over my head and the surrounding trees were disorienting. My vision clouded as tears began spilling from my eyes. I didn't know what to do. If I was capable, I'd explore to find the easiest way out. But that wasn't an option. I knew better than to stray away from the main trail and risk getting lost. I had to go back the way I'd come.

I realized I needed to do something with my ankle. I remembered a First Aid class I'd taken last year that taught not to remove your boot so it would compress the injury. But I had on shoes, not boots. I screamed in frustration. The shrill noise echoed off the rocks, fading to silence. After a few deep breathes, I decided to buck up and get myself out.

I shrugged off my pack to grab my pocketknife, thankful I had one. I checked my cell phone for service, but wasn't surprised I had none. I'd lost service at the base of the mountain. I found a couple sticks within reach and cut off a strap from my pack.

I locked my jaw and gritted my teeth as I focused on the process of forcing the sticks between the sides of my swelling foot into my shoe. Sweat dripped from my nose and my arms trembled as I tied the sticks in place. It was difficult with my injured wrist. I gasped from pain with each knot. In the end, it kind of looked like a brace.

The sun was dropping behind the trees. The damp ground was soaking through my clothes and I felt a huge bruise forming on my hip. I was shivering and knew I was in danger of going into shock.

I swallowed the pain and slid back into my pack. I crawled on my right hand, left elbow, and knees along the base of the boulder I'd fallen from. I didn't see an apparent way up. I'd have to make my own path. The right side looked a little better than the left.

I bulled my way up, through brush and over jagged rocks. Branches scratched my face and pulled my hair. My pack kept getting hung up, forcing me to finagle my way through. I was a bug in a web, struggling to get loose.

I came to a spot where I used my right hand and leg to pull and push myself along by gripping the trunks of some young trees. I'd just made it through when a branch boomeranged, hitting my hurt ankle. I automatically screamed from the excruciating pain. After a few tears and deep breaths, I locked my jaw and kept going, which was my only option.

I made it out of the hole and saw the footpath. The scree was to my left. At a diagonal approach, the incline wasn't too steep. The brush was not as thick, but the decaying and blooming carpet was slimy. I felt safe closer to the ground and continued crawling.

By the time I made it to the footpath, I was wet, covered in gunk, and exhausted. But I couldn't stop, not yet. I'd rest later. I crawled my way up the several feet to the main trail. I felt a sense of triumph pulling myself onto the bench I'd sat on earlier. I slipped off my pack.

The sun had disappeared behind the trees and the warmth gone with it. I was surprised so much time passed. It didn't feel like it took that long.

The temperature was dropping and a slight breeze was chilling me to the bone. Shivering uncontrollably I slipped off my wet sweatshirt and put on the dry jacket. I checked my cell phone again, still no service. Twice I searched every pocket of my pack for a lighter or matches. I slammed the pack on the bench, angry I didn't have something with me to start a fire. I grabbed my last bottle of water and twisted it open, contemplating my next move.

The trees were losing their color against the skyline and the few clouds were turning orange. Soon it would be dusk. I didn't want to be stuck in the forest at night. But the later it got, the more real that possibility became, one I refused to panic over. I still had a long way back. That would take several hours, which inevitably meant I'd have to do some walking in the dark. I wished I'd at least packed a flashlight.

I began to wonder how long it would take before someone came looking for me. Sarah would wait until tomorrow to worry, if at all, since she knew I was mad. I had the next couple days off, so my boss wouldn't notice. I'd talked to Mom on the way up here. She knew I went hiking, but not where exactly. She'd get worried if I didn't call her sometime soon. She'd have the entire state searching for me by the next day. I had to get myself back to my car. There was no way I wanted a search party sent out on my account.

I scanned the area for something I could use as a crutch. I thought I'd spotted a pretty good stick lying on the ground just off of the trail. Then I saw it.

I was on the bench about to put my water bottle back in my pack when I noticed something out of place. At first it didn't register, but my eyes snapped back and focused in on a large tannish animal with four legs, a long tail, rounded ears, and whiskers.

The mountain lion was perched in an attack position atop a huge boulder a little farther along the main trail. The trail veered to the left circling around the enormous boulder. I would have passed the rock on my right if I'd continued a few more yards.

I didn't know how long the mountain lion had been there watching, hunting me. My shivers from the cold turned to tremors of fear as my fight or flight instincts kicked in.

There was bear mace in my pack. I just wasn't sure which pocket I'd repacked it in. The closest weapon was my, now very small, pocketknife, which lay next to my leg. I had pulled the knife out thinking I might need it to clean the stick I planned to use as a crutch.

The mountain lion was huge and beautiful. Its face a perfect copy of the ones I'd seen in zoos and magazines. She had white fur on her muzzle. At least I assumed it was a "she" with the black mascara like fur lining her fierce yellow eyes.

She crouched there as if she were stuffed and on display,

staring at me. I didn't dare take my eyes off of hers. There was nothing between us except fifty or so feet of open air.

I don't know how long we had the staring contest but I had to blink, which was a mistake. Her tail twitched, her weight shifted back slightly, then forward as she took one giant graceful leap for me.

Everything slowed as I watched her bear down on me. The white tufts of fur on her underbelly moved gently against the wind as she descended. Her ears lay back as her front paws reached for me with claws like little black daggers. She revealed four white fangs and a pink tongue when she opened her mouth to attack.

I grabbed my knife and thrust it out in front of me, never losing eye contact with my assassin. I was going to die a horrible, painful, disgusting death that would be in the headlines of the local news.

The feline was almost on top of me when something shot out towards her from behind me, a much larger brownish animal with an all black tail. It was another mountain lion. The force from this new cat as it crashed into the other landed them both across the trail and down the mountain. My view was blocked by the brush and clump of trees. It sounded as if they'd fallen into the hole I'd just crawled out of.

The pain from my injuries didn't matter anymore. Absolute panic had my adrenaline going full force. I stood and fell with my first step. My ankle refused to bear my full weight. I got back up, grabbing my pack in the process, and limped down the path.

I was moving like the doomed extra in a cheap horror flick, the slow one you knew was going to die. The two mountain lions were screaming and tearing at each other, a horrible vicious sound that terrified me to my soul. I reconsidered outdistancing them.

I spotted a small dirt cave along the trail formed by the undercut of the bank. I shuffled through the curtain of roots into the shallow area barely deep enough for my small body. The roots dangling from above provided me with pretty good cover. I sat on my knees with my left ankle cocked out at an angle. It had more than doubled in size and the pathetic brace was coming loose. I didn't care. I felt no pain. But my ankle wouldn't bear my weight.

Terrified, my senses were on high alert as my heart pounded blood through my veins. I was glad I still had the pocketknife in my hand. I had a much better chance of defending myself from within the small cave. The mountain lions would have to attack me from the front, through the roots.

Trembling I listened to their ferocious screams and snarls. Bushes thrashed and twigs broke as they tore at each other. It sounded like they were only a few feet away. But I couldn't see any sign of them when peeking through the roots. I prayed they'd kill each other, or at least forget about me. My mind raced. I thought, *What if they both attack me?* The idea of being ripped apart by two mountain lions made me sick.

After what felt like hours, the forest grew quiet. My relief from the silence was short lived. Not knowing where the two predators were was more frightening than hearing them fight. I listened hard, hearing only my own breathing and pulse beating in my temples.

The roots obscured my view making it dark in my little cave. I had to lean forward and move roots aside to peek out into the darkening forest. I debated whether I should try for my car while adrenaline still downplayed my pain, or stay put. I might be more vulnerable to an attack on the trail, but if I stayed I'd freeze to death. I decided to go for my car.

CHAPTER 3

I crawled from my cave and found a stick to use as a cane. The pain was intense, but tolerable. The stress of my situation helped dull the ache. It was dusk when I finally started down the trail, the sky amber and black. Soon it was dark, but at least the almost full moon provided some light.

It was impossible not to think of lurking dangers. The wind had picked up, bending trees which cast moving shadows. The shuffling of leaves, chorus of cricket and hoots of several owls were amplified by my fear. I thought I heard growls a couple of times which spiked my fear, but nothing ever happened. At one point I caught the stench of a skunk.

I couldn't remember what the low was forecasted to be. I didn't think it was supposed to drop below freezing but couldn't recall for sure. My jaw began to ache from chattering teeth and my breath left puffs of vapor that disappeared with the wind.

I was sweating, a cold sweat from fear and pain and my clothes were damp from the ground. When I reached mile marker five I cursed in frustration. I thought I was farther along, that I'd just missed the last couple markers. I was cold and my adrenaline was wearing off. My ankle throbbed and every step hurt worse and worse. I'd been hobbling along the trail for over two hours and was exhausted.

I came to a fallen tree in the middle of the trail. Gently I began to climb over the trunk, lifting my leg with both hands. I lost balance and fell, tangling my backpack on a thick branch. It was dark. I couldn't see in the shadows. I tried to slip my arms from the pack, but couldn't.

My shivering intensified, making it hard to move. I twisted my body trying to break lose. I heard a tearing sound and my right arm broke free. Suddenly I fell from the pack to the ground.

I was on the Centennial Trail that followed the Spokane River. A trail I liked to jog along. I felt the heat of the asphalt through my shoes. The bright sun was alone in the deep blue sky and I could see the fuzzy bluish-purple silhouettes of mountains far off in the distance. The fragrance of the river was strong as it meandered toward a small dam that I knew existed downriver. I squatted, balancing on the balls of my feet, and grabbed a handful of the hot coarse gravel next to the trail. I let the tiny colorful rocks filter through my fingers and fall to the ground.

"It's time," said an angelic female voice.

I stood spinning around searching for whoever had spoken. I was alone, but didn't feel alone. There was another presence.

"Who's there?" I called.

"You mustn't be afraid," the same voice said.

I saw a bright light down the path, a comforting light that called to me. I began walking toward the light.

"No," called the voice. "Do not follow the light."

But I wanted, needed, to follow the light. It was warm and safe. I felt a hand on my shoulder. I turned, no one was there. I turned back around but the light began moving, shrinking. I ran to it, but it kept moving farther and farther away. The warmth was leaving. In panic I raced after the light. The river began to fade, then the trail and trees. Soon I was alone in blackness. I felt a hand on my shoulder again. This time it didn't leave, but still no one was there.

I was in a void of nothing for a moment, before intense pain woke me from the nightmare. I heard the crackle of a fire and smelled smoke before drifting into blackness again, only to be awakened to the hiss of water on coals. In a fog I felt myself being moved by strong arms.

"No," I whimpered in an attempt to struggle as I remembered where I was and why my body hurt. But my efforts were feeble. My arms were tight against my stomach and wouldn't move. My eyes wouldn't open. I was so weak.

Somewhere from the darkness I heard a man's voice say, "It's okay. I'm going to get you some help."

I don't know why, but I sensed he was sincere and was going to help, not hurt me. I felt one arm wrap around my back and another slip under my knees. As soon as he lifted me, my lungs found air as I screamed. The movement shot bolts of pain through my entire left leg. It felt as if my foot had been ripped off. The pain was so excruciating that I blacked out. The next thing I knew, my head was against the stranger's chest as he carried me along the trail. I fought to stay awake, to keep from slipping back into the calling darkness.

I focused on the beauty of the night forest. Trees were latticed together in webs of branches swaying to the music of the wind. Everything was black, highlighted in silver by the moon and stars. Deep shadows lurked everywhere.

I was being carried fast and wondered if my rescuer was running. The pace was steady as I rocked back and forth in a soothing rhythm. But each movement sent a sharp stab of pain into my ankle, which now helped me stay awake. Once or twice it felt as though my rescuer jumped, but I never felt a heavy landing. I heard a loud thumping noise and realized my head was against his bare chest. I was hearing his heart.

So he didn't have a shirt on, which was odd. But I didn't have the energy to debate with myself whether that was something I should be concerned with right then or not. His chest was warm and he smelled good, a musky masculine scent.

"We're almost to the road," he said, his voice vibrating deep within his chest. I wondered how long I'd passed out. It seemed like I was only awake for a few minutes.

Slowly I let my eyes drift up to his face. Through the moonlight I saw strong features. He had deep set eyes with a high forehead, a strong brow, a straight nose, and his cheekbones cast a shadow down his face.

"My ankle...," I whispered weakly, my mouth was dry and voice raspy.

"I know. I fixed the splint while you were out," he said, in what seemed like an irritated voice. Maybe he was tired. I was amazed he carried me so far.

I let my head rest against his chest and listened to his rhythmic breathing and the THUMP-thump of his heart, which I also felt softly against the side of my face. It wasn't long before we reached the trailhead turnout. I didn't see any other vehicle but my silver car in the parking area.

"There's my car." I tried to point but couldn't move my arm. I remembered that my keys were with my pack, which I suddenly realized I didn't have. I was just about to say something when he unshouldered the familiar bag.

He tossed the pack onto the hood of my car. While still holding me, he unclasped my keys which were attached to the backpack with a carabineer hook. He unlocked and opened the passenger side door. Gently he placed me on the seat.

I watched him jog around the front of the car to the driver side. He flung the bag into the back and plopped down on the seat. He started my car, turned on the lights, flipped the heater on high, and began to drive us down the mountain. He did all this without once looking at me or uttering a single word.

"Let the heater warm you up. I think you're still shivering because your clothes are damp. But I don't think it's necessary to take them off." His eyes focused straight ahead.

I got the impression he was mad but didn't understand why. And there was no way I'd be taking my clothes off.

I didn't have a chance to think about his attitude problem because my attention was instantly focused on my stinging flesh under the constant blast of heat. My fingers were red and stiff. It took a few minutes before I could move my arms. I suffered as I began to warm up. It felt like I was sticking my hands and face into boiling water. I clenched my jaw trying to keep my teeth from chattering and from crying.

After a while my shivering slowed and the stinging began to fade. But my ankle still let me know it was injured. My wrist was feeling a little better. I could bend it forward slightly without too much discomfort but I noticed it was also swelling. My headache was making me nauseous in the moving car. The thought of throwing up was humiliating. *Please, no. Please, no*, I repeated over and over to myself until the watering in my mouth and sick feeling went away.

"Where are we going?" I asked. My throat felt like sandpaper.

"To the hospital in Chewelah," he answered.

Now I was certain he was irritated, his tone obviously rude. I was confused. I didn't know what his problem was, or what I should say. This stranger had rescued me, but he seemed put out by the whole ordeal.

It was another several minutes before I asked, "What's your name?"

"Derrick," he answered.

"Thanks," I whispered. Attitude or not, he did help me.

Derrick didn't acknowledge he heard me at all. We rode the rest of the way to the hospital in silence.

I stole a more observing glance toward his direction. Through the yellow hue of the dashboard lights, I could tell he was handsome. His long hair hung straight and loose around his bare shoulders. His skin was a darker complexion, his arms and shoulders toned just enough to cast shadows highlighting them. Derrick stared straight ahead. I figured he was in his early twenties.

How did this gorgeous guy who smelled amazing, and didn't seem to mind the cold, find me, rescue me, only to end up being pissed-off? Where was his car?

I couldn't figure out what was going on. My thoughts were murky and head was still throbbing. I decided not to think anymore as I gazed out my window up at the night sky. The moon was high in the sky, and I could make out the two Dippers and part of Orion. It was easy to find Orion's belt, but for the rest of him I was at a loss.

We began passing more and more mailboxes the closer we got to town. The dash revealed it was almost ten, earlier than I thought it'd be. A couple more turns and I could see the glow of Chewelah in the night sky. I always found it interesting how easy it was to tell where a town lay by the glow it cast. I looked south and could easily tell where the next town was. No wonder stars were so much clearer out here. They didn't have the illumination of the city lights to dilute their beauty.

We arrived at St. Joseph's Emergency Room. Derrick parked the car close to the entrance. Without a word or a second glance, he got out of the car and shut the door behind him. I watched as he walked toward the hospital wearing only jeans. His straight hair hung loose over his muscular back almost to its middle. His feet were bare. He never looked back.

I didn't know what to do. Was he getting help? Now I was irritated. I wasn't used to being treated so rudely; not that anyone ever treated me like a princess, but usually people were courteous enough to tell me what they expected. But as quick as it came, the anger left. He did save me after all.

I had a stubborn streak and decided I was done accepting help from Derrick, crippled or not. I grabbed my backpack from the backseat and found my cell phone. I sighed in frustration when it wouldn't turn on. The battery was dead.

I found my wallet and decided not to wait for help. I'd get into the hospital on my own. I opened the door, gasping as I lifted my hurt leg out and onto the ground, which was the first time I saw the rewrap of the brace around my ankle. Derrick must have found better sticks because these two where smoother and almost identical, much better than the twigs I'd scavenged. He used the same strap to tie them in place.

My ankle had now swollen three times its normal size. It didn't even look like I had an ankle. I figured it was broken.

Once both of my legs were out of the door, I realized I was stuck, yet again. I couldn't walk. I knew there was no way my ankle would take my weight. I really didn't want to crawl. I could hop on my right leg, but with the pain in my head, that idea was not very appealing. I searched for another option.

The long one story cement building was brightly lit and either side of the entrance was landscaped with trees and ornamental shrubs. Only a few cars were parked in the shadows at the far corner of the parking lot. There was no one around I could ask for help. In fact, if it weren't for the lights shining through the ER's doors, the place looked closed.

As I sat there, contemplating my limited options, a nurse with a wheelchair exited the ER pushing it my direction. I was relieved it wasn't Derrick.

"Hello, Miss Mathews. My name is Susan," the nurse said once she was close enough for me to hear without yelling.

"Hi," I said, embarrassed but thankful.

Susan helped me onto the wheelchair and draped me with a heated blanket that felt almost as good as a warm bath.

I was surprised how strong Susan was for being an older woman. She easily maneuvered my hundred-and-ten pound body from the car to the wheelchair. Her gray hair was pulled back in a tight bun and her glasses hung on a multicolored beaded chain around her neck. She wore dark blue scrubs with a white lab coat and her name, SUSAN SMITH RN, was displayed on a simple black and white name pin below her left shoulder. She smelled like lavender.

As Susan wheeled me toward the hospital, it occurred to me she knew my name, which I hadn't revealed yet, not to her or Derrick.

"Um, Susan," I began. "How'd you know my name?"

"Mr. Dennison informed me of your situation as he signed you in." Her voice reminded me of Mr. Rogers.

We entered the emergency room and Susan parked the wheelchair next to the check-in desk. I wondered how Derrick knew my name as I watched Susan walk around to take a seat in front of a flat-screen computer monitor. I figured he must have gone through my wallet when he found me. I looked around the small waiting room, but didn't see him anywhere.

Susan interrupted my thoughts and began asking routine questions to find out who I was and about my health history. I pulled my ID and medical card from my wallet and handed them to her.

"Can I use your phone?" I asked while she typed my information into the computer.

Without taking her eyes off of the monitor, she handed me a cordless phone receiver. "Dial nine first," was all she said.

I dialed the number to my parent's house and got the answering machine. Guilt filled my stomach. They must be out looking for me. I left a brief message and tried my mom's cell.

"Hello." Mom's voice came through the receiver sounding professional. I knew she didn't recognize the number.

Before I said anything, my voice cracked. "Mom" was all I got out before the tears began to fall. I was able to sob to her that I had an accident. That I was at a hospital in Chewelah and needed them to pick me up. I left out the part about the mountain lion and Derrick.

I could tell by the background noise Mom was in a public place as she talked to me. Somewhere in our conversation I found out that she and Dad were downtown having dinner, not out looking for me.

I was sorry to have interrupted their plans, but relieved they hadn't been freaking out the past few hours. There was no way I wanted to deal with the embarrassment of explaining to the cops that I'd fallen. I was humiliated enough without having to get the police involved.

I handed the phone to Susan, who asked my mom a few more insurance questions and then gave her directions to the hospital before hanging up.

I caught my reflection in the window as Susan typed away. I looked like crap. I didn't recognize myself at all. My hair was a tangled mess with leaves and twigs sticking out all over. My face was covered with blood and mud, except for a few clean streaks where fresh tears had made their way down my cheeks. I noticed a cut on my forehead and felt a large bump. I must have hit my head when I was trying to get loose from the tree. I lifted the blanket to see my clothes which were caked in mud. I let out a long depressed sigh. I was a disgusting mess.

When she was done, Susan parked me in the empty waiting room area, which had several blue chairs along the perimeter and a few in the middle. Each wall had a pastel water color painting of flowers except for one wall, which had a large flat screen TV instead. Magazines and tissue boxes were placed atop the several end tables. I sat alone wondering how Derrick had found me and where he went.

It wasn't long before Susan was wheeling me into a large rectangular room that smelled like rubbing alcohol. The room was divided in half with a wide path down the middle. Five examination areas were positioned on one side of the room against the wall, with another set of five examination areas on the opposite wall. All of the partition sheets were open, exposing matching hospital beds, heart monitors, blood pressure gauges and other pieces of medical equipment.

"Someone will be with you shortly," Susan said as she parked me in the closest examination area, locking the wheelchair in place before leaving.

It was way too still and quiet. If I wasn't so exhausted I would have been freaking out. The emptiness and dim lighting made it a perfect setting for a scene in a slasher movie.

"Hi, Erica. I'm Dusty," a male nurse said, making me jump.

"Sorry. Didn't mean to scare you," he said. "Nice splint."

I just smiled, not feeling the need to explain.

"So, you took a fall while hiking?" Dusty asked sticking a thermometer in my mouth before shining a little flashlight in my eyes.

I nodded yes as an answer.

Dusty took my blood pressure and checked the thermometer. "Your vitals look good and it doesn't look like you suffered a concussion. Is it okay if I take off your shoes, so I can take a look at that ankle?"

I nodded and he removed the shoe and sock from my right foot. When he moved to my left foot, he very gently cut the strap and removed the sticks, then began to unlace my shoe.

"Do you go to school around here?" Dusty asked. I knew he was trying to keep me distracted from what he was doing.

"Um, no. I started Gonzaga last Fall though," I answered bracing myself for the pain as he began to slowly ease the shoe off of my foot.

"I went to Gonzaga for a while, before going through WSU's nursing program," he said. "What do you plan to study?"

"I don't know yet," I answered.

"Undecided. I started out thinking I was going to be an accountant, changed majors after my first year," he paused and gave me a "get ready" look. "I'm going to cut off your sock, okay?"

I nodded again. He was careful. I barely felt the scissors against my skin. I gasped at the sight as he peeled away the filthy fabric. My foot began to swell and turn purple quickly matching my ankle.

"Wow. That doesn't look good," Dusty said. "Now, what about the rest of your clothes? Do you need some help? Or if you'd be more comfortable I can get a female nurse."

Dusty was polite and cute. He was clean shaven with a square jaw and his light brown hair was cut short. He had an out-of-place barcode tattoo on the inside of his right wrist, compared to all the dragon and skulls that covered both forearms. I suspected the tattoos went all the way up his arms, maybe even his back and chest.

I thought about his offer as I watched him place a white cotton hospital gown with small faded blue dots on the bed.

"I think I can manage," I said with a smile when he turned back to face me, waiting for an answer.

"Would you like something for the pain?" he asked.

"Yes, please," I answered.

I didn't care if he was a guy or girl. I just didn't like the idea of anyone helping me undress. Dusty gave me a nod and told me he'd be back in a minute. He closed the curtain to give me some privacy. The wheels made a soft hiss like a snake as they followed their tracks, the only sound in the large room.

It didn't take long before I regretted not asking for some help. I was able to take off my jacket which dropped chunks of mud onto the white tiled floor. I tossed it to a lone blue plastic chair butted up against the wall next to the bed. But when it got to my jeans, I was having difficulties.

It was all I could do to keep the curses under my breath when the blood rushed down my leg into my foot as I pulled myself into a standing position. I leaned against the bedrail with all my weight on my good leg, fumbling to get my pants off while trying to keep my balance.

I'd unbuttoned and unzipped my jeans when I heard Dusty from the other side of the curtain. I could see his silhouette.

"Ready?" he asked.

"Not really," I answered. "Umm, maybe I could use a little

help."

Dusty slipped his head through where the two curtains met. My expression must have been pretty pathetic because he smiled. Dusty gave me a couple white pills that I washed down with a small Dixie cup of water. Then he helped me with my pants, being careful around my hurt ankle. I kept on my black bra and matching undies. He helped me put on the gown. When I slipped my right arm through the sleeve, Dusty froze.

"What's wrong?" I asked, pulling the sleeve the rest of the way up onto my shoulder while he still held my hand. I followed his gaze to the underside of my right forearm, to where I had a star shaped birthmark about the size of a quarter. He just stood there like a manikin. I started to feel uncomfortable and pulled my arm a little, giving him the hint to let go.

"Sorry," he stammered. "I just thought… Um, never mind." He let go of my arm and helped me up onto the hospital bed. The crisp white sheets and plastic mattress felt wonderful.

When he was done, he smiled at me and said, "Everything looks good." But his body language had changed. He examined my wrist and the cuts on my face, all the while asking me questions about my fall. I figured it was to keep my mind occupied while he worked. He even asked me a couple of strange questions like, "Did I sense the danger before I fell?" and, "Did I feel someone guiding me?" That question disturbed me a little, because of the dream, but I told him "no" and explained I was a klutz. Before I knew it, he had me ready for x-ray.

Dusty wheeled me to the x-ray room. It was an odd experience being wheeled around on a hospital bed, but I was happy to be able to stay on the same bed.

I was left with the technician, a skinny younger woman who wore frameless glasses and short blond hair. Even though I was starting to feel the numbing effects of the painkillers, it was an excruciating process. I couldn't help the wincing as she arranged my ankle into various poses. She would apologize and hurry behind the protective wall as I struggled to hold the position until she gave me the okay to relax. We went through six positions. My wrist didn't hurt nearly as bad when she took its x-rays.

Soon I was wheeled back to my little curtain enclosure where Nurse Dusty helped me to feel comfortable while I waited for the doctor. He draped me with a heated blanket, except for my swollen foot which stuck out from the bottom. My foot rested on a firm pillow so that it was slightly raised. I gawked at the purple body part that no longer resembled any ankle. It was a ballooned puffy purple mass of flesh. I would have never dreamed my skin would stretch so much.

Dusty had a wash-bin of lukewarm water and cleaned me up a little. He seemed more relaxed as he dressed the cuts on my face and hands. I figured I must have imagined his change in attitude earlier, and realized I was pretty lucky to have him all to myself, since there were no other patients around. He seemed to be giving me his undivided attention and even brought me a brush and helped pick debris from my hair.

When the doctor arrived, Dusty left. He introduced himself as Dr. Hardy. Immediately I liked him. His compassionate mannerism and gentle touch made me feel like he sincerely cared about me as he asked questions and softly poked and twisted my limbs.

Dr. Hardy felt along my torso and listened to my breathing with a stethoscope. During the examination, he explained that my ankle had a grade-two sprain, and that my wrist was slightly sprained as well. I had a bump on my head, but other than that I would be fine, just sore for the next several days. I was thrilled to hear my ankle wasn't broken.

By the time Dr. Hardy left, the pain killers were really working. I barely noticed Dusty slip back in through the curtain. As I drifted to sleep, I thought I heard the sound of a camera, but didn't care. I welcomed the coming darkness and the escape of sleep.

CHAPTER 4

I drifted in and out of consciousness until I could keep my eyes open. It was 9:47 a.m. according to my alarm clock.

I was in my bedroom. The simple pink and brown striped curtains that matched my bedspread were pulled open. I remembered getting the set for Christmas a few years ago. The sun beat down on me through the window. The warmth felt good.

I listened to a song bird in the tree next to my window as the cobwebs cleared. I'd slept through everything: my parents arriving at the hospital, the ride home, being carried to my room. I noticed a set of crutches next to my nightstand. I still wore the cotton hospital gown.

With great effort I sat up. Every muscle protested my movements bringing tears to my eyes and unavoidable whimpers of pain. I'd been placed on an old cream colored blanket which now had dirt stains on it from my hair. I was gross. I smelled of smoke and was covered in blood and mud. I needed a bath. I tossed off another old blanket and got up from my soft twin bed and suffered through new waves of agony. Feeling like a 100 year old woman, I grabbed the crutches and began to hobble to the bathroom which must have alerted my mom that I was awake, because she beat me to the door. Mom followed as I made my way to the hallway bathroom.

The second floor of the house encompassed three bedrooms, two bathrooms, and a linen closet. The layout had the master bedroom and spare room on one side. My bedroom, the upstairs bathroom, and linen closet were on the opposite side. A long rectangular hallway with hardwood flooring was placed in between with a large stairway opening that had a simple wooden guardrail around it. So if I wanted to go to my parent's room I'd have to walk around the guardrail. Each end of the hallway area had a window with a short three shelved bookcase that spanned from wall to wall below it full of books.

Mom unwrapped the bandages from my ankle and wrist while I sat on the lid of the toilet. She explained I would need to stay off my feet as much as possible for the next couple weeks, which meant a lot of sitting and strict usage of the crutches. She told me she'd already picked up my pain prescription and bought a brace from the pharmacy earlier that morning.

My wrist was bruised but the swelling had gone down. It hurt a little when I rotated it. My ankle was already looking better. The bruising was darker but it was only twice its normal size, and my foot just slightly puffy.

After insisting I was capable, Mom left me alone while I took a long hot bath. Actually I took two baths. The first was focused on getting clean. And after I drained the dirty water, the second was a nice hot soak.

I was bummed I'd have to gimp around with crutches. But I was thankful to be alive, thanks to Derrick, who I couldn't get out of my mind.

After my toes and fingers were prune-like, it was time to get out. I was only partially dressed before Mom was in the bathroom. She helped me into the new black Velcro ankle brace. I let her help me, but was starting to get a little irritated.

"What happened to my clothes?" I asked, referring to what I'd worn hiking.

"We tossed them, but your shoes are out in the garage," she answered as she rewrapped my wrist.

I followed her down to the kitchen, familiarizing myself with the crutches. I descended the stairs putting most of my weight on my right foot and using the banister as leverage, all under the watchful eye of my mom.

My dad was reading the paper at the breakfast table. I greeted him with a smile as I sat down. The smell of bacon filled the room as Mom was busy at the stove. Soon she set the table with French Toast and all the fixin's.

When I was halfway through my plate, Dad laid down the paper resting his elbows on the table and folding his hands.

"What happened on that mountain?" he asked in a calm, but straight-to-the-point voice that meant business. My dad was a very kind man who rarely lost his temper, or used this tone.

"I was hiking and slipped," I answered obediently. "I fell and landed wrong." I didn't tell him about the mountain lions. I didn't see the need to make the situation worse. He never liked it when I went hiking alone. I looked down at my plate and ate as if I was starving. As long as my mouth was full, I didn't have to speak.

"Who is Derrick?" Dad asked, taking me by surprise. I realized I should have mentioned him. Of course they knew about Derrick.

"I don't know."

"Were you up there with him?" he asked.

Quickly I understood what he was getting at. I began to feel defensive. I was 18, close to 19, going to college. I could be with whoever I wanted wherever I wanted. It was really none of their business. But instead I answered, "No, Dad. He found me on the trail. I don't know who he is or how he found me. But he saved my life." I would have died up there if not for him. I had no doubt about that.

Dad didn't ask any more questions. He just stared at my face, making me very uncomfortable. I think he was waiting to see if I'd fess up to anything. Which I'm sure I would have, if there was anything to fess up to.

"Sweetie, we're just glad you're okay," Mom said sitting at her place with a cup of coffee, She'd barely eaten anything. She reached out and held my hand before saying with a smile, "You're probably going to need to stay home for a while, longer than just spring break. I can't see you climbing three flights to your dorm. And you're not going to be able to work in that cramped little shop with those crutches."

My parents didn't like the idea of me working and going to school and threatened I'd have to quit if my grades slipped. So far I've always been a 4.0 student, and college hadn't changed that. They paid for all my college and living expenses, which were not cheap. We weren't poor, but far from rich. I just hated asking for money, so having a job helped me feel less of a mooch.

"Dad and I can talk to the University next week," Mom said quickly.

I knew she was right. I couldn't work with crutches in that small coffee shop. Joe would have to hire someone to take my place. Part of me felt relieved to have a valid excuse to leave. I could always find another job. But the other part felt like that job was the only link keeping me and Sarah together.

"You're probably right," I answered in a whisper.

Mom patted my hand. I knew she would be happy I was home for a while. Dad too. Being an only child, they hadn't handled the whole empty nest situation very well. Mom took it worse than my dad.

"It's for the best," Dad said before turning his attention back to the paper, flipping to the sports section. And that was the end of our talk.

After breakfast, my ankle began to ache. Mom followed me back up to my room. Mine was an average sized room that just fit my mismatched furniture I'd had since I can remember.

Mom handed me a dose of pain killers with a glass of water. Before she left, she gave me a big hug and pulled the curtains closed to block out the sun. I was napping within minutes.

The fierce yellow eyed mountain lion was lunging for me. I felt the hilt of the knife in my hand, but I was frozen with fear. She never took her hungry eyes away from mine. I knew I was going to die, when the black tailed mountain lion crashed into her. I heard them fighting and screaming, the awful screaming over and over until it abruptly stopped. Then the black tailed predator was over me, my knife gone. The massive beast glared at me with large black eyes and released a snarl opening its mouth. I saw large sharp fangs before it lunged for my neck.

I sat straight up drenched in sweat, trembling and heart racing. My hand shook as I took a drink from the glass of water atop the nightstand. There were three tiny disfigured ice cubes floating in the clear liquid.

I kept telling myself over and over it was just a dream, but it felt so real. Gently I lay back down on the bed trying to avoid the pain which was so sharp and deep. It was like invisible fingers pinching each muscle I used.

I replayed what had happened yesterday. Not the falling, almost being eaten, or freezing. Not about my parents, or how I was going to tell Sarah I couldn't work, but about Derrick. How did he find me? Why was he such a jerk? Why did I keep thinking about how great he looked, and smelled?

His name was Derrick Dennison. I remembered the last name from Nurse Susan. I tried to figure out why he would take off without saying anything to me. I remembered him walking toward the hospital. He never looked back. I blamed the fact that I couldn't get him out of my head on the mystery surrounding his rescue.

I was such a gross mess when he found me. The sight and smell of me had to be repulsive. I was no beauty queen. I bet Derrick had a beautiful girlfriend or wife waiting for him at home.

I sat up again and looked at my reflection in the mirror over the dresser. I had several scratches on my face and an angry black goose-egg on my forehead. I stared at myself, turning my face side to side and piling my mop on my head. It didn't help.

I flopped back down, pushing through the pain. I shouldn't feel sorry for myself. I was lucky to have parents who loved each other and me, and my health. Not everyone could look like Angelina Jolie. At least I didn't look like Jabba The Hut.

The phone rang. I began reaching for the receiver on the night stand, but one of my parents must have answered it before the second ring. I got comfortable the best I could and drifted back to sleep.

Several hours later, Mom woke me. She had a steaming bowl and pills. I ate the chicken noodle soup in bed while she sat at my desk.

"Sarah called," she said.

"What'd you say?"

"She wondered where you were. I told her you would call her later. I didn't tell her what happened."

"She's going to be mad I can't work for a while," I said, shaking my head. She was going to have to cover most of my shifts until Joe found someone else.

"Sarah will understand if she is as good a friend as you say she is." Mom never did care for Sarah, especially after we graduated high school. I figured it was the gothic style Sarah sported now. Maybe Mom was scared I'd start piercing my face and wearing dark make-up. She didn't have to worry though. I hated attention. I'd never wear anything that shouted "look at me".

When I finished, she took my bowl and gave me another dose of medication. I was glad to have the medicine even though it knocked me out. It kept the pain away. I fell asleep, but woke to the same nightmare. I decided maybe the pills were not such a great idea after all. Eventually I fell back asleep and was wakened late the next morning by Mom gently shaking me.

"Morning, Sweetie. Sarah is here," she said. "Do you want me to send her up?"

"No. I'll go downstairs. I need to move anyway," I answered. "Tell her I'll be there in a minute."

The main floor of the house had a simple layout, a big square. If you were to enter the house through the front door, you'd walk into the foyer with the stairs that led to the second floor right there. The right led to a dining room and behind it the kitchen. The left led to a formal living room and behind it a den that we also used as a TV room. Behind the stairs was a small hall that led from the spare room to the kitchen, which was where you'd find the half bathroom and laundry room.

Sarah was at the kitchen table with a cream soda. Her eyes

widened as she gasped from the sight of me.

"I guess I should have brushed my hair," I smiled flinching slightly from the unexpected pain in my ankle as I made my way to the table. I leaned the crutches against the wall and sat down. There was a pitcher of orange juice and some fruit on the table. I poured myself a glass and grabbed a banana.

"Your mom said to tell you she went to the store. If you need something, call her." In a concerned voice she asked, "What happened to you?"

I saw the worry on her face, her eyes glossy with tears. She cried easily, the starving children commercials always made her shed a tear or two.

Sarah usually toned her appearance down when she knew she'd be around my parents, today she looked more EMO than Goth. But she still had a couple rings in her brows, a diamond stud in her nose, and a silver ball tongue ring. Her long layered blond hair was swept forward over her right eye, pinned with a Hello Kitty clip. She wore a black tee-shirt and jean mini-skirt. Her neon green eye shadow matched her tights. I was in a Mickey Mouse PJ set I'd had since I was fifteen. I hadn't even brushed my teeth yet.

"I went hiking and fell. But don't worry. I'm fine," I reassured.

"What about your face? Dimples, you look like you were in a boxing match."

"It looks a lot worse than it is," I said smiling trying not to move the healing cuts too quick. "I was rescued by a really hot guy though," I said to lighten the subject.

"Really," Sarah said with a complete change in demeanor. Guys were always her favorite subject.

After a lengthy discussion of describing Derrick, the way he looked, smelled, and acted, we agreed he probably had someone else he was committed to. I think Sarah was trying to be nice, not adding to my insecurities. She played match maker a time or two trying to hook me up, which never seemed to work out. They were all good looking and smart, but I was never attracted to them. In fact, I couldn't remember the last time I had the "hots" for a guy, if ever.

"So how long before you're back to work?" Sarah asked, taking me off guard.

Looking down at my hands, my throat tightened. It felt like we were breaking up or something. Before I could answer, Sarah said, "You're not, are you?"

"Sarah....," I began, but she cut me off.

"I'm going to move into an apartment with Larry," she said.

"What?" That was a shock. "I thought he lived in Seattle." Sarah met Larry online and had been chatting with him for about a month. I didn't know much about him, just that he was a few years older than her and lived on the other side of the state. His Facebook pictures reminded me of a Goth Tom Cruise.

"I didn't know you two were even dating," I said unable to control my surprise. Apparently I was more concerned about our dying friendship than she was.

"We're not," she blushed. "We've been Skyping each other

every day though. We have so much in common." After a pause she said, "Dimples, I really like him. He wants to move over here. He could have your job until he finds something better." Her eyes were filling with excitement as she spoke.

"Oh, great," I said, my chest heavy. She didn't seem upset at all, almost happy.

"Dimples," she said noticing my lack of enthusiasm. "Only if you quit for good, no big deal. Okay?" She was excited about the possibility. I saw it in her eyes. But this was a big deal. I had no idea she was this serious about him. It was like I didn't know her anymore.

"What about school? And what does your mom think?" I asked.

"I already checked into it. EWU lets freshman live off campus. I've found a bunch of apartments with roommates on Craigslist. It will be great," she said. "Mom could care less." Sarah was an only child too, raised by just her mom. Her dad took off when Sarah was three. Once Sarah graduated, her mom took a job as a flight attendant. They barely saw each other.

"Sure, Sarah, talk to Joe. Larry can have my job if he wants. I'm not going back," I said swallowing the lump in my throat. Sarah pretty much had Joe wrapped around her little finger. She ran the coffee shop not him. If she wanted Larry hired, Larry would be hired.

She took out her hot pink smart phone and swiped the screen, turning it on. "So, Dimples," she said as she texted, "what about you? You gonna stay here till your foot is better?"

The change of subject helped. I tried to hide the hurt as I explained I'd probably stay home for a while at least.

Her phoned chirped. "Wow. He said yes," she said, a smile spreading across her face.

"Larry?" I asked, already knowing the answer.

"Yep. He said he could move over here and start working in a few days." She was smiling, a Cheshire cat smile.

"Great. Um, I'm not feeling so hot. I need to lie down," I lied, wanting to be alone.

"Sure, Dimples. You rest. See ya later." She gave me a gentle hug. I watched her leave before I moved. I couldn't help but feel like that would be the last time I'd see her. She'd be okay. She made friends easily. I on the other hand... Depressed, I took a half dose of pain killers and went to watch TV. It still knocked me out, but at least I didn't have the nightmare.

The bad thing about being forced to relax is your mind wanders. Derrick relentlessly consumed my thoughts, which did help me forget about Sarah. I even tried to look for him on the internet. I searched the name Derrick Dennison on Facebook and Myspace, but nothing. Then I tried the white pages around the Chewelah area, still nothing came up. When I searched just the last name Dennison, at least twenty names popped up. I was not quite desperate enough to start calling random numbers looking for him. Besides what would I say? He obviously didn't want to talk to me.

By Sunday I had come up with two acceptable scenarios to

the mystery behind Derrick's rescue. The first being he was high on drugs out in the middle of the forest, which I doubted because he drove fine. Or, I figured it was totally plausible that he was out doing some kind of jock thing testing his mettle, which was the picture I leaned towards. That he happened to see me knocked out on the trail which would explain how he found me. I didn't have an explanation about the lack of a vehicle. Drugs might explain his ability to carry me so far so fast, but I didn't like to go there.

CHAPTER 5

It had been over a month since my accident and I was better, only a slight pain if I over worked my ankle or twisted it funny. I was still living at home. My parents worked it out with the school that I could finish the semester at home since it was over soon. I had until the middle of summer to decide if I wanted to stay at home my sophomore year or live in a dorm. .

I finished my last class for the day and was on my way home. I decided to swing by Joe's Hot Shots for a coffee. I changed my mind when I saw Sarah's car, but Larry in the window. They were working the lunch rush. Sarah and I texted back and forth a couple times since my accident, but that was all. She and Larry found an apartment they could afford without roommates. They were now a couple. *Duh*, I'd thought when I read that text, which was over a week ago.

Instead I went to Starbucks and bought an iced vanilla latte. The sun was out, and the temperature unusually warm. It was a beautiful day, a day to be outside. I drove to the park next to my house. With my advanced algebra book I found a clean bench and started studying. While enjoying the warm rays, I escaped into a world of numbers and formulas.

I was engrossed in a complicated word problem and barely noticed the bench shift from someone else's weight. I didn't bother to look up...until I noticed the scent. It was the same heady aroma that haunted me day and night. I snapped my head toward the source. There he was, Derrick, sitting next to me, staring straight at me.

I couldn't believe my eyes. I blinked twice to make sure it was really him. Derrick had become a fantasy, a dream. But here he was in flesh and bone. My heart rate tripled. I struggled to control my shock.

My earlier recollections were nothing compared to what he looked like at that moment. He was Native American, his skin bronze and his eyes dark with straight black eyebrows over long lashes. He had a strong jaw line and high cheekbones with a clear complexion. He wore a simple white t-shirt and faded blue jeans. His black hair was pulled back into a tight braid that started from the top of his neck and hung just below his shoulder blades.

We stared at each other for a moment. I wished I'd put on some makeup, or at least some lip gloss. My mop was pulled up in a loose ponytail that I'd folded into itself. I wore my favorite sweats and a dusty green shirt, which at least brought out the green in my eyes.

Derrick was the first to speak. "How's the ankle?" he asked. His voice was deep and sexy, not the impatient, irritated voice I remembered.

"Oh, um, well...it's better, I guess," I sputtered, at a loss for words.

Heat rushed to my face. I tore my eyes away from his and looked at the ground. There were so many questions I wanted to ask him. So many I'd gone over night after night. But I couldn't remember a single one at the moment.

"I'm glad to hear it." he continued. "I probably should have called or something. But I had to see you."

I looked at him, confused. Did I hear him right? He had to see me?

"Um, okay. You need something?" I asked, trying to keep my voice calm.

"No. No. I guess not," he answered. His eyes looked sad. I got the feeling he was nervous too. I remembered one of my questions. "How did you find me?" I asked in a rush before it faded from my thoughts.

"Which time?" he asked pulling his lips back into a smile that made me blush, again. He had straight white teeth.

"When you found me in the woods," I stammered, feeling stupid.

"I'll tell you about that a different day," he frowned. "But I remembered where you live from your driver's license. I was just there, but you weren't home." He suddenly looked uneasy, "So I decided to look for you. I didn't think it would be so easy."

I debated whether to insist he tell me more. But, I didn't trust myself. I was afraid I'd say something stupid. I'd never been so perplexed before. Plus I was embarrassed by my involuntary reactions brought on by his presence. My red face was surely noticeable.

After a moment, he interrupted my thoughts and said, "I think we should talk."

I nodded in agreement.

"You have a beautiful smile," he said softly.

Heat flooded my face as I blushed even deeper. I had to be the same color as a ripe tomato. I hadn't realized I was smiling. I didn't say anything. I just looked off toward the playground in the center of the park, seriously wondering if I was daydreaming. Then I remembered some of the more romantic dreams about him and me which were totally embarrassing. I suddenly wished I was somewhere else, anywhere but here with him. I was sure he could read my every thought like a movie. But then I recalled the hospital...his attitude.

"So you don't want to tell me how you found me in the woods. Fine." I'd found some courage. "Then why don't you explain why you just left me at the hospital? Why were you such a jerk? What was your problem?" I looked him straight in the eyes.

"Honestly Erica, I don't know," he stared past me. "But I'm sorry."

I was stunned. I didn't know what to think, or say. He sat at the other end of the bench, resting both arms on his legs. I began noticing the outline of the muscles in his forearms. I told myself to knock-it-off and sat up straighter putting both hands in my lap. The shock of him being here was wearing off. I needed explanations, not to be distracted by how great he looked and smelled.

He scooted closer to me. "May I?" he asked slowly reaching for my hand. I was hesitant at first thinking his request was weird, but I lifted my hand to his and he gently took hold. His hands were warm and rough, but not harsh. They felt strong. My heart beat against my chest as feeling of desire overwhelmed me.

Slowly, he folded his fingers through mine. Only in my dreams would I have thought I'd be here with him, like this. Derrick gently placed my hand on the bench.

"Erica," he started, "there are some things I need to tell you. Some things about me that are, well, not quite normal. I guess."

"Okay," I said, hoping he wasn't some sort of pervert or criminal, or psychic...that would be my luck. He probably *could* read my every thought. That horrific idea made me blush again.

"I have a condition," he started, but was interrupted by loud thumping of a stereo system that pulled into the parking lot, about a block away from where we sat.

As if to remind me of my insecurities, four beautiful women in skin tight jeans and tops hopped out of a candy-apple red Jeep Wrangler.

I watched the women walk towards a picnic table not far from where we sat, laughing and carrying Subway sandwich bags. Two were blond, one was brunette, and the fourth had black hair. They were busy amongst themselves, and didn't notice us until they were almost to the table. Once they did, they were silent, and walked a little straighter.

I wondered what we looked like to them. Me, all awkward and boring sitting next to someone who could be a supermodel. Any one of those women would be a much better match for Derrick. Then I scolded myself. What was I thinking, "match". I didn't even know this guy. I didn't have any idea what was going on. Why was I reacting so intensely to this man?

Afraid to look at Derrick, I stared at the women. I was sure he'd be gawking at them. I was. When I did finally look at him I was surprised to see he was staring at me.

He wanted to tell me something important. I sensed it. His mouth opened and closed a couple of times as if to begin speaking. But he explained nothing.

Frustrated, in the voice I remembered from the mountain he said, "Maybe I should go."

But I didn't want him to go. I was afraid that if he left I'd never see him again. Before, I was only able to remember him as a dream. He didn't seem real, but he was real, and he was here with me.

"I'm okay. You can stay," I blurted a little too loud, the brunette looked our way.

He shook his head slowly, "No, I should go. I can give you a ride home if you want."

"Sure," I said clinging to any reason for us to spend a little more time together. I would walk back to the park later to get my car.

Derrick stood and helped me up, his touch sparking flames of desire. He led me to an old Ford parked on the street. It was black with chrome accents and lifted about two feet. In the back window were two decals. On the left was a dream catcher and on the right a bugling silhouette of an elk head.

One of the women at the picnic table let out a long catcall whistle. It wasn't for me. I glanced at Derrick. He didn't seem to notice, his forehead was knotted with tension.

Derrick opened the door for me and to my surprise, effortlessly lifted me into the cab. I couldn't help but wish he'd hold me a little longer. I thought back to the night I first meet him, his bare chest and beating heart. Then I remembered again how rude he was.

"Why were you angry that night?" I asked once he got into the truck. "What did I do?"

"It's complicated, Erica." He inserted the key into the ignition but didn't start the truck. "I learned some news about myself, about my family. But I wasn't angry at you. I was angry with the situation. I'm really sorry if I upset you," he apologized again.

I waited for him to explain more. But instead he started the truck and drove us away from the park leaving me with more questions than answers.

Too soon he was pulling into my cul-de-sac. My mom's car was in the driveway, but my dad was still at work. I was positive she'd hear the loud rumble of Derrick's truck. I searched the windows of the house, trying to spot her face behind lacey curtains. Finally I did. She was peeking at us through the window of the front door.

"Will I see you again?" I asked, surprised by the desperation in my voice.

He looked at me, his lips pulling back into a smile before asking, "How about tomorrow, around this time?"

"Sure," I smiled back.

We sat in his truck for a little longer. I just wasn't able to find the willpower to open the door. After few awkward moments he said, "I guess I should get going. I have to work in a couple hours."

"Oh sure, okay," I said feeling stupid and fumbling to open the door.

"Just a minute," Derrick said getting out of the truck. He made it to my door before I was out and helped me the rest of the way down. Again his touch sent a deep yearning throughout my body. He walked me to the front door where we stood for a minute.

"I'll see you tomorrow," he said before abruptly turning to leave.

"See you tomorrow," I echoed quietly before he reached his truck.

I watched and listened as he started the beast and drove away. After I no longer heard the engine I went into the house. Of course my mom wanted to know everything as soon as I was inside. She didn't even wait for me to close the door.

"Tell me who your new friend is," she insisted with a huge grin on her face.

I tried not to make a big deal out of it. So I made sure I

wasn't facing her when I told her it was Derrick. I didn't want her to see me blush.

"There's not much to tell, Mom. He's the guy who found me the night of my accident. I think he was checking up on me to make sure I was okay." I felt her flinch from the memory, "We hung out at the park down the street for a while, and then he brought me home." I paused a minute before adding, "He's coming over again tomorrow."

"Oh really, that was him?" she was prying. "Is he nice?"

I didn't want to tell her that he was mesmerizing and left me bewildered.

"He seems pretty cool," I answered trying my hardest to sound normal.

"Where you going?" Mom asked as I started back out the front door.

"To get my car," I answered shutting the door behind me. I didn't want to talk to her about this. I was confused, eager, scared, and mad all at the same time.

My mom had been popular in school. She made friends easily and had a hard time understanding why I didn't have more friends, or a social life. She always encouraged me to meet more people. She assured me college would be a fresh start and I'd meet tons of new people. Well, that didn't happen.

On my walk I replayed the last hour. I'd pinched myself several times during our time together, so I knew I hadn't been daydreaming. Derrick was amazing and mysterious. His scent drove me crazy. It was a smell I couldn't quite place, maybe a hint of musk, sawdust, and fresh air. I wondered if my reaction was normal, if this was how girls were supposed to feel when they crushed on someone. But the whole wanting to hold my hand thing and admitting there was something wrong with him, was weird. In fact, it was downright creepy.

When I made it back to the park, the girls in the red jeep had left. I drove my car home and went up to my room where I stayed until Mom called me for dinner. I had to admit, having home cooked meals was a nice change from cafeteria food.

We sat at the table, said grace, and began eating my mom's famous meatloaf. It was as if I'd never left. I wondered if my parents kept this same routine while I was living at the dorms.

"Derrick Dennison met with Erica today," Mom said avoiding my glare.

So then I had to relay my time at the park to Dad, which he seemed much less excited about than my mom, even though there was barely anything to tell.

After I helped clean up dinner and watched a little TV, I went back up to my bedroom intending to do some studying. But all I could think about was Derrick. Finally I gave up and just went to bed. But I couldn't even escape him then. My dreams were full of Derrick.

CHAPTER 6

I tossed and turned all night. According to my clock, I was waking every hour. I had classes in the morning and needed sleep. But every time I closed my eyes I saw him, smelled him, felt him. Then I'd remember he was coming over tomorrow and get nervous, definitely not sleepy. It was like I'd suddenly become super obsessed. Everything made me think of Derrick.

Sometime in the early morning I fell asleep because I woke to the beeping of my alarm, which was set for 7 a.m.. My first class started at 8 a.m. I made it to class on time but was tired and distracted, way too focused on the clock. For the first time ever, I drifted off to sleep during an English Lit lecture. I woke with a start to classmates around me packing up their notes and books. Finally at noon I was on my way home.

I pulled my hair up in a barrette and put on some mascara. I found some rootbeer lip-gloss and put that on too. I tried on a dozen different outfits, all of which I realized were basically the same, just different colors. I finally chose a pair of khaki capris and decided on a lavender sleeveless sweater. I liked the soft colors in contrast to my dark hair. I even clipped on my gold necklace with a charm of a white dove that I'd gotten for my seventeenth birthday. I've always liked doves and thought the white ones were the prettiest of all birds.

Dad was still at work. I ate a late lunch with my mom before she left to run some errands, and decided to wait for Derrick in the living room. I attempted to read one of my mom's woman magazines.

It was almost 2:30 p.m. when I heard Derrick's truck. My heart started beating faster and my skin pricked with goose-bumps. I was excited and scared all at the same time. I listened as his truck idled briefly in front of the house before the engine stopped. I opened the front door at the same time he reached the top step. My heart was still pounding, but at least my skin smoothed down.

"Hi," I said, unable to stop the smile that followed.

Derrick stood at the door wearing a similar outfit as yesterday, but his tee-shirt was black and his hair hung loose. I couldn't help but stare. He cleared his throat and I realized he was waiting for me to ask him in. Blushing, I opened the door as wide as it would go and moved aside so he could pass by me.

"Anyone home?" he asked.

"No, Dad's at work and Mom went to town. She should be back in a little bit. She wants to meet you." I had a suspicion her errands were conveniently timed to give me some time alone with Derrick.

"Oh, great," he said nervously as he walked by me. I tried not to be obvious as I caught his scent.

"What kind of cologne do you wear?" I asked shutting the

door behind him.

"I don't," he answered giving me a funny look.

I led him to the kitchen wondering how his scent could possibly be just him. He sat on one of the stools at the island. I grabbed a couple of sodas from the fridge. "Thanks," he said as I handed him one. We drank in silence while my mind raced trying to figure out something to say.

"Erica, I need to tell you some things, but I don't know how to start," he said with a frown.

I saw tension in his expression. His mood suddenly turned serious, as if someone flipped an attitude switch. It made me feel a little uneasy.

"I can't stop thinking about you, dreaming about you," he said softly.

I didn't dare tell him "ditto", but I blushed as he continued.

"I don't even know how to tell you what's going on without sounding like a complete lunatic and freaking you out." His voice was full of stress. He now had my undivided attention as I stopped admiring his good looks and listened to what he was trying to say.

He hesitated before blurting, "I dreamt of where to find you that night in the woods. I had the same dream, well nightmare actually, for a week straight. I tried to ignore it, telling myself it was all just a damn dream, but that night I had to come to you. It was unlike anything I'd ever felt before. I was in physical pain if I tried to resist."

His eyes told me he was serious. He was telling me the truth.

So much for my own jock scenario.

I was a lot nervous now. I wanted to believe he was joking. But I knew he wasn't. Was I supposed to say something, laugh? I had the feeling laughing would be the worst thing I could do at the moment. I saw suffering on his face and heard the strain in his voice. Then I realized maybe he *was* psychic and began to panic as I focused on his shoes not his bulging biceps.

He took a deep breath and continued, "I panicked when I saw the mountain lion. I knew that if I didn't do something you'd be killed..."

"Whaat?" I interrupted. That statement punched me hard in the stomach sweeping away all other feelings. I hadn't told a soul about the almost attack, and what did he mean "saw".

"You saw me?" I whispered suddenly feeling dizzy. I felt cold and began to shake.

"Here you better sit down," Derrick said in a worried voice. He got up and helped me to the stool where he'd been sitting. Then I heard my mom's car pulling into the garage.

"Do you want me to leave?" Derrick asked quickly.

"No, she'd wonder what happened, and I don't even know what's going on. I don't understand..." I tried to wrap my brain around what I'd just heard, trying to remember if I saw any signs of another human being on the trail.

"I'll explain. I promise," he said as he took my face in both of his hands gently lifting my chin so that he was looking straight into my eyes. "Trust me."

How could I resist? There was something so urgent in his voice, and pleading in his eyes. His touch sent flames through my body. "Okay," I whispered as he slowly let go and moved to the only other stool next to me. It was like he had some kind of magical power over me.

Mom came into the kitchen with an arm full of groceries. "Hi, I'm Molly and you must be Derrick," she said as she set her colorful hand sewn reusable grocery bag on the counter, "our family's hero."

"Well, I don't know about hero, more like being in the right place at the right time," Derrick said in a smooth voice as he reached out to shake her hand.

Derrick and my mom were having a conversation, but I was lost in my own thoughts of what he just revealed. I felt Derrick nudge my knee with his. I tried to refocus and pay attention to what was going on.

"Derrick, where do you go to school?" Mom asked.

"I don't," he answered.

"Do you work?"

"Yeah. I've worked at the lumber mill in Usk since I was sixteen."

"Are you a member of a tribe?" Mom was looked a little embarrassed after asking that question. She never did think before she spoke. She always said the first thing that popped into her head.

"Washtucna Tribe. We have a small reservation north of here, about an hour-and-a-half drive or so."

Then Mom asked, "Do you want to stay for dinner?"

"Oh, I don't know," he answered. This question caught Derrick off guard. Maybe he wasn't psychic.

"We are having barbequed New York steaks. I bought an extra just for you." My mom can be very persuasive when she wants to be.

"Okay. Thanks," Derrick said, forcing a smile.

"Derrick, let's go out back," I said to get him alone so I could get some answers.

I lead him through the backdoor of the kitchen. An eight foot wooden fence around the yard gave us privacy. A couple old maples would soon be shading most of the area once their leaves opened. Against the back fence was a two tiered flower garden with freshly planted purple petunias and yellow marigolds.

Derrick followed me to a cement patio. We sat next to each other at the wicker patio set. The stiff maroon cushions matched the umbrella placed in the middle of a rectangular glass table. The day was warm with the sun starting to drop in the sky. I barely noticed how nice the afternoon was.

As soon as we were seated I asked, "Do you want to explain to me what you meant by 'saw the mountain lion' Derrick? I haven't told anyone about that." My voice cracked from the memory.

He took my hand and instantly I felt better. Very slowly he leaned forward, his face just inches from mine. "I don't think now is a good time, Erica. I promise I will explain everything, but I need to be able to in private, without interruption."

In a shaky voice I asked, "You promise? You promise to explain?"

He nodded, "Yes, I promise."

It was difficult to maintain a conversation. I talked a little about my recent move back home from the dorms. He talked about his job at the lumber mill. Both of us avoiding the obvious topics that needed discussion.

Eventually we just sat there in silence. He held my hand, his skin almost hot. I looked at our hands and noticed how much darker his skin was than mine, and his hand so much bigger. His nails were short. It looked like he bit them. So he's a nail biter, I smiled to myself.

My eyes slowly traveled up his arm. I noticed the small humps where his veins raised slightly under tight skin. My eyes continued up until they found his face, where our eyes met and locked. I didn't care anymore that he knew my secret. I think I would have told him anyway.

I never believed in love at first sight; it always seemed like a cliché. But I had no other explanation for the intensity of my emotions at that moment for this man I barely knew. Our peaceful moment was interrupted when my dad came through the backdoor to the patio. He was getting stuff ready to light the barbeque. Dad refused to use propane. He said the only way to cook on a grill was to use briquettes.

The afternoon passed quickly. What had been several hours felt like minutes. I watched Dad set the bag of charcoal briquettes down and walk towards us to meet Derrick.

Nervously I introduced them, "Dad, this is Derrick. Derrick, this is my dad, Bill."

"No don't get up," Dad said to Derrick, "It's nice to finally meet you." He shook Derrick's hand. "Thank you for finding Erica and taking her to the hospital. Her mother and I are very grateful. If you ever need anything, don't hesitate to ask."

"You're welcome. I'm just glad she's all right," Derrick said.

I remembered it sure seemed like a problem that night. But maybe he was struggling with some issues. A ball of worry grew in my stomach when I remembered him mentioning a "condition". Hopefully he wasn't sick. He sure didn't look sick. I hated being so clueless.

Dad gave us a smile and turned back toward the barbeque. Dad was never one to ask me a lot of questions. I think he asked too many question at work as a Bank Manager, prying into people's private financial lives. We watched as he arranged the black briquettes into a pyramid and douse them with the starter fluid. I felt the *whoosh* of flame after he threw in a lit wooden match igniting the inferno.

I had to hand it to my dad. He is an awesome cook with a barbeque. My parents joined us on the patio to eat the steaks and potato salad.

"Derrick, what are your plans for the summer?" Mom asked after swallowing a bite.

I kept my focus on my food, but my ears were listening.

"Not too much, just work. My family and I go huckleberry picking at the end of July, but besides that, nothing big planned," Derrick answered.

"Oh, do you still live with your parents?" she asked.

"Just my mom and younger sister, my dad was killed when I was eight by a drunk driver." Derrick's voice didn't reveal any emotion.

"I'm so sorry," Mom said, her voice full of empathy. She could relate. Her dad died when she was about my age in a car accident. No alcohol was involved, just a tired old truck driver who fell asleep at the wheel. Grandpa's little Toyota never had a chance. Her mom still lived in New Mexico. She stayed in a retirement community and was very happy. She wouldn't even consider moving here with us.

My dad's parents died when I was twelve. Grandma suffered from cancer for about a year before she passed. My dad went to see her in Arizona just before she died. Then less than a month later, Grandpa died. Dad had been sad for a long time afterward.

We finished dinner with less serious chatter, my dad asking Derrick about sports, which Derrick wasn't really into.

When dinner was finished, Mom brought out dessert, an angel food cake topped with strawberries and whip cream. I love strawberries, so I ignored my full stomach and helped myself to a huge piece. Derrick took what I thought to be a rather small piece for someone so large. I was just slightly embarrassed by my much bigger portion. After desert, my parents cleared the table and left us alone again.

"I should probably get going," Derrick said looking at his watch. I glanced at mine. It was after eight thirty. Where'd the day go?

"By the time I get home, it'll be pretty late, and I have to work early in the morning. I should try to get some sleep."

"On a Saturday?" I interrupted.

"The mill runs all week. We alternate shifts." Our eyes locked again as he cupped the side of my face with his warm hand. "I'll call you."

I blushed, but didn't move. I wanted to stare into his eyes forever. They were dark, like a large drop of black paint, it was impossible to distinguish the pupil from the iris.

As we walked through the house he told my parents "thank-you" and "goodbye". He hesitated at the door briefly before turning to leave.

I watched through the living room window as he drove out of sight. He was such a mystery, a handsome wonderful mystery that captured my heart. Maybe I was going crazy.

CHAPTER 7

I was having a hard time finding energy to get out of bed. It had been almost two weeks since I'd seen Derrick. The days he had off conflicted with the days I had classes or testing. I thought back to the first time we talked on the phone, the night after the BBQ with my parents.

"Derrick, what did you mean about seeing the mountain lion?" I asked. There was a long pause, and for a moment I wondered if he'd hung up, but then he started explaining.

"Our people, Natives in general, have legends that go back to the beginning of life, to the beginning of the world. They are all different in story, but similar in meaning. I have spoken with the Council of my tribe and they've opened my eyes to many things recently. Um, they're eager to hear about us too," he said.

"Eager to hear?" I didn't like the thought of other people talking about me, especially people I didn't know.

More softly he continued. "My family and I don't really follow any popular religion. We don't belong to a church. But you know how some people believe in guardian angels. Well, we believe that we are guided and protected by guardian spirits, pretty much the same thing I guess."

"Sure," I said, letting him know I was still listening after another long pause. I got the feeling he was struggling with what to say.

"Well, my mom was concerned for me after witnessing one of my nightmares. The one about you in the woods, before I knew it was you. I never saw a face, or body. It was just a feeling of someone or something in danger. She went to the Council, and they met with me that same day. They all agreed I was having visions and told me to listen. Not that I would have been able to ignore it that night. The pull was unbearable. It was like a magnetic force and if I went the wrong direction, every inch of my skin began to burn as if exposed to some kind of chemical gas.

"So I listened to whatever it was that guided me to you. And when I saw you there, unconscious... I had no idea that I would feel so protective over you. It was insane. I would kill or be killed without knowing your name or having ever spoken to you.

"You'd hit your head on a rock. I watched you laying there for a while trying to figure it out, who you were, what was going on, what I should do. At first I was going to call the police. But there's only the one sheriff now, and he'd take too long. I noticed the frost and knew it was getting cold, so I started a fire and set you next to it..."

"But you knew about the mountain lions," I interrupted.

"Yes."

"How?" I asked, trying to make sense of what he was and

wasn't telling me. "Why didn't you help me sooner?"

"It's complicated. I can't tell you everything, not yet. Not on the phone anyway. Erica I will explain everything soon. I just can't screw things up."

"Derrick, this is so weird. I mean…us. Sometimes I think I'm dreaming. Or that I've gone completely mad."

"It's a lot to take in. Let's just leave it at that for now," he said.

We talked at least once every day since, and found that we had a lot of the same interests and tastes. But we never discussed that night on the mountain again. He still owed me an explanation.

"Erica. Don't you think it's about time to get out of bed?" Mom said coming into my room opening the curtains. I shielded my eyes from the bright light. "Really, it's past noon…unless you're not feeling well." She checked my forehead with the back of her hand.

"I'm getting up," I sighed kicking the covers off. She gave me a stern look and left, leaving the door open.

I took my time getting dressed. Finals were over. I finished early and was officially on summer break. Derrick was working overtime at the lumber mill and couldn't come see me. He did reassure that the good part of all this overtime was the fact he'd have a few extra days off. I missed him. It was as if a piece of me was gone, which hardly made sense since I'd just met the guy. I literally ached to see him. My dreams didn't help. They just left me longing for more.

I made my way down to the kitchen. Mom was at the sink.

"If you're hungry, there's a sandwich in the fridge," she said with her back facing me.

"Thanks," I said. I wasn't hungry, but I grabbed the sandwich anyway feeling a little guilty I missed lunch, especially since she and dad were leaving for their anniversary getaway to Hawaii tomorrow. They'd postponed their trip after my accident.

"Great sandwich, Mom," I said trying to lighten the mood. "Need some help packing?"

She turned toward me after hanging the dish towel over the oven door handle. "Sure, how about after you're done?" She relaxed and smiled. I smiled back. I was determined to make the rest of the day pleasant.

I kept busy helping Mom pack. She and dad planned to leave late in the morning on a flight from Spokane to Seattle, where they were going to stay overnight, then fly to Hawaii early Saturday. Their vacation was for twelve days. They were coming back June 20, the day before my birthday.

"What do you think of this?" she asked holding up a black bikini.

"I think you'll give Dad a heart attack," I said, my face blushing.

"Well it has been twenty-five years, and I'm pretty proud of the fact I can still wear one of these without scaring away everyone on the beach," she laughed.

"You should be, Mom. You're one of the most beautiful people I've ever seen," I said honestly. She had a better body than most twenty year olds.

I didn't look anything like her, or my dad. She was tall and thin with curly red hair that she kept cut short. Mom had a naturally beautiful face dusted with faint freckles. Her eyes were blue, my dad's brown. He was tall and lean with sandy blond hair. I was short compared to them. I barely reached five-foot-five. I was thin, but not in the sexy curvy way as my mom. My face was round with two deep dimples, one in each check. Neither of them had dimples

"Oh, thanks, Sweetie," she said giving me a hug.

"Your dad is not too thrilled about having Derrick stay here overnight when he barely knows the guy," she said as I handed her a stack of summer dresses to put into the suitcase.

"I know. But he doesn't have anything to worry about. Derrick would never do anything I didn't want him to do. Plus it saves him gas money."

"I've never seen you so interested in someone before. You mope around all day and only light up when you talk about him," she said pulling me down to sit beside her on the bed.

Mom was more understanding about my feelings for Derrick than Dad. We'd had several talks about Derrick, especially the night I'd asked her to talk to Dad about having him stay for a few days. At first Dad had said "no", but then Mom reminded him I was in college, almost nineteen and legally an adult. Eventually he caved, but very reluctantly.

"I really like him, Mom," I said. "I even think I might be in love..."

"A little early for that, Sweetie," she interrupted.

I didn't want to argue so I said, "Maybe, but we definitely have a connection," without going into detail. I wanted to get off the subject of me and Derrick.

"I guess Sarah and Larry are getting along pretty good," I said, blurting out the first thing that came to mind. Sarah and I barely talked anymore, but she did text me the other day of how great things were going.

"Mmmm. Well, that's good news," Mom said. "I know you two have had a falling out, but it might be for the best." She gave me a squeeze before going back to her packing.

"Yeah, maybe," I answered. I had mixed feelings. I cared about Sarah and hoped she and Larry worked out, but things had definitely changed between us. I didn't miss my old job one bit. And when I thought about it, I didn't really miss Sarah either.

"I'm certainly glad you agreed to quit that Bistro job," Mom said.

I nodded not sure what to say. I hated not earning my own money. But my parents were giving me an allowance that more than covered my gas, fast food and then some. We had a lengthy discussion where in the end it was agreed I will do additional chores around the house to "earn" the raise in allowance.

"Sorry, Erica, but I really am glad," Mom said, probably reading my emotions.

"I know, Mom. I didn't really like that job much anyway," I said giving her a hug, knowing that would make her feel better.

I helped her pack the rest of their bags, not talking about much more than how best to pack. Then we took the bags downstairs and made dinner together. When Dad got home from work, they went over their itinerary with me as we ate, which included snorkeling, hiking, dolphins, and a helicopter tour. We watched Jeopardy before going to bed, my dad and I were competing for the highest score. He won.

The next morning, Dad woke me on his way downstairs. Mom was already in the kitchen. After a quick breakfast, we were on our way to the airport. Mom gave me some last minute information in the car.

"I left the name and number of the hotel in Seattle and the one in Honolulu on the tablet by the phone. I probably won't call you from Seattle, but I will call you as soon as we get to Hawaii." She paused. "Are you sure you're going to be okay by yourself?

"I asked the Johnson's across the street to keep an eye on things," she said without waiting for my answer.

"Mom, please don't worry about me," I said rolling my eyes. "I have been on my own before, remember." It seemed like she and Dad forgot the eight months I lived in the dorm. "Besides, Derrick is coming over, so I won't be by myself the whole time." I noticed Dad cringe when I mentioned Derrick. I ignored him.

I dropped them off at the airport a little after ten. We said our good-byes with a few tears shed by my mom, then I went back home. The house was clean and the fridge was packed. Mom went completely overboard. I had enough food to last three months.

It was early and I was restless. Derrick was working and it would be several hours before I could talk to him. I was hoping he'd be able to come over tonight instead of waiting until the morning, but it depended on when he could get off of work. I didn't want to read, and didn't want to watch TV. I decided to go on a walk.

Once I shut the door behind me, I heard the muffled sound of the phone ringing from inside. I thought about answering it, but changed my mind. My parents were on a plane and Derrick was at work. Whoever was calling wouldn't be anyone I'd want to talk to. I made it to the end of the block when I realized I'd left my cell phone in the house. I didn't bother going back for it. I wouldn't be gone long.

It was warmer than usual for early June. The sun was high in the sky. I didn't have to worry about sun block. My skin never burned. I never even had a tan. No matter how long I baked in the sun, my skin stayed the same milky white.

After a couple of blocks, I found the familiar trail that led from our housing development to a small urban park that was about three square miles. The entire park was pretty much level with old growth trees and native brush grasses. It was secluded, nothing like the other city parks around the area. It almost felt like being out in the woods.

A couple hundred feet inside the perimeter of the park, I couldn't see any surrounding houses or streets. There was a main dirt trail that crisscrossed the park, dividing it into four parts. But there were a lot of smaller trails snaking their way through the trees.

The park was usually busy with joggers and walkers, but today it was empty. I was alone except for a couple younger teens that passed me on bikes.

I was enjoying myself, and there was no hurry. I looked for things to distract me so time would pass quickly. Ignoring the food wrappers, cigarette butts, and other various litter scattered about, I listened to the birds and the hum of traffic far off in the distance. I heard the shrill scream of a siren as it got louder then faded. The still air was tainted by the smell of skunk.

The canopy of branches shaded the trail like a natural umbrella. But there were plenty of spots where the sun's rays broke through, sending columns of light to the ground. I made it to the end, which was another housing subdivision, and turned back around. Before long, I stopped in the middle of the park to rest on a fallen tree.

The shaded parts of the tree were slimy from the morning dew. I found a dry spot in the sun and ignored the coarse bark poking my butt and thighs as I relaxed in the heat. I was lost in thought daydreaming about Derrick holding me, kissing me.

After a few minutes, I was ready to leave. Before my first step the hair on the back of my neck stood straight. I glanced around, but didn't see anything out of place. I was alone. The woods were quiet. But a feeling of danger was spreading through me.

I started towards home at a jog. A moment later I was running as the sense of danger increased. My heart raced. Something terrible was out there, but I didn't know what.

I dared a glance back when my foot landed on the edge of a rock and rolled my ankle. I fell hard. Without wasting a moment I was up ready to flee, but froze. From the corner of my vision, behind me a hundred yards, I made out a figure in the shadow of the trees.

Within seconds it was running towards me at an unbelievable speed, weaving in and out of the trail. It was as if the figure had taken flight, hovering just above the ground.

Do not run. Stay in the sun. I heard from inside my head.

The voice was the same angelic voice from my dream, from when I lost consciousness on the mountain. I was in a sun beam at least ten feet in diameter. I fought my instinct to run and stood still as the figure approached. I didn't really have time to consider my options in the few seconds it took for the thing to reach me.

Trembling I watched the figure slow to a walk and stop at the edge of my circle of light. It was a man. Even with the oversized hood shading his face, I could tell. He wore a black cloak with a pair of muddy work boots poking from beneath. His arms were folded so that each one slid into the other's sleeve. He was at least two feet taller than me. A rope tied around his waist revealed how abnormally thin he was.

Slowly he unfolded his arms and slid off his hood. Shrieking in horror, my hands went to my mouth. The sight of him sent another jolt to my already racing heart. He had sharp ugly features, a large mouth with thin lips, a hooked nose, and thick black eyebrows over sunken red eyes. Unable to take my eyes off his face, I saw tiny black veins that branched beneath white translucent skin. His hair was slicked back.

Slowly he grinned, revealing white teeth and fangs. My legs went weak and I fell to my knees.

"Hallo," he sneered in a voice as vile as he looked.

Shaking uncontrollably I stared at him. Evil and danger radiated off of him like the heat from a blazing fire. The world began to go fuzzy. I forced myself to breathe deep. I gagged. He smelled like rotting eggs and death.

Tears began to trickle from the corners of my eyes as I struggled with the realization of what was happening. This thing was real. A vampire. I knew it in my soul.

"You are beautiful," he said in a German accent.

"What do you want?" I whispered barely loud enough for my own ears.

"Imagine my surprise," he sneered ignoring me. "I was underground over there," he said, pointing toward the end of the park where I'd turned around, "next to the trail, waiting for nightfall. I am on my way to Seattle, you see. Our searching is more intense as the deadline draws nearer. A precaution for nothing...or so we thought." I had no idea what he was talking about. He stood still, nothing moving but his lips. "I heard you walk past me the first time, and thought it odd I couldn't smell you. But when you passed me again and still no scent. Well, My Dear, I rose early just to meet you."

"I followed the noise only a clumsy human can make, and saw you sitting there. But still I could not smell you. When you sensed me and ran, I knew it was you." In a smile of anticipation he sneered, "I cannot believe my luck, that it is I who will kill you. I who will kill The One."

I didn't say anything He was psychotic and evil. But he stayed in the shade. I pieced together that if the sun things was true, the drinking blood thing was probably true as well. Slowly I stood on shaking legs, as my courage began to surface. I would fight.

"I am so rude. Let me introduce myself. I am Frederick," he said holding his hand out as if I were stupid enough to shake it. He was careful not to cross the light barrier.

I didn't move. He jerked his hand back and gave me another vile grin revealing his teeth that were brighter and sharper than any I'd ever seen before.

"Mmmmm," he said. "Shocking isn't it? By your reaction I can tell you are ignorant to this situation," and with a hiss he added, "which will allow me to complete this task easily. You are unaware of the threat you pose. Of the glory I will reap. I will enjoy this immensely. Your eyes will do as proof, but I won't take them too soon. You will want to see how creative I can be." He shifted revealing a very long dagger strapped to his waist.

I slightly wondered why he would use a knife to kill me before panic ravaged my body in violent tremors. The sun was moving. My sanctuary of light was shrinking. I searched for another ray, but there were none close enough. All the sun spots were shrinking as the sun began to fall below the tree line. Frederick would have me within minutes.

"Help. Someone, help me please. HELP!" I screamed. I screamed at the top of my lungs surprising myself how loud and high pitched my voice could go.

Frederick laughed. "Do you really think anyone can stop me?" he said before gliding to a boulder bigger than me. He picked it up with both hands and crushed it, as if the rock was one large Ritz cracker.

"Anyone who comes to your rescue will be killed," he said, his accent more pronounced. He gave me a look of wickedness, daring me to scream again. I swallowed my scream.

Frederick seemed impatient waiting for the shade to reach me. I watched as he paced back and forth. On trembling legs I stood my ground, unwilling to go down without a fight.

"Why?" I choked, barely above a whisper.

He acted as if he didn't hear me. But then Frederick said, "Now why would I tell you, and give you leverage? I think the less you know, the better for me."

He turned and stopped in front of me. "Hurry up. Hurry UP," he hissed. Then Frederick reached for me. Once his hand met the sunlight it ignited into flame. Momentum brought his hand only inches from my face.

Automatically I flinched away, stumbling backward. Time went in slow motion as I realized part of me was outside the light beam. I saw Frederick's eyes, eager and excited, as he skirted around the sunlight. I flung my body forward, but not before Frederick was behind me and able to grab a handful of hair. I screamed as the clump pulled loose from my scalp.

Falling to my knees I touched the raw flesh, my hand was covered in blood. I struggled to stay conscious as the warm rivers of blood wound their way down my scalp and neck. Frederick tossed the patch of hair aside. Long strands of hair fluttered to the ground. He shook loose a few remaining pieces of hair from his burned hand. His skin was charred and black. Smoke curled into the still air. The smell was horrible, more of death than rotting eggs. I swallowed repeatedly to keep from puking.

I pressed against the wound on my head to stop the bleeding and watched as his injuries healed. The charred skin began to crack. The cracks grew wider replacing the damaged flesh with translucent new skin. Seeming not to feel any pain or discomfort, Frederick started pacing again, clearly agitated.

I barely fit in the circle of light. I sat hugging my knees to my chest. I had a few minutes left, if that, before the sun disappeared behind the trees. A sense of calmness overcame me. My fear and pain faded as I prepared myself for the inevitable. But then I heard a familiar sound, a familiar engine.

My short spell of calmness was replaced with a new kind of panic. It was Derrick's truck. I didn't want him here. He had to leave. He'd be killed. Everything happened so fast; I never had a chance to come up with a plan.

Derrick's truck charged down the trail toward me like a black beast, skidding to a stop just a few feet from me. I screamed for Derrick to leave, screamed for him to run, to go. The truck was never turned off. The guttural idle of the engine muffled the noises of the fight to come.

Derrick's eyes met mine briefly, full of anger and fear. The door flew from the frame crashing into a tree several yards away, as he sprang from the truck. I watched Derrick morph into the dark eyed mountain lion of my dreams in mid air. His clothes exploded from his changing body before he hit the ground. Derrick let out a fierce growl and was between me and Frederick, hunched, ready to spring.

Frederick grabbed his knife, hesitated briefly, then turned and fled avoiding the few remaining sun spots. Derrick took off after him. They were a blur of motion. Derrick didn't have to avoid the sun and quickly caught up to Frederick. He leapt onto the vampire's back, forcing him to the ground.

They were a summersault of cloak and fur. Then it looked as though Frederick stabbed Derrick and tried to run. But then Derrick was back on him. I listened to Frederick's dying screams as Derrick tore him apart, until one last cry was stopped short.

Frozen in place, my sunlight gone, I watched Derrick saunter toward me. His head hung low, but his dark eyes never leaving mine. Derrick stopped just in front of me. He lifted his head, his posture normal for a mountain lion, yet our gaze was level. I saw the same dark eyes. The same eyes I had stared into so longingly a couple weeks earlier.

I reached out to touch him but he avoided my hand. I watched him go back to his truck. He was near the driver's side when he morphed back into his bronzed body. I stared, unashamed as he turned off the truck's ignition and grabbed a pair of jeans from behind the bench seat. Once he shrugged them on he turned and sat on the chrome nerf bar, resting his elbows on his knees and burying his head in his hands. His long black hair hung like a curtain hiding his face from my view.

It seemed like a long time before I could move, my brain trying to catch up with reality. I was in shock as everything I'd known was challenged. I had plenty of time to comprehend the idea of vampires in my shrinking cell of light. But this was too much. I was fighting for my sanity.

It was dusk when I went to Derrick. I reached out and touched his warm bare shoulder with my cold trembling hand. "Derrick?" was all I could mutter.

He brought his head up and our eyes met. Slowly I reached out, brushing a few strands of loose hair from his face.

"I'm so sorry," he said. "I wanted to tell you. I tried, but then I couldn't." He dropped his eyes, looking at the ground.

I rested my hand on his head then let it fall to beneath his chin. Gently I lifted his face so he'd look me in the eyes.

"I have no idea what's going on. Maybe I'm dreaming. But I know one thing's for sure. You saved me, again...and it, it doesn't matter. We can figure things out," I said. He was all I cared about. My sanity could wait.

He stood and held me, pressing my face against his bare chest. I breathed in his scent, listening and feeling his strong heart beating. We held each other for a moment before he asked in a strained voice, "Erica, are you all right?"

"I, I think so," I stuttered.

He let go and turned my head to look at the bloody mass of flesh and hair. "You sure?"

"Right now, that's the least of my worries," I tried to smile.

"I need to finish this, then we can go," he said.

"What do you mean?"

He didn't answer. I watched him grab an old red metal gas container from the bed of his truck and walk to where Frederick lay. Derrick began piling the pieces of Frederick. Hesitantly I walked closer to see why.

I let out a choked gasp. The once small pieces of Frederick had grown. The pieces were slowly moving and combining, like spots of mercury. Derrick doused the small pile he'd made with the gasoline and lit it. The fire let out a plume of black smoke that smelled like Frederick's charred hand but a hundred times worse. It was too much. I turned and barely made it to a tree before violently emptying my stomach. When the heaving stopped, I went back to the truck while Derrick fed the fire with all the remaining pieces of Frederick.

"Did you get them all?" I asked when he came back.

"Yes. I'd be able to smell any parts that were left no matter how small," he said. There was no expression in his face.

With the fire still smoldering he helped me inside the truck. I watched Derrick retrieve his door and toss it into the truck's bed. I overheard him grumble, "That's going to be expensive."

The trail was barely wide enough for his truck. Motor vehicles were not allowed, and there was nowhere for him to turn around. He backed all the way out.

Staring out the window I said, "Strange that no one reported the fire."

Derrick didn't respond. He drove us the short distance to my house and pulled into the driveway. He turned the engine off. After a moment of silence, I let myself out of the truck.

CHAPTER 8

I fished my keys out of my pocket and unlocked the front door and stepped inside. I flipped on the foyer light, and turned to close the door expecting Derrick to be behind me.

"Are you coming in?" I asked Derrick, finding him standing on the porch looking up at the night sky.

"I need to get some...socks," he said leaving the porch.

"You're coming back?" I asked, desperation flooding through me. What if he left?

He turned giving me a tired smile. "Yes, I'll meet you inside. Go do what you were going to do. I just need a minute."

I watched him walk to his truck before closing the door. I went upstairs to my bathroom.

While brushing my teeth I stared at my reflection in the vanity mirror. My eyes were red and swollen. Dried blood was crusted down my neck. The collar of my white shirt was stained crimson. My head didn't hurt as much as I though it should, probably shock dulling the pain.

When I finished my teeth, I found a cosmetic mirror and angled it with the vanity to see where Frederick ripped out my hair.

On the back of my head was a spot about the size of my fist matted with blood and hair. There were a few dime sized bald spots, but nothing that would be too noticeable. Lucky for me, Frederick grabbed my hair from the ends, not near the scalp. I shuddered at the thought of what could have happened.

The knees of my jeans were muddy and my palms and arms road-rashed. A nice long cleansing shower sounded wonderful. I tossed my bloody shirt into the garbage and the rest of my clothes into the hamper. The bathroom was full of steam when I finally stepped into the pre-warmed shower. The water stung the wounds on my head and other cuts, some of which I didn't realize I'd had until the water hit them.

Changing my mind, I made the painful shower quick and dressed in a pair of old sweats and long sleeve tee-shirt. Unable to think of anymore excuses to keep me upstairs, I went to find Derrick.

He was sitting at the breakfast table, his back to me. I stood in the dining room watching him. He'd put on a black shirt. His hair was loose. It looked like he'd run a brush through it. His feet were still bare, no socks.

I took a deep breath and softly walked to the sink. I filled two glasses with water and sat next to him. He didn't move or say anything. He just sat there, staring out the back door window.

As I drank my water I thought back to the park. Everything was surreal. I knew what I'd just been through really happened. The pain was real. But it seemed like a movie, like the events happened to someone else and I was the silent observer.

Unable to take the silence any longer I said, "Derrick, tell me what's going on. How did you do that?" My voice came out as shaky as I felt.

Derrick looked at me. "How is your head?" he asked.

"It doesn't hurt too much. I shouldn't have a huge bald spot anyway." I tried to smile.

In a sullen voice that matched his face, he started to explain. "I heard legends of shapeshifters, but never gave them too much thought. I would listen to the stories, but that was all I had thought of them as, stories.

"That day on Chewelah Peak was the first time I'd ever transformed. I had to hurry that night. I knew something horrible was about to happen. The force of the pull was excruciating. I couldn't move fast enough.

"I drove my truck to the base of the mountain. But then I ran to where you were. Somehow I knew it would be quicker than driving the windy roads." He reached for my hand, "I ran so fast, Erica. When something was in my way I'd just jump it, sometimes yards at a time. It was…amazing." I could see in Derrick's eyes the wonder of the experience.

After a brief pause he continued. "I ran as fast as I could. I saw the cougar on the rock, but I couldn't see you. She was watching something, the something I needed to save, waiting to pounce. I saw her tail twitch. She was ready. But I was still too far. Before I knew what had happened I was on four feet, racing through the woods. I leapt for her. We crashed into the brush. I didn't want to kill her, I tried not to hurt her, but she wouldn't stop attacking me. Then I realized she couldn't hurt me. I let her tear at me, scream at me in frustration. Eventually she gave up and left."

Derrick took a deep breath. I tried to catch his eye, but he wouldn't look at me. He stared into the backyard as he spoke. "I went back to the trail, searching for what it was that brought me there. I still sensed you were in danger, but I had no idea what you looked like, if you were human. I...I changed back into myself but had no clothes. I figured I should be dressed. I ran back down to my truck. I always have a spare pair of jeans. It really didn't take very long."

Derrick looked at me and attempted to smile. The memory was still vivid to me, probably to him as well. "On my way back, I suddenly had a sense of urgency...but I was close and found you easily, like a magnet to metal. You were an unconscious heap of hair and mud. I went to you. It looked like you fell over the tree,"

"My bag got hung up in the branches," I interrupted. "I think I'd gotten loose but fell knocking myself out." My skin broke out in goose bumps as I remembered the light in my dream, the sense of safety. I really had been close to death.

"You were caked in mud and blood," Derrick said, "but you were alive. I wasn't quite sure what to do. I picked you up, and that was when I realized you were so cold. I didn't feel the cold at all, even with nothing on. But you were like ice. I started a fire. When you woke up, that's when I figured I'd get you to the hospital and let them take care of you. I didn't know what was happening to me, who you were, what I was doing there.

"I was surprised how much stronger I'd become. It was no effort at all to carry you, you were light as a teddy bear," he said finally looking at me. "I never got tired."

"I knew to trust you. I didn't want to fight you," I said, "I was in agony, but not once thought you were going to hurt me." I looked into the depths of his eyes.

"This, whatever it is that's going on," I said, dropping my gaze to the table as I became frightened. "We'll get through it together...right?" If he left and I never saw him again, I'd go crazy.

I felt his hand under my chin. Gently he turned my face to his. Tears spilled down my checks. "Yes," he said wiping them with his thumb. "I will never leave you. I know this sounds crazy, but this whole situation is insane," he paused for a moment and leaned toward me. "I love you and nothing, nothing, can keep me from you." I heard the determination in his voice and saw the truth in his eyes.

"I love you too," I said rejoicing and knowing what was coming. I closed my eyes and felt his warm lips on mine. Our kiss, gentle at first, grew intense. His large hands were on my sides, and guided me to his lap. My hands found their way to his back pulling him closer. His mouth opened slightly. I followed his lead. His taste sparked a desire in me. I adjusted my legs to straddle him.

"Erica," he moaned against my lips. His body was hard and hot. My hands tangled in his hair as his kisses moved to my neck. Derrick's hands found their way inside my shirt. His callused fingers left tingling trails of excitement up and down my back. It was just us for the moment, the confusion of the day gone.

"Erica, we are meant to be," he whispered against my lips.

The phone rang. It was a slight interruption that we ignored, until my mom's voice called from the message machine. "Erica, pick up the phone. I know you're there. Erica. I'm waiting."

Reluctantly I got up. "Hi, Mom," I answered a little out of breath.

"What's wrong?" she asked.

"Oh, I, uh...I just ran downstairs," I lied.

"Well then. I called to let you know we made it to Seattle all right. We took a taxi and are at the hotel. Our room number is 315."

"Okay. Thanks." She was lying too. Mom rarely lied, but I could tell when she did, she always over explained. I figured one of the neighbors, probably the Johnsons, texted them about Derrick's truck.

"Derrick came over a little bit ago. He was able to get off early," I confessed.

"Oh, really. That's...nice. Is there anything you need to tell me about?" she asked.

I was right. Her tone changed. "Well, Derrick had a little accident on the way here and the door to his truck was damaged."

"What happened?" she asked. "Everyone okay?" she asked again before I had a chance to answer.

"A deer hit him," I fibbed, "and no one is hurt." There was awkward silence, until I realized this situation could work to my advantage. "He can't drive though. I don't know how long it will take for him to get it fixed. He might have to stay a few extra days."

"Oh, I don't know, Erica."

"There is the spare room."

"I'm glad everyone is all right. I've gotta go. We can talk about this later," she said. "Goodnight...and be safe."

"Goodnight, Mom, and don't worry about me. Have fun." I said before hanging up.

I looked at Derrick, still sitting in the chair, and smiled. I'd just had my first kiss, and it was fantastic. I wanted to kiss him again, but wasn't sure how to get the process started.

Derrick stood, downing his glass of water in one drink. "That reminds me. I'm going to check on my truck. I got the door in place, but want to make sure it'll hold till morning."

"Okay. Of course," I said turning red. Reality hit me again. There were real issues that needed addressed. I'd also experienced my first vampire attack.

Derrick gave me a crooked smile as he walked to me. He picked me up and gave me a kiss I eagerly accepted. Leaving me a little breathless, he set me down and went outside through the kitchen door that led to the garage. I listened as the garage door opened, still in a daze.

My stomach growled. I realized I hadn't really eaten since breakfast, and whatever had been in my stomach was gone. I was starving. I found some spaghetti in the fridge. While dinner warmed in the microwave I set the table for two. Waiting for him, I wondered if Derrick might need some help.

I found him working on his truck in the driveway. The street lamp and garage provided enough light to see. The door was back in its place. "Is it fixed?" I asked.

"No. I'm just trying to get it to stay put. I'll have to get in and out through the passenger door."

"I guess you're a lot stronger than you thought," I said, observing the mangled metal that sort of resembled a door. I noticed where the door had been ripped off of its hinges. The window was gone.

Derrick let out a deep sigh. "That'll have to do until I can find a new one." He didn't sound satisfied with the results. He started putting his tools into a small black metal toolbox. I handed him the last tool, a wrench from the ground.

"Hungry?" I asked following him around the truck, watching him slip the toolbox behind the seat.

"Starving."

"Good. Let's go eat."

Back inside, he washed his hands at the kitchen sink. Then we ate.

"This is really good," Derrick said taking a second helping.

"Thanks, but I can't take the credit. Mom made it."

We avoided the subject that hung in the air. I think we both needed a little more time to let the madness sink in, or at least I did. I wanted to be able to talk to Derrick without freaking out too much.

After dinner he helped me clean up. Then we sat outside on

the patio, watching moths swarm the porch light. I was exhausted, physically and emotionally drained. But I was not going to bed before Derrick explained, even though I was terrified by what he might say.

I slapped at a mosquito when Derrick spoke, "Erica, I think we should probably talk about earlier."

I nodded, not sure if I was ready to hear what he had to say or not, but determined to try.

Derrick's face turned hard. "I'm not sure where to begin, but since you saw me change, I think it is okay to tell you everything. Screw the Council's permission."

I flinched from the intensity of his sudden anger. I felt tension radiating from him as his body stiffened.

"I'm kind of pissed at myself that I listened to them, waiting to talk to you. If I would have just told you sooner, then, well maybe things would have been different, and you'd have been prepared. They were worried you wouldn't believe me. That if I told you too much too soon, it'd risk our tribe's safety. But since now you've seen *me* and a *vampire*. I don't really care what they think."

"Derrick," I said softly, "if I hadn't seen the vampire or watched you change, I don't think I would have believed you."

"That was why I hesitated telling you anything. I didn't want you to run for the woods, writing me off as a psycho." Derrick stopped for a moment and let out a long sigh, his shoulders relaxing. "I could have changed in front of you. I could have prepared you. Maybe you wouldn't have gotten hurt. Erica, if I'd have been a minute longer…"

"But you weren't. You were there in time," I said ready to argue. "It wasn't your fault."

"You're actually taking this all in pretty well. I'm kind of surprised you're not sitting in a corner babbling to yourself."

I smiled. Derrick had no idea how close I was to losing it. Watching him, marveling in his extraordinary ability, had helped. I loved him and he loved me, and as long as I focused on that, I told myself I could handle anything.

"You ready?" Derrick asked.

I nodded, knowing it was really him who was finally ready.

"This is a long story. Maybe we should move into the house. You look like you're a little cold," he said helping me to my feet.

He was right. I was getting cold. "You're not at all cold... hot or cold doesn't bother you?"

"No, I seem to be fine in any temperature."

I followed him into the house wondering how it would feel never to be cold or hot. I couldn't decide if it would be a blessing or curse. Past the dining room I took the lead and led Derrick to the living room.

Before we left Albuquerque, my parents had a huge moving sale. They sold basically everything besides our bedroom sets. Mom kept her great grandmother's Birdseye Maple seven piece set she'd inherited, and I kept my simple mismatched furniture. They'd offered to buy me bedroom furniture when we arrived to our new house. But I was attached to my stuff, and I wanted to have something familiar in an unfamiliar place. Mom decorated the new house with vintage Victorian pieces. The den had a huge flat screen TV and microfiber couch, my dad's only contribution to the decorating scheme.

As soon as I saw the firm sofa in the living room, I decided we should be more comfortable. I led Derrick to the den. We sunk into the brown couch. I leaned over to the table lamp and flipped it on before I curled up next to Derrick. He shifted his body so that he could see my face.

"Do you remember when I told you my people had legends?" Derrick asked.

"Yes," I nodded.

"Well, when the British came to our lands, they brought with them more than disease and hardship. They brought with them demons...what we now call vampires.

"The vampires feasted on our people because their blood was pure and free from pollution...free from disease. I'm not a very good story teller, but let me tell you the legend as I've been told," he said.

"Okay," I answered, nervous.

"Before the settlers our tribes would band with brother tribes to fight against larger common enemies, to protect our lands, women, and children. The Washtucna Tribe was large and strong. We had respect. The rivers were full of fish, mountains plenty with game, and bushes ripe with berries.

"We lived in peace for many, many years." Derrick shifted and pulled me closer. He cleared his throat before starting again.

"One early spring morning our people received a messenger named Yellow-Arm from the Colville Tribe, our closest neighbor. Yellow-Arm was exhausted. He could barely speak. He'd run all night, fifty miles, up over Chewelah Peak..."

"The mountain you found me on?" I interrupted.

"Yes, the same," he answered before continuing. "Yellow-Arm was finally able to tell of a foreign enemy that was headed east. Their Medicine Man saw in a vision an attack by a great unknown evil and that the Washtucna tribe held the only hope to end this evil. Within an hour our warriors were on their way. Many of them had never fought before and were eager to prove themselves. But they were too late. When they got to the Colville village, it was burned to the ground. Bodies were torn to pieces and scattered across the village. Yellow-Arm screamed in grief as he spotted a woman's detached hand still clutching a dagger. He grabbed the hand and stabbed himself in the heart, holding the hand to his chest while he died. It was the hand of his wife.

"The Washtucna warriors returned home quickly, running the entire night, but again they were too late. Our camp had been attacked. Some of the people escaped into the forest...maybe a hundred. Only a quarter of what had been. The survivors told the warriors that they were attacked at night by men and women with fangs like snakes, skin of the dead, and haunting red eyes. They told that the attackers were demons. They were too strong, too quick, and too evil to be anything but."

I watched him speak, his expressions and voice revealing the intensity of the story. It was as if he had lived through the experience, the pain and anger fresh in his eyes.

"They told the warriors how the demons tore at their loved ones flesh, ripping them apart as they drank their blood." Derrick abruptly stopped talking. I felt his heart hammering against his chest. A growl escaped his throat.

"Derrick," I said, "are you okay?" There was something wrong.

"I'm fine, just...just give me a sec to focus," he answered, standing to pace the room.

It was only a few minutes, him walking back and forth breathing deeply, before he sat back down pulling me to him again.

"I can feel it in me when I think about them, the vampires. I feel the cougar wanting to emerge," he said. "I really have to concentrate to settle it down sometimes."

"You're okay then?" I asked, placing my hand on over his heart, feeling its more normal rhythm.

"I am," he said. "Ready for the rest?"

"Yes," I whispered.

"Are you sure? You know this is a lot for one person to take in all at once, Erica. It took me changing forms to believe this story. I'm worried about you."

"It is a lot. But I deserve to know what's going on. So finish," I said with a little more force than I meant to.

Derrick didn't seem to notice, or didn't mind, as he started where he'd left off.

"The Chief's son, Sikyahonaw, was now Chief, because his father was one of those killed in the raid. Sikyahonaw was driven mad with grief and anger. His tribe's Medicine Man was one of those who had been spared, and he pleaded with him to call upon the spirit guides to help avenge the massacre.

"The Medicine Man meditated and asked his spirit guide for help. The next night he performed a huge ceremony using all those who remained of the tribe. He called upon the highest of all the spirits to help Sikyahonaw's spirit guide...to give him the power and skill to kill the demons and protect the people.

"After the ceremony, Sikyahonaw transformed into a huge blond Kodiak bear, larger than any had ever seen. He roared and ripped apart trees. The tribe was scared and they hid in the forest. When morning came, they found Sikyahonaw naked next to the smoldering fire asleep. When he woke he told the people the spirits had given him a great gift. He could take the shape of his spirit guide. But on the full moon, he would take the form of a demon hunter.

"It would be several days before the next full moon. Sikyahonaw practiced his phasing from bear to man. Sikyahonaw's strength and senses increased as a man. He had the warriors fight him in his human body, sometimes all at once, but he never received a scratch.

"During the night of the full moon, Sikyahonaw waited for the moon to show itself. When it did, he took the form of a Mingan, or Werewolf. He hunted the vampires by following their scent. He traveled like lightening, racing to find them."

I flinched in surprise. Werewolf? When did they come into this? I opened my mouth to ask, but Derrick started talking.

"It didn't take long for Sikyahonaw to find the demons. Not only was their scent strong, they had slaughtered everything in their path, leaving a rotting trail of flesh and bone. Once Sikyahonaw came across fresh kills, he knew he was close.

"Sikyahonaw found the demons when the full moon was at its highest. There were a dozen of them, dressed in leather and fur, taking the clothes from those they killed. At first the demons didn't fear the werewolf. They even mocked Sikyahonaw before attacking him.

"Sikyahonaw was overtaken by his primal instinct to kill. He ripped them apart. Some demons tried to flee, but he tracked them down and killed them, until there was only one left. Sikyahonaw saved this last one. He forced it to talk and learned that the demons had one creator called Master who made them through his bite. That the small band of demons crossed the ocean on a ship to search the new land. They feasted on Native people because their blood was pure, unlike any they had before. Sikyahonaw tortured this last demon to keep it talking. When dawn broke and the sunlight hit it, the demon burst into flames.

"Sikyahonaw changed back to his human form. He could still smell the stench of the demons he'd killed. He followed the scent and found the demon pieces putting themselves back together, at least the parts that had not been burned from the sun. Sikyahonaw searched for all the remaining body parts as he retraced his trail, placing them in the sunlight. By the time he made it back to his first demon kill, it had completely reformed and escaped.

"Sikyahonaw vowed not to return home until he'd killed that demon. Sikyahonaw traveled through villages tracking it. He spread the word of the demons to other tribes and how to protect their people through spirits. When they wouldn't believe him, all he had to do was change into his spirit guide form.

"During his travel Sikyahonaw found a wife, who waited for his return while he tracked the demon. Finally the full moon appeared and Sikyahonaw changed into the Werewolf. He found the last demon on a ship bound to cross the ocean, going back to its Master. Sikyahonaw killed it and returned home with his new bride. Sikyahonaw had many children and his people rebuilt their village. The demons never came back."

I waited making sure Derrick was finished before saying, "Until now."

"Until now," he agreed running his fingers through my hair.

"Was Sikyahonaw related to you?"

"Yes, he was my father's father by six generations. His first son with his new wife was able to make the transformation, and a couple generations after him. But since then, I am the first to change into the body of my spirit guide for over a hundred years."

Derrick paused before explaining, "The Chief presides over the Council, kind of like a strong mayor over a city council. My dad was Chief of our tribe. When he was killed, I was too young to take his place. As I get older, I learn more, and eventually the Council will place me as Chief."

"Do you want to be Chief?" I asked curious.

"It isn't as simple as *want*," he struggled to explain. "It is part of my responsibility, of who I am. I love my people and want to see us succeed, to keep our heritage and culture while adjusting to the world around us."

He held me as what he said sank in. Tired, I laid my head on his chest, listening to his heart. "Do you change into a werewolf too?" I asked, already knowing the answer.

"A few days after I changed into the mountain lion, there was a full moon. I transformed into a werewolf, just like the legend said I would. I started to hunt automatically, and came across a vampire scent down by Oregon. I didn't find the vampire and it was hard for me to leave the trail, but I was able to come back home. The Council wants me to be careful until we learn more. They don't want me to track vampires yet. They want to ask the spirits for guidance and talk to other tribes to see if they have had any problems. They're worried about a trap."

"I wonder what this all has to do with me?" I asked through a yawn., Before he could answer I asked, "Does it hurt? Can you transform whenever you want?"

"No it doesn't hurt. It feels...weird, like popping your joints. When I change back into my human form my skin is a little itchy, but that's all. I've practiced, and have way better control over changing into my spirit guide form. I didn't try to fight the werewolf experience. I just went with it. It felt like the moon was charging me somehow, filling me with its energy. The Council, my sister and mom watched. They said I scared them...that the very sight of me would send an army running." He smiled as he spoke.

I felt his body tense. "But I don't know if I could keep myself under control around vampires, not after what just happened. Earlier my instincts took over when I killed that thing. *I* didn't know what to do, but my *spirit guide* knew exactly the right places to bite and tear.

"The Council told me other tribes learned that vampires could only be killed through burning them, either with sunlight or fire, and that every last piece had to be destroyed or they would find a way to put what they could back together then dig underground and hibernate until their bodies grew back."

I shuddered at the thought. But that explained why Derrick burned Frederick with gas. There really weren't anymore sun spots.

"What's the difference?" I asked, not sure why he'd be a mountain lion except on the full moons. "I mean, if you can kill them in your spirit guide form, why do you change into a werewolf?"

"It is said that the Moon Spirit was upset that vampires come out only at night making people afraid of the dark. She consulted with the Great Spirit, and it was agreed that on the full moon, we'd have extra power fed by her...the Moon Spirit, but only on the full moon when her power is at its greatest. When I was the werewolf, the instinct to hunt was so intense...I had to go. Like when I had to find you," he explained.

"Derrick" I asked, "why would a vampire come here now, especially after so long?"

"I have no idea. I just hope I can protect my people...and you."

He pulled me up to him, kissing me softly on the lips. We snuggled on the couch, kissing and holding each other.

"You tired?" I asked through another yawn.

"I could go to sleep."

I gave him a tour of the house, showing him the spare room where he'd be sleeping. The spare room was sparsely decorated with white walls, a blue comforter and matching curtains.

I got ready for bed while he grabbed his bag from his truck. Lucky for him, he packed his stuff the night before. He planned on coming over straight from work, just like I'd hoped. I sat on my bed hoping I could stay awake long enough to tell him "goodnight".

Apparently I had spaced out because he startled me when I noticed him suddenly at my door, watching me. I wondered how long he'd been there, but only for a moment. As he began walking to me, eager goose-bumps covered my skin and my heart began to race.

He sat on the bed next to me and leaned in slowly, his scent and arms soon engulfing me. We shared a kiss more passionate than any we'd had yet, a kiss that kept us busy for several minutes.

"I'd better go," he said in a ragged whisper against my lips.

"Yes, you probably should," I answered breathlessly, even though my body hungered for more.

With a sigh, he stood and took his turn in the bathroom. I

braided my hair before lying in bed. I always liked the way the braid left my hair wavy after sleeping on it all night, and thought Derrick might like it too. I listened to the hum of the shower while I lay in bed realizing I'd have to be careful how I placed my head, my scalp was tender and sore. I heard the water shut off, and I listened to the squeaking of the floorboards as Derrick made his way to the bedroom across the hall.

I was exhausted, but sleep didn't come easily. And when I did finally fall asleep, I dreamt of Frederick in horrible gory nightmares. He was the demon in Derrick's story, tearing apart Yellow-Arm's wife and all those other helpless people. I woke myself from one nightmare screaming as Frederick tore me apart. Derrick must have heard because he was in my room holding me tight, telling me I was safe as I woke. I did feel safe in his arms, so he held me the rest of the night while we slept together in my tiny bed.

I woke before Derrick and was able to slip from between his arms without waking him. I made my way to the bathroom and freshened up before going to the kitchen to make some breakfast. My hair was wavy just like I'd hoped. After poking around, my scalp was a little tender but not nearly as bad as I thought it would be. I still had my scratches and cuts, which were also sore. Even though it was going to be warm, loose jeans and a long sleeve tee-shirt were a perfect option for the day.

I looked forward to making Derrick breakfast. I made pancakes and brewed a pot of coffee. Derrick came down to the kitchen just as I finished setting the table. I could smell him before I heard him, his heady scent calling to me.

I looked his way and had to do a double take when I saw him. He entered the kitchen wearing only dark cotton plaid pajama pants. His hair hung loose around his shoulders, slightly mussed. His chiseled chest and arms were glowing in the morning sun. My eyes followed his stomach to his hip line that disappeared beneath the waist of his pants. I resisted the urge to attack him.

"Good morning," I said seating him at the breakfast table and placed the full plate of food in front of him. I sat next to him with the same food, but a much smaller amount.

"This looks great," he said digging in. "Thanks."

I had to give myself a pat on the back. It did taste good. Maybe I inherited one of my mom's talents after all. I did help her a lot in the kitchen, so it made sense. Derrick and I were both hungry and ate our breakfast in silence. When we were done, he helped me with the dishes.

"So, what's the plan for today?" I asked nervously.

"Well, I think I'll search for a new door, if that's cool with you?"

"Sure, you can use the computer in the den, or I can get my laptop. Whatever you want."

"I can use the one in the den," he said pulling me into his arms. He gave me a long enticing kiss tasting of maple syrup and coffee, a kiss that I eagerly accepted.

The moment was interrupted by the phone, which I finally

answered when I heard my mom's voice calling for me from the answering machine, "Erica...its Mom...Are you there?"

"Hi, Mom. How's Hawaii?"

"Oh we haven't left Seattle yet. Our flight was delayed. Is Derrick still there?" she asked.

"Yes, Mom," I smiled after him as Derrick left the kitchen.

"How's it going?" she pried.

"Great, we hung out on the couch last night. Um, I'm not sure what we're going to do today."

"Okay. Just checking in. Dad sends his love. We'll call again when we get there"

"You guys have fun and don't worry about me. I'm fine," I said before hanging up.

After I finished getting ready for the day, I found Derrick in the den searching the net. I quietly watched as he looked for a door. He was in luck because one of the local salvage yards happened to have the door he needed. He bought the door with his credit card and we planned to take my car to pick it up the next morning since they were closed on Sundays.

I fiddled with some books pretending to be busy as I worked up the nerve to ask him some more questions, questions I didn't think of until that morning, after my nightmares.

"Derrick, can I ask you something?" I tried to keep my voice calm.

"Sure," he said raising one eyebrow slightly higher than the other.

"Well. I'm not quite sure how to ask so I'm just going to be blunt. Can you be killed?" My voice cracked and my throat tightened, the worst of last night's nightmares coming back to haunt me.

He seriously thought about my question before he answered. "In my human form I think I can, but not easily. My reflexes are faster, my strength is ten times what it was if not more, and my senses help me stay alert. I don't think I can be killed while I'm in my spirit guide form or as a werewolf, but I don't know for sure."

"How about yesterday? How did you know where to find me? How were you able to show up at just the right moment?" I barely noticed the tears falling from my eyes.

He walked to me and I buried my face into his chest holding him tightly. "I was so afraid you'd be killed when I heard your truck. I was terrified for you. Afraid I'd watch you die. Die because of me," I sobbed.

Gently, he pushed me back by my shoulders and I looked up into his deep dark eyes. "I would die for you Erica. If you were killed, I'd be lost. I don't know if I could survive without you," he pulled me back into his chest. "It's like the closer we get to one another, the deeper the connection."

We held each other tight as he explained. "I was at work and had a vision that you were in danger. I could actually see your face full of fear. Again, I knew that something terrible was about to happen. I tried to call, but you didn't answer your home or cell phone.

"I was in my truck and on the road within a few seconds. I didn't even clock out. I drove so fast pushing my truck to its limit. I think I did a hundred-and-fifteen all the way here. I was lucky traffic wasn't heavy because I blew through a couple lights. It was like before...I knew where you were, even though I had never been there. I found the trail and didn't even slow down. I knew I was getting close and that you were about, well to be hurt"

I had a few more questions but decided they could wait. I let out an embarrassed giggle when we finally let go of each other, his blue tee-shirt had a large wet spot from where my tears soaked into it.

"Sorry," I apologized. He just grinned.

We spent the rest of the day inside, not really doing much besides being near one another. For me, I needed to make sure I wasn't having a dream that I'd wake from. I was still having a hard time believing everything that had happened. That night Derrick spent the night in my bed again, holding me while we slept.

CHAPTER 9

The next morning I drove us to the wrecking yard. They had Derrick's door waiting for him at the front office, so it was a fast trip. We swung by an auto parts store where he bought a few more things. Then we were back at my house.

He took off the damaged door and threw it into the bed of his truck. I mowed the yard while he worked. When I finished, I sat in the grass watching him, helping him when he needed it. Before long he had the new, used door in place.

"Good job," I said.

The door looked like it belonged there, except that it was a burnt orange color that clashed heavily with the shiny black paint covering rest of the truck.

"I'll paint it at home," Derrick said more to himself as he sat down next to me.

"You painted your truck?" I asked, a little surprised.

"Yeah, my mom bought me this truck when I turned sixteen. It was pretty beat up, but it ran. I pulled out a few dents, jacked it up a couple of feet, added some bells-and-whistles and a coat of paint. Only took me a summer," he said proudly.

My dad always took our cars to the shop. I don't think he even changed the oil. I had a sense of pride that my boyfriend was not only some sort of superhero, he was also a mechanic.

We headed back in the house just in time to hear the phone ring. I answered knowing it could only be one person, "Hi, Mom."

"Oh Sweetie, it is so nice here. You are coming next time. The weather is great, and the hotel is perfect." Her voice was happy as she chattered away.

"That's great, Mom," I said when she finally gave me a turn to talk.

"Well, I was just checking in, letting you know we finally made it. I'd better go. Our table just became available. Love you and call me if you need to."

"Love you too, Mom. Tell Dad, 'hi'," I said waiting for her to bring up Derrick's name.

"I will. Bye, Sweetie," she said.

"Bye," I said hanging up, a little surprised. Maybe they were finally accepting I was a big girl.

"How long have they been married?" Derrick asked.

"Um, twenty-five years," I answered making a mental note to send them an e-card to their cell phones on the special day. They were going to spend their actual anniversary in Hawaii since they postponed their trip. Originally, Mom was going to have an anniversary party at the house. But I think Dad liked the way things turned out, that they were spending their special day alone instead of with a house full of guests.

"That's cool. My mom and dad were married right out of high school...They were high school sweethearts," his voice melancholy.

"I'm sorry about your dad...You must really miss him," I said, not quite sure I should have.

"Yeah, it's been twelve years since the accident. From what I remember he was a good dad. He took me fishing and hunting. He worked hard at the mill, and worked even harder for the tribe." There was a touch of sadness in his voice.

I gave him a hug, which he returned before going back out to fiddle with his truck. I figured he wanted to be alone for a while.

Later that day I went to work in my mom's flower garden while Derrick surfed the net inside. Apparently our internet was much faster than at his house, so he wanted to research vampire legends. Weeding was one of my new chores, which I didn't mind. I found it relaxing. I guess I've always liked to play in the dirt, or so my mom would say.

I was off in thoughts of me and Derrick, his story of Sikyahonaw, how he came to be, who he was, what he was. I was startled out of my daydreaming when I heard Derrick say, "Please don't stop. Your voice...your voice is amazing."

I was shocked that he was there. And by the look of it, he'd been there for a little while, watching me. He was sitting on one of the patio chairs with his legs up and a half empty glass of water.

"What?" I asked a little confused.

"The song you were singing. Erica, you have the voice of

a...an angel," he said, "I had no idea you could sing like that."

It took me a minute to figure out what he was talking about. Then I realized I had been singing a tune, something I tended to do when cleaning the house, washing dishes and I guess gardening.

"Was I singing?" I asked turning red. "How long have you been there?"

"Long enough. I wouldn't have said anything, but you stopped. I want to hear more." His face lit with a sexy grin.

"I don't remember what I was singing. Besides, I couldn't now anyway, not with you watching me."

With a frown he begged, "Pleeease."

I got up and walked to him, the knees of my jeans dirty, and I sat on his lap. I placed my gardening gloves on the table and kissed him.

"I'm not really that great," I said.

"You don't give yourself enough credit. Seriously, why can't you ever take a compliment? You are absolutely gorgeous, and you have the most beautiful voice I've ever heard."

A little defensive I said, "Sorry, I guess it's hard for me to hear those things. I've never thought of myself as...pretty, and definitely not talented. I've always..." I hesitated. I didn't know how to say how I felt without sounding pathetic, "I've always thought of myself as ordinary, boring. And, I guess I've always known I'm kind of a nerd when it comes to books and school." Sports were never my forte. I was way too clumsy.

"What about your voice?" Derrick asked encouraging me to

talk more about myself, a subject I'd rather avoid.

"Um, I guess in grade school the music teacher wanted me to sing, but I had stage fright. At the yearly Christmas concert I'd always freeze up. I'd just stand there feeling sick." I remembered being six, standing in front of the choir at the microphone, frozen. The other kids yelled at me to sing. The music teacher never to asked me to do a solo again.

"Can you please sing something for me, just for a minute...so that I can hear you a little more?" His eyes were giving me a puppy-dog look. He even folded his hands together like he was begging.

"But really, I don't remember what I was singing," I objected.

"It sounded like a waltz or something. You weren't saying any words. It was just tones, just a beautiful mix of humming and tones."

I tried to think of an excuse, any excuse to get out of it, but I couldn't. I decided to suck-it-up and give it a try. Finally I decided on a song that reminded me of Cinderella dancing at the ball, since I felt like Derrick was my Prince Charming. I took a deep breath and blushed as I started. But after I got going, it wasn't so bad, except trying to focus on the melody. Derrick wrapped his arms around me and held me while I sang to him. I figured we looked ridiculous, but I didn't really care, which was nice. When I finished, Derrick clapped and I blushed even deeper.

"Do you really like to hear me sing?" I was skeptical.

"Yes," he said kissing my neck until his lips found mine. Derrick softly asked, "You have absolutely no idea how beautiful you are...do you?"

I looked away as heat flooded my face. I wouldn't call myself beautiful, especially compared to him. He gently lifted my chin and stared deep into my eyes. "You *are* beautiful, Erica," he whispered as he tucked a loose piece of hair behind my ear. A tear rolled down my cheek. He kissed it away. I tasted the salt when his lips found mine. I was the luckiest girl in the world.

The next couple of days were great. We spent a day at Riverfront Park, Spokane's main downtown public park. We had a fun lazy day of people watching and feeding the ducks. We went on a gondola ride in a glass cabin that took us over the Spokane Falls. It was a little unsettling watching the angry water crashing against the rocks just below my feet. The idea of plummeting to my death was a constant impression until we were back on land, after which I thought the experience was pretty cool. We went to an arcade where we raced each other in go-carts, which Derrick won, and played a round of miniature golf, that I won.

We spent our time together talking, laughing, and just hanging out. In the evening we'd watch a movie or spend time together out on the patio. We were inseparable. Instead of getting sick of each other, it was the complete opposite. We couldn't spend enough time together. At night we slept in my bed talking until the wee hours of the morning with lots of kissing interruptions before finally falling asleep.

It was Wednesday night and we were waiting for a table at Luigi's, the best Italian restaurant in the area. We sat on an iron bench outside the building. The smell of fresh bread, garlic and steak was making my mouth water as I looked through the takeout menu to pass the time. I had just narrowed my possibilities down to three dishes when I heard a familiar laugh. I turned and easily spotted Sarah in the crowd leaning against the building.

"Dimples?" Sarah mouthed, catching my eye.

"Hey, Sarah," I said as she made her way toward us. She was pulling Larry behind her.

"Oh my God, it's so good to see you," she squealed giving me a hug. She smelled like coconut and her blond hair was in a loose French braid. I hugged her back being careful not to get poked by her many earrings. She was dressed less flamboyantly than I remembered...neither Goth nor EMO, more normal but still in a way that drew attention. I couldn't help but notice her Coach purse and Miu Miu boots. I remembered the boots from a Nordstrom catalogue she had showed me at the coffee stand, black with embroidered red roses. They were over a thousand dollars. I'd have bet her tiny sequined outfit was designer as well.

"You remember Larry," she said stepping back so he could step in.

"I don't think we ever officially met," said Larry in a deep velvety voice. His brown hair was thick and wavy. He still reminded me of Tom Cruise. He wore a casual black silk suit with a silver tie. He reached out his hand for me to shake. Before I was able to take it,

Derrick stood and took Larry's hand instead. I noticed a barcode tattoo on the inside of his wrist. It seemed familiar, but I couldn't recall why.

"Derrick," Derrick said in a "don't mess with me if you know what's good for you," voice.

Derrick was taller and outweighed Larry by at least fifty pounds. Not seeming surprised, or offended, Larry said, "Larry." They shook hands and stepped back. Sarah sat down next to me taking Derrick's spot. I felt the tension in the air.

Unfazed, Sarah said, "I can't believe we ran into you. How are you?"

"Umm, pretty good I guess," I said a little nervous.

"Devealson, party of two," called the restaurant hostess.

"Oh, that's us," said Sarah. Devealson must have been Larry's last name because Sarah's was Thompson.

"You two should sit with us," said Sarah. "There is so much for us to catch up on."

"Oh, um, I don't know," I said. Noticing Derrick's posture, I didn't think it would be a good idea. Before I could say anything Sarah yelled to the hostess, "Make that a party of four." Standing, she took my hand and began pulling me after her. Once through the door, the four of us were handed off to a beautiful olive skinned brunette wearing a red Luigi's polo and black slacks. "Please follow me," she said with a slight Italian accent.

We followed in single file as she weaved us between full tables to an empty one in the back corner of the small restaurant.

Every table was round topped with a white tablecloth, delicate china, silver and a small lamp. The dim lighting provided a romantic ambiance.

"Can I bring you anything to drink?" asked the server after handing each of us a leather bound menu.

"A bottle of your best Merlot," said Larry.

I looked at Sarah. Neither of us was old enough to drink, nor was Derrick. Sarah mouthed the words, "It's okay," and gave me a wink.

Before the server turned to leave, Sarah was giving me the rundown on her life since Larry moved to Spokane. They have tons in common and are in love. They plan on spending a couple weeks in Las Vegas at the end of the month. Sarah explained that Larry was extremely wealthy, that the whole working at Joe's Hot Shots was a ploy to make sure Sarah wouldn't be after his money. Neither one of them were working at the moment. After their vacation they planned to move back to Larry's estate in Seattle. Derrick and Larry sat in silence. Derrick wore a scowl and Larry a smug smile, probably proud of how Sarah elaborated on his affluence. Sarah was able to get all that information out before the Italian beauty arrived with the wine and to take our orders.

Sarah and I ordered the lasagna. Derrick ordered steak. Larry ordered the prime rib special, "I like it rare," he said.

Once the server left, there was an awkward silence at our table. The only noise was the chatter of other restaurant patrons and the clinking of silverware on china.

"So, what's new with you?" Sarah asked abruptly.

"You remember the guy who rescued me when I fell on the mountain?" I said. "Well, this is him." I smiled looking at Derrick, reaching for his hand under the table. I was surprised to see the hardness on his face. He took my hand, but something was wrong.

"Oh yeah. I remember. So you two hooked up after all," Sarah said with a smile. "What do your parents think?"

I was a little shocked she brought them up at all. "They're fine I guess."

"How long will they be in Haw...?" she stopped herself and promptly took a drink of her wine, changing the subject slightly. "You have anything planned this summer?" I noticed her head beading with sweat, even though it was cool in the restaurant. Larry was silent, watching us from behind his glass of wine.

Derrick stood helping me to my feet. While still holding my hand he answered, "She is spending the summer with me."

I followed as he led me from the table. Glancing back I saw a shocked Sarah, her mouth open watching us leave. Larry sat there, not a look of concern on his face until my eyes met his, and then he smiled and winked at me.

"What's wrong?" I asked Derrick once we were in his truck. He pulled into traffic before answering.

"There is something wrong with him...with Larry," Derrick said. "Sarah too. I'm sorry, Erica, but I had to get you out of there."

"It didn't feel right to me either," I said. "Sarah was off. I mean she's always been a chatterbox." Then it hit me, "How did she know my parents are in Hawaii?" Last time we spoke I'd told her they rescheduled their vacation, but I didn't tell her when. That was why she was acting nervous. "What the hell, Derrick. Why would Sarah be keeping tabs on my parents?"

"I don't know, but something is definitely wrong with those two," he said. I watched him for a moment and could tell he was calming down. His shoulders relaxed and his grip on the steering wheel loosened.

He pulled onto a main road which was full of businesses and fast food restaurants.

"Hungry?" he asked.

"Very."

"How about a Big Mac?"

"Sure," I smiled. It wasn't the romantic dinner we planned, but just being with Derrick was good enough for me. He had to go to work early the next morning and was on the schedule the next couple of days, but then he had Sunday and the entire following week off. Derrick requested to use his vacation, and his boss gave him the go-ahead to start the following Monday. Since tonight was our last night together for a while, we wanted to make it special.

Pulling into the parking lot, we could see into the restaurant through the large windows. It looked as if all the tables where full and kids were running wild from one end to the other. We went through the drive-thru, and took our food back to my house.

"That was pretty good," I said throwing away the garbage.

"Good ol' Mickey D's," Derrick said coming up behind me. It

was night outside and I saw him through the reflection of the window. He saw me too, and smiled before turning me around.

I looked up at him, into his dark eyes, and as if he were reading my mind, he bent to kiss me. His lips were soft on mine at first, but our kissing grew harder. My heart raced and a soft moan escaped my lips. He lifted me onto the counter with his lips on my throat sucking and kissing.

My hands were behind his head, my finger entangled in his soft black hair. I moved my legs to wrap around and pull him to me. His breathing heavy, he pulled my hips to him. I felt him against me growing with desire. His hungry lips were back on mine.

Suddenly aware the windows were open and it was light inside, I breathed, "We should go upstairs."

Without taking his lips off mine and with me still wrapped around him, he picked me up and carried me up the stairs. He pushed the door open with his foot and laid me on my bed. I pulled him down to me.

My hands were under his shirt, slowly caressing his back and sides. Suddenly he stood and took off his shirt. I sat up, my hands around his lower back as I kissed his hard stomach. He reached down and I let him slip my shirt off as he gently pushed me back with his body and lay on top of me.

"Oh, Erica," he moaned. "You are so beautiful." His hand was at the top of my shorts. I could feel him fiddling with the button. Soon I felt the button open and the waist of my pants loosen. My hands shot down to stop him from going further.

"I can't," I said, embarrassed. I wanted to. He was everything I wanted and I was burning with desire, but I just couldn't.

Derrick rested his head on my chest, his breathing ragged. He kissed my chest before rolling over onto his back.

"I'm sorry," I whispered.

"Don't be."

"Does it bother you that I want to wait?" I was nervous asking him this question. I knew he loved me. I never felt any anger or frustration from him when I let him know to stop. This was the farthest we'd ever been, but I was too embarrassed and scared to let him go farther, even though I wanted him to.

I rested my head on his chest waiting for an answer, listening and feeling his heart pound deep inside.

"No," he said in a husky voice. "Actually, I think I want to wait too."

His answer took me off guard. "Really?" I asked lifting my head to look at his face, to make sure he was being serious.

"This may be a shock to you," he said as a grin spread across his face, "but I've never...um. What I mean is that...well, I've never gone all the way."

I was stunned, which must have showed on my face because he began to laugh.

"You can pick your jaw up off the ground...now," he teased.

"Oh, wow," I whispered. I had just assumed he'd be more experienced. He was older, but only by a year and a half. But he was so hot. He had to have had plenty of opportunities.

Derrick obviously noticed my confusion because he took a deep breath, "I've gone out with girls. But it was always the same. I'd usually get setup on a blind date. We'd have dinner and talk, but nothing more ever happened. It didn't feel right, and I couldn't force it, although I did try once. I went out with this one girl. I think I was seventeen...anyway we made out in my truck. I went with it, telling myself I should just man-up, but it felt wrong. I think I made her mad when I told her we needed to stop. It took a while for her to talk to me again. But now she's married with a kid, and we're cool." He pulled me closer to his face and whispered against my lips, "I guess I've been waiting for you."

I met his lips with mine and kissed him hard and deep. I shifted my body over his with my legs straddling his waist. Everything for me was new, all these experiences, but knowing Derrick was a virgin too; well, that was just a total turn-on. He sat up and softly caressed my neck and chest with his warm soft lips.

"Erica," he whispered close to my ear, "marry me."

I froze. "What?" I squeaked, taken aback for a second time within ten minutes, but this was much more surprising. Maybe I misunderstood. "What did you say?"

"Marry me," he said sitting up, with me still on his lap.

I felt sick to my stomach realizing I heard him right the first time. Slowly he lifted me off him, and moved to sit on the chair at my desk. He simply sat there and waited, watching me as I tried to digest what just happened.

"Erica, I love you and you love me...right?"

"Yes," I whispered. I'd had fun playing house the last several days. I liked to cook for him, do all the stuff a wife might do, but get married?

"I know it's soon, too soon actually, but I can feel it in my entire being, my heart, body, and soul, that we're meant to be together. I've never been so sure of anything before in my life. I need you like I need air to breathe. I've been thinking about us a lot lately. And I was going to have a ring and flowers...but now felt like the right moment."

He walked over and knelt on the floor in front of me, taking my hand in his. In a loving voice and glossy eyes he said, "I love you and I want to spend the rest of my life with you. I want to make you happy and grow old with you. I want a home with a white picket fence and a yard full of kids if that is what you want. My whole motivation for living is to make you happy. I've never felt so whole, so at home, as when I'm with you. Please, Erica, be my wife... Will you marry me?"

"Um, I...m- m-marriage?" I stuttered.

Which was not what he'd hoped I'd say because in a more serious tone he answered, "Yes, marriage. I love you and I want to be with you *every* day." Then slowly Derrick moved next to me on the bed. Reserved, he said, "You don't have to say yes."

"It's not that I don't want to be with you," I said moving onto his lap, wrapping my arms around his neck. "You know I love you. You took me off guard," I whispered as I moved closer to kiss him. He wasn't responsive, which hurt.

He got up from the bed and left without saying a word. I heard the door to the spare room shut. I was dumbfounded. I didn't know what to do. I loved him, but wasn't sure marriage was the right thing to do.

Officially Derrick and I'd only been together for almost a month. But, in that time has anyone ever experienced what we had? I couldn't stand to be away from him, so wouldn't marriage be a way to keep us together, every day? What would my parents think? What would his mom think? Should I really be so concerned with what everyone else thinks, or should I just follow my heart? I struggled with these and many more questions alone in my room until I narrowed them down to my true concern.

It was a long while before I went to find Derrick. I spent the time thinking about what happened to me since the mountain lion attack and what I wanted in my life. Slowly I opened the door and found him lying on top of the blue bedspread, an arm resting over his eyes. I watched him. How many times had I just stared at him, admiring him, thinking how lucky *I* was to have someone like *him* to love and want *me*.

"Derrick," I whispered.

He didn't move. I went to his side and gently sat on the bed. I knew he was awake so I started talking.

"Derrick, I love you. I want to be with you. And I realize it shouldn't matter what anyone thinks. It's our life, not theirs. But, I don't want you to marry me, only to regret it later." My voice cracked at the end and a tear slid down my check. "What if in a couple years you realize I'm not the beautiful singer you think I am now...and you resent me?"

Derrick moved his arm away from his face and sat up. "You're worried that I would regret marrying you?" he asked. I only nodded because I couldn't speak. My throat was tight with a sob I was controlling. Saying my fear out loud was much worse than thinking it.

He leaned in and softly wiped my tear with his thumb. "I don't know how I will feel in a year or ten and neither do you. But now, it is killing me to have to leave tomorrow not knowing what the hell is going on. Your friends earlier, well my instincts, the same that brought me to you before, tell me they are no good." Derrick tensed when he mentioned our encounter Sarah and Larry.

Taking a deep breath, softly he said, "But that isn't why I want to marry you. I'd just ask you to live with me. I want you to marry me because I love you, and know with all my being we are meant to be together. I hope for a future where we grow old together, safe and happy. I'm sorry, Erica, I shouldn't have sprung this on you," he said. "I love you and will wait...if that is what you want."

"No," I choked out, "I don't want to wait...I want to be with you now. My heart tells me to say 'yes', my brain tells me to say 'no'. But honestly, the past few weeks have thrown logic right out the window," I managed to say with a smile.

We were staring into each other's eyes. "I love you, Derrick. So much it hurts, and more than I think should be possible. I can't imagine a future without you. I didn't know how empty I was until your love filled me. So my answer is...yes. Yes. I will marry you. The sooner, the better." I threw my arms around his neck and kissed him hard and long so he could feel my sincerity. That night I fell asleep in his bed.

I woke late in the morning to the bright sunlight shining through the open curtains. I was alone in bed, Derrick's familiar smell and breathing gone. I found a note in the kitchen telling me he went to work and that he loved me. He signed it, "your fiancé". I grabbed a bowl and poured some Cheerios. It was the first time in several days I was apart from Derrick. I felt very alone.

After I showered and picked up the house I was bored. So I decided to send my parents a HAPPY 25th ANNIVERSARY e-card to both of their cell phones.

I had some hard decisions to make now that I was engaged. I was pretty sure my parents wouldn't be thrilled that I was getting married. And I didn't know if they'd still pay for my college. Derrick and I talked about Gonzaga before falling asleep last night, and he offered to move into town with me while I went to school. But I wanted to explore my options. Since I was still online, I decided to search for other universities to see what was near the Usk area, and explore what class options were offered online. I was pleasantly surprised with what I found.

The City of Spokane had a couple community colleges. I did some calculations and found that I would save money by enrolling in one of the community colleges to finish my Liberal Arts Degree. And several of the classes were offered online. I'd only have to commute a few days a week if we lived closer to Derrick's work.

This news gave us an alternative to Derrick quitting his job and moving. He was close to his family and his responsibilities to his tribe were important to him. His dad had a hefty life insurance policy that left his mom a lot of money and she owned her own catering business, so she didn't need help financially. But Derrick felt responsible for taking care of her and his little sister. I didn't want him to leave his life there, even if it was just for a couple years.

Speaking to my parents was going to be tough. They'd be disappointed. But I also knew they'd come to love Derrick and eventually respect my decision. If I really thought about it, I wasn't too disappointed about not going back to Gonzaga if it meant I got to stay with Derrick. I didn't even know what I wanted to major in. I was pursuing a general two year degree to see what I liked, hoping I would find something career worthy, which was exactly what I could do at the community college. Yes, the more I thought about it, the more I liked the idea.

We would have to just tell my parents and explain that we are in love and getting married is the right thing for us to do. Sounded simple, yet I had a feeling it was going to be anything but simple. Ever since Derrick walked into my life, things had become so complicated yet certain. Everything felt like a fantasy, science fiction, but the way he made me feel was worth all of it. The world was changing around me, but I was meant to be with Derrick. I'd do anything to be with him.

I finished looking up school information and started

browsing different on-line wedding stores, daydreaming about my future wedding when I realized that Derrick would have to tell his mom, whom I had never met. All of my insecurities flooded back. What if she didn't like me? What if she doesn't approve of the marriage? Would Derrick break off the engagement? I didn't care about dresses anymore. I was terrified of what she'd think about Derrick getting engaged to a woman she'd never even met. At least my parents had had dinner with Derrick. I'd never even talked to his mom over the phone. I've always called Derrick's cell. Just then my cell phone went off. It was Derrick.

"Hi," I said.

"Erica," his voice was distraught. My heart began to beat faster. Something was wrong.

"Derrick, what is it?"

"Erica, I'm coming to get you now. Pack some things. You're coming home with me tonight."

"What's going on?" I asked definitely freaking out.

"Apparently it's not over. It's just beginning. Erica, you're in danger."

"Danger?" I whimpered.

My heart fell to my stomach as Frederick's face appeared in my head. A face and experience I'd conveniently locked in a box secured with heavy chains deep inside my subconscious.

"I'll explain when I get there. I'm only about thirty minutes away, so hurry."

He hung up, leaving me there holding my phone to my ear.

CHAPTER 10

My dresser drawers were ajar and clothes strewn everywhere, as I debated what to pack. I wasn't sure how long I'd be gone, or what type of outfits I'd need. Did the Dennison's live in town, in the forest, on the river, or near fields? Crap. How did I miss this tidbit in out nightly talks? After the third time of going through my dresser and closet, I realized I was making way too big a deal out of packing and grabbed layering clothes. I decided on a medium suitcase with enough stuff for five days.

I heard the rumble of Derrick's truck just as I finished putting away the mess. Soon he was thundering up the stairs and in my room, pulling me into his arms. I hugged him back, a little shocked.

"What's wrong?" I asked, more frightened.

"I'll explain later, just get your stuff together. I'm going to get my things then we'll get out of here," he said. Derrick left his clothes and stuff in the spare room planning on spending his vacation with me.

I picked up the pace, and had most of my things together by the time Derrick was back in my room. When he entered, the light hit him just right. I couldn't help but notice, no matter how inappropriate for the situation, that he was looking damn good in his work clothes. His jeans hugged his thighs just enough to notice the muscles beneath. The dirt and grease stains on his white tee-shirt added to the curves beneath. His biceps flexed as he nervously helped me zip my suitcase closed. And, he smelled slightly of sawdust and oil, which combined with his unique scent, was a masculine smell that instantly made me want him. Instead of attacking him I hurried to the bathroom to pack a bag of girly stuff. I had to get away from him to stay focused.

By the time I met him in the living room, Derrick already loaded his truck with my suitcase and his duffle bag.

"Do you need to let anyone know where you are?" he asked.

"Not if I get cell service at your place."

"Okay...good. Don't worry about your phone though. You can always use my cell...or the landline phone."

As I watched him lock the front door I asked, "Should I drive my car?"

I could tell he hadn't thought of that. He'd probably assumed I'd be riding with him. After a moment he nodded and answered, "Maybe that would be a good idea."

Derrick closed the door and we were heading toward the driveway when I said, "Why the rush Derrick? I need something from you...please tell me something."

"I don't know much. But I've never seen my mom so upset. I ran home for lunch and she met me in the yard telling me to get you, to bring you home as fast as I could." We stopped by my car and

Derrick opened the driver's door. "I was able to find out that a couple of the Council members just got back from a trip south. Apparently they stopped by to visit Mom and freaked her out big time. She said they wouldn't tell her anything in detail, except that you and possibly all of our lives were in danger."

He pulled me into his arms, "That's all I know...but Erica, I've never seen my mom this way. I think the Council will be waiting for us at the house. Whatever they have to tell us is going to be big," he said letting go and helping me into my car. "Be sure to follow me. Call if you lose me."

"Okay," I said as he shut my car door. I grabbed my cell from my purse and turned it on, grateful that the battery was fully charged. I backed out of the driveway and waited for him to get turned around. Then we were off.

Following Derrick out of the city was a huge pain. I had to stop at a couple of lights that he made through. So he would pull over to wait for me. Then a few times a car cut between us. But his truck was tall enough I could easily follow, even with several cars between us. Once we were on the highway heading north, driving was less stressful but long. I had plenty of time to let my mind wander. "It's just beginning", "you're in danger", Derrick had said to me, words I certainly didn't want to hear in the same sentence.

What could it mean? Why would I be in danger? I'm not special, not anything like Derrick, who turned into animals to fight vampires. I figured it had something to do with Frederick, but he was dead. I shuddered from the memory. Frederick had thought I was someone else though, so maybe that had something to do with whatever was going on. I was making myself crazy with theories. After swerving to miss a dead porcupine in the road, I focused on driving more and theories less.

It was twilight and the sun was setting. I turned on my radio and didn't think about anything else but the road and lyrics to the songs that played. I surfed radio stations searching for songs I knew so I could sing along, avoiding all commercials. I was doing a pretty good job keeping myself from speculating, until I saw the WELCOME TO USK sign through my headlights. I couldn't avoid what was coming.

The town of Usk wasn't much bigger than a few blocks. There were a couple of restaurants, a local grocery and hardware store, and a gas station. The air became fragrant with the smell of freshly cut lumber. The source was obvious when I passed a large lumber mill, which I figured was where Derrick worked.

It was pitch black outside, no moon or stars. And once we were on the country roads, the only lights were from our vehicles. All I could see was Derrick's taillights and the reflective devices along the road and on mailboxes.

Soon we turned right onto a driveway. The mailbox had white stickers spelling DENNISON on the side. We were there. I began to shake. Not about the possible danger to my life. No, I had a whole new problem. I was about to meet Derrick's mom, for the very first time. I couldn't even remember her name. I began to hyperventilate. I forced myself to take deep even breaths. I felt sick and was thankful my stomach was empty, or else I was sure I would have puked.

The driveway was dark, long, curvy, and bumpy. I took it slow, probably slower than I needed to, but I was not in a hurry to get there. Finally I saw some lights through trees. I followed Derrick's truck to a garage where he parked along the side. I could see why. There were two cars in it already. I pulled up next to his truck and shut off my car, but I didn't get out. I held onto the steering wheel trying to steady my breathing while resting my head on my hands.

I heard my car door open.

"You okay?" Derrick asked.

I nodded, lifting my head to meet his gaze.

"What was your mom's name again?" I asked in a panicked whisper.

"Is that what's got you so worried?" With a sigh and a smile he said, "Her name is Karen and my sister's name is Miya." He reached out a hand to help me up.

"You'll be okay?" he said reassuringly after looking at me closer under the garage light.

"I think I'm going to throw-up," I whispered as I stood, my legs feeling weak.

Derrick pulled me up into his arms. "You're just nervous. Don't be. My mom has been looking forward to meeting you. I'm sure she'd have preferred different circumstances...but it'll be fine. And my sister's been pestering me to meet you. Every time I see her she's asking 'when you bringing Erica?'" he said trying to make me feel better.

I let him hold me. Being in his arms was working. I began to relax. I inhaled his scent which gave me some distraction from meeting his family. I doubted he could smell bad at all, even if he didn't bathe for a week. There was something about him that drove me wild.

Derrick took my hand and led me to the front of his house, where I noticed more cars parked. We walked a cobblestone path lined with solar lights and took a few stairs to the front porch.

I realized he lived in a log house with a covered front porch spanning the entire front. There was a porch swing at one end with a rocking chair next to it. There was another rocking chair at the other end of the porch next to a huge square window. I could see some furniture inside the house, but no moving bodies.

Derrick led me to the porch swing instead of through the front door, which was a surprise.

"Let's take a minute before we go in," he said nervously, which sent a new wave of panic through me.

"I thought you said they'd like me?" I said as he sat pulling me down next to him.

"No...I mean, yes. Yes, they will like you. I'm sure my mom and sister will love you. I'm a little nervous about the Council. I was right. Those are their cars," he said pointing to three cars that I could barely make out parked at the end of the yard. "The fact that three Council members would show up in the middle of the night, waiting for us, means something serious is going on."

I glanced at my watch. How did it get so late so fast? I jumped when I heard the sharp slam of a screen door. When I looked up I saw a beautiful dark eyed, chubby faced girl running toward us.

"Derrick, Derrick, you're home!" she squealed as she jumped on his lap. She found a comfy spot and stared at me. "Hi," she said shyly.

"Hi," I said back, my voice a little squeaky.

I'd never had a boyfriend, so I'd never had the experience of meeting the other family. I tried to tell myself this was no different than if it were just one of my friend's families. But it was different. I couldn't trick myself no matter how hard I tried.

"Erica, this is Miya," Derrick said squeezing one of her cheeks.

"Ouch, knock it off," she said punching him in the stomach.

I couldn't help it. I laughed and it felt good. They laughed too. It was a great tension reliever.

"Come on you guys. Everyone is waiting. Mom made some food. She told Jack that you two needed to eat before any talking," Miya explained as she got up tugging Derrick's arm to follow her.

Derrick looked at me and I gave him a little nod letting him know I was ready. I followed them into the house, not quite as panicky as earlier, but still nervous.

As soon as I stepped through the door I smelled food, and it smelled delicious. My stomach grumbled loud in eager anticipation. I couldn't tell what it was exactly, just a mixture of aromas that instantly made my mouth water. I also smelled coffee and...pipe tobacco?

A striking woman with short black hair came to greet us. I knew immediately it was Derrick's mom. Derrick had her eyes and smile.

"Mom, this is Erica," Derrick said stepping aside so she had a full view, "and Erica, this is my mom, Karen."

"Hi, Erica. It is nice to finally meet you," she said giving me a gentle hug.

"Thanks...um, me too," I said returning her hug, certain she could feel me shaking.

"I bet you two are hungry," Karen said taking me by the arm and leading us closer to the smell.

My stomach growled again, louder and longer this time. I looked at Derrick horrified. He just gave me one of his sexy crooked smiles and patted me on the shoulder.

Miya was skipping in front as I was led into a dining room with a large picnic table and two pull out benches. Derrick guided me to a spot to sit. The table and benches were coated with a clear sealer that made the surfaces soft. The designs the grain of the wood made were beautiful, almost like abstract art if you looked in any single place long enough.

"I hope you like chicken," Karen said to me.

I nodded to her that I did.

"I've kept it warm in the oven. Derrick, will you give me a hand?" Karen said as she headed towards a door.

"Sure," he answered following her.

I watched as they left the dining room through a swinging wooden door. I couldn't help but want to walk through the door myself. It was one of those doors I'd only seen on TV or in a restaurant.

Miya gave me a huge grin and skipped in after them leaving me alone. I heard them talking, but couldn't make out any words.

I glanced around and instantly fell in love with the house. It was rustic, but homey. The main walls were polished logs, while the inside walls were drywall painted in soft earthy tones. The floors were cherry hardwood, much darker than the log walls. The living room and dining room were open with vaulted ceiling and exposed log beams. A huge fireplace with a river rock mantel occupied one corner. A dark leather sofa and loveseat set with a natural wooden coffee table between them was placed in the living room area. I saw a set of stairs leading up and down and realized there must be at least three levels.

I jumped when Derrick suddenly came through the swinging door with two huge plates of food. Miya followed with two glasses full of a dark liquid, and Karen followed Miya with a wicker basket of bread. My stomach revealed its neglect, again.

"Wow! This looks great," I said as Derrick set one of the plates down in front of me and took a seat to my right.

"Thank you, Miya," I said as she handed me a glass, which I realized was a wine glass.

"You two eat up. The Council wants to talk to you when

you're finished," Karen said placing the bread on the table. "Come on, Miya. Let them eat." She gently pulled Miya up from the table.

I smiled as I watched Miya follow her mother. I could tell Miya wanted to be with her brother.

"Let's eat," Derrick said as he picked up his fork.

"This looks excellent."

"Mom's a great cook," Derrick mumbled between bites.

I grabbed my fork but didn't know where to begin. There were whipped potatoes topped with gravy, a vegetable medley with fresh herbs that smelled so good, and roasted chicken breast that was golden brown and juicy. I decided to start with the potatoes. I took a drink from the wine glass which confirmed the liquid was wine, not my favorite. Derrick noticed my reaction and left. He came back with a glass of water.

"Try to drink the wine if you can. It will take the edge off...help you to relax," he said handing me the water. "This should help."

As we ate, we tried to keep the topic light. I didn't want to speculate what was going on, not with my morbid imagination. "Was that the mill you work at?" I asked, referring to the only one we passed on our trip.

"Yep. That's where I work. It's a good job. I like to work with my hands and the time goes by fast because I'm always busy, plus I get to put my mom and sister on my benefits package...and the pay is great," he said.

"How'd you like the drive up here?" he asked.

"What do you mean?"

"Well, if I'd known you were a blue-hair driver, I'd have made you ride with me," he teased. "I think you drove forty the whole way here. The speed limit on the highway's sixty."

"I was watching for deer," I tried to sound insulted as I punched him in his thigh.

"That excuse will only work once. I was trying not to lose you, until I realized your headlights were the only ones not passing me."

He laughed a little harder, and so did I. It was a good laugh. We both felt better after.

We finished the rest of our dinner jabbing each other with jokes about slow driving. I ate all the food on my plate, and was stuffed. I still had a full wine glass. I didn't like the taste of wine. My parents usually let me have a half a glass on special occasions, probably knowing I wouldn't drink it. Derrick chuckled as he watched me chug it all in one drink, then chase it with what was left of my water.

The wine warmed my body and my head felt lighter. Derrick was right, soon I was feeling more relaxed. I hated attention and had a sinking feeling I was about to have a lot of it.

"Ready?" he asked.

I nodded that I was, and followed Derrick into the kitchen with my empty dishes. The kitchen was amazing. I knew Karen ran her catering service from home, but had no idea how cool a kitchen could be. It was a chef's dream kitchen straight from a magazine, with stainless steel appliances and countertops everywhere. "Wow," was all I could say.

"Where is everyone?" I asked while helping Derrick put the dishes in the dishwasher. I assumed Karen and Miya were in the kitchen, but it was empty.

"Out back," he said motioning toward the window above the sink. But the only thing I could see in the window was my reflection. I noticed that some of my hair had escaped from its clip.

"Where's the bathroom?" I asked, needing to freshen up.

"I'll show you," he said. I followed him through the kitchen to a narrow mudroom. There was a door to outside, and one other. He pointed to the other door. "In there. Meet me in the kitchen when you're done," he said. I could tell he was stressing again, his shoulders were tense.

"Are you okay?" I asked, taking his hand.

"Let's just get this over with," he said giving my hand a little squeeze. He kissed the top of my head and headed back to the kitchen.

I tried to fix my hair, combing it with my fingers and patting it with water. But it looked frizzy, and kept sticking out in weird places. I gave up trying to make it look nice and twisted it into a French roll. Then I stared at my reflection for a while. *What am I so nervous about?* I kept asking myself. Whatever had Derrick worked up, couldn't be good. But he didn't know what was going on either. The more I thought about it the more worried I became. I pinched my checks to give them some color and went to find Derrick. He was in the kitchen leaning across the island.

"You ready?" he asked handing me a purple windbreaker that wasn't mine.

"Are we going somewhere?" I asked taking the jacket.

"Everyone's waiting for us outside and it's a little cold. This is my sister's, but I think it will fit you."

I was a little embarrassed that a twelve-year-old's jacket would fit me, and hesitated before putting it on.

"She's big for her age. What can I say. Mom feeds us well," Derrick said patting his rock-hard stomach.

"Ready?" he asked again.

"I guess," I said zipping the jacket, surprised it fit me just fine.

I had no idea what was going on or about to come. Derrick's edgy reactions about this meeting had me worried. Whatever was waiting for us, I felt wasn't going to be good.

I followed Derrick through a sliding glass door in the dining room, which was hidden behind long cream colored drapes, onto a cement patio. Over the patio was a pergola strung with white lights. The glow from the lights was in strong contrast to the night, making the pergola look as if it had translucent black walls.

I was glad for the jacket when the chill hit my bare legs. The cold didn't seem to affect Derrick. He didn't show any sign of discomfort.

Derrick led me from the patio to the yard. I stumbled over an uneven piece of ground. Derrick turned and caught me before I fell forward. "Thanks," I said. "I guess my eyes need a couple seconds to refocus. I can barely see."

"Really?" he said. "I can see fine." He held me by the waist, his hands warm. I could barely make out his features in the now distant glow of the lights. I stepped in closer, laying my head on his chest. He wrapped his arms around me. I took solace in our moment which was interrupted from a laugh not far away.

Derrick took my hand and soon I saw our destination. A camp fire glowed in the distance, and the smell of smoke filled the air. I made out Karen, Miya and three strangers. As I walked closer I distinguished a faint hint of tobacco smoke, a distinct smell, not like cigarettes at all. The smell reminded me of my papa who would smoke his pipe while relaxing in his oversized La-Z-Boy chair. It's funny how smells can bring back such vivid memories.

Once we were close enough for the group to notice us, Karen said, "Okay, Miya. Tell everyone good night."

"But, Mom," Miya complained.

"I let you stay up this late. Don't make me regret it," Karen said in a stern voice, one that I would have obeyed for sure.

Miya got up reluctantly, gave her mom a kiss and said "Goodnight" to the group.

I heard a mixture of "goodnights", "sleep-wells", and "sweet-dreams". I simply waved as she turned and slowly walked towards the house. We were about fifty yards from the house.

"Um...this is Erica Mathews," Derrick said introducing me to the group.

He continued by introducing the Council members to me. "This is Bill." An older heavyset gentleman gave me smile and a nod. "This is Amy." A thin middle aged woman with long salt-and-pepper braids framing her face smiled at me. "And this is Jack. He's the Tribal Elder." A very old man with long white hair and a leathered face carved with deep wrinkles gave me a grunt and nod while holding a pipe to his mouth.

"Hi," I said in a voice they probably couldn't hear.

Derrick and I sat next to each other in the only two seats available.

"Coffee or hot chocolate?" Karen asked me and Derrick.

"Coffee," answered Derrick.

"Hot chocolate, please," I said, not a fan of coffee.

I watched Karen walk to a metal pushcart with a large portable coffee pot and teapot. She filled Derrick's mug with coffee and scooped cocoa into another mug, then poured hot water from the tea pot. I watched her to avoid making eye contact with the Council.

"Marshmallows?" she asked giving me a beautiful smile, so similar to Derrick's.

"No thanks," I answered. She brought Derrick and me our mugs and we both told her "Thanks".

My mug was super hot. I watched the steam rise from the dark liquid in thick wispy waves that disappeared several inches above the mug's brim. It would be a while before I could take a sip without burning my mouth.

It was silent for a while before Jack finally spoke. "Your

mom tells us that you've already told Erica about Sikyahonaw."

"Yes," Derrick confirmed quickly.

Jack continued. "She also tells me you killed a vampire while in your spirit guide body," his voice more curious. "Tell us about it."

I tensed, unable to help my reaction. It was uncomfortable knowing someone else, several someone elses, knew our secret. I didn't like it. I sat silently keeping my eyes down as Derrick recounted what happened. He told the group how he had a vision while working and that he was guided by some force. The closest he could come to describing it was like a magnet. He told how he drove to exactly where I was trapped in a shrinking circle of sunlight, which was the only thing keeping the vampire from killing me. He replayed his transformation, the fight, the way he knew where to bite and pull, and how he burned the vampire pieces. He told them he could smell every last piece. He finished with telling them that he took me home.

The group sat in silence listening to Derrick's every word. He told a good story, but I was the only one who flinched when he recounted the horrible parts I'd tried to forget. An awkward silence followed.

"What about the girl?" Jack asked.

"She saw me change and kill the vampire...She accepts me, what I am," Derrick quickly answered.

"After we learned of your transformation, Derrick," Amy began, her voice soft, "we have been looking into our and other Native histories and legends. We wanted to know why now, after all this time that you would be able to call upon your spirit guide for help, without even knowing you were doing so."

Amy took a moment and continued, "Our people try to retain our culture and heritage, but some is lost and there are blank spaces that leave unanswered questions. Tribes bicker between one another for land and resources," she chuckled a little, "an ongoing problem since the birth of our peoples. But, when it comes to the interest of saving our identities and protecting our people, we put those differences aside."

Amy explained, "Jack and I just got back from a long trip visiting other reservations and speaking to their Councils and Elders. What we've discovered is very disturbing," her soft voice grew hard as she finished.

My anxiety intensified as I listened. I had to know what they discovered. But at the same time I didn't want to know because it could be bad, bad for me and for Derrick. My gut instinct, my sixth sense, was screaming bad news coming.

"And what is that?" Derrick asked leaning toward Amy, his forehead knotted with stress. I wanted to reach out to him, to touch him, comfort him. For him to comfort me. But I was too embarrassed in front of all these people, especially his mom.

Bill began to speak in short quick sentences. "Amy and Jack were away. I did some research here. Seems you aren't the only one making the change. Suppose it's genetic. You musta got it from your daddy." Bill's voice was raspy and his words were frank and to-the-point. "But from what Jack tells, there are some other tribes experiencing the same thing. Some of their young men changed to their spirit guide form. Not too long ago. You still the only one to have gone Werewolf."

Bill took a pause and shook his head. "'Parently this changing business is causing some headaches. One reservation over there on the coast had a young man transformed who'd supposedly come from another man. No one had any idea he'd come from the Chief's line. Guess it come out that a onetime affair ended with a mixed up pregnancy. Shocked all parties involved."

He gave a grunt and then in a much more serious tone he finished. "The problem is...we didn't know why this stuff's happening now. That is 'til you ran into that there vampire."

Amy started were Bill left off. "You are the first to see, or even kill a vampire for many generations. The other men, like you, claim to be able to smell them. Say that they smell like death...like a rotting carcass. We don't think it is a coincidence. We think the changes and the vampire's presence are connected."

Derrick nodded in agreement.

I wondered why they smelled like rotten eggs to me, but before I could come up with an idea, Amy continued her explanation.

"What we've been able to determine through research, discussion, and meditation, is that they are looking for something..." Amy looked me straight in the eye, "or someone."

I was grateful that I was already stiff with cold and nerves, or else I'd have given away my shock. Why was she looking at me?

What the heck did I have to do with this? I never even heard of these legends, or histories. Which, by the way, what was the difference between the two? I've read books and watched movies about werewolves, vampires, and stuff, but so has everybody else. I didn't have any special information about them. I looked down at the mug in my hands watching the steam that still rose from the liquid and away from piercing eyes.

Amy continued. "We had to look hard into our legends and histories, and other tribes' about where the vampires had come from. Our Sikyahonaw legend touches on this subject briefly, telling us that vampires traveled across the ocean and moved west before the settlers. From that legend we knew how to kill them and that their weakness is sunlight. But we didn't know much about them specifically. In fact we still don't know much about them. But we do know vampires hunt humans and drain them through the bite, drinking the blood. If a vampire does not kill the person by draining them, the victim is killed by the venom within a few minutes. We learned that from another tribe whose legend told of a daughter. Their spirit guide was able to kill the vampire, but not before it bit the daughter. She died a few hours later in pure anguish."

Amy took a long pause and sipped from her mug. I began to wonder if the conversation was over, but she began talking again. "There was one history we found very interesting from a reservation far south of here. It was an affair between their Chief's eldest son, Joseph, and a very pale faced witch with no name. They say that her beauty was surpassed by none. Her skin was soft and milky white.

And that her voice could enchant the deaf."

I noticed Derrick tense and sit up straighter.

Amy took another sip from her mug before she continued. "The affair was only for one night. Joseph was obsessed with the witch as soon as he saw her. He spent the night with her despite the fact he had just married months before. The Chief said his son loved his wife very much, that when she agreed to marry him, he was happy beyond words. His devotion to his wife was absolute. Only enchantment could have led him astray."

Amy took another long pause before she resumed. I had a feeling the pauses were meant to be suspenseful, which was working. I thought Derrick was a good story teller, but Amy beat him hands down.

"The witch met with the Chief, Chief Harlan, the next day under the condition that their conversation would never be shared until the time was right. Chief Harlan agreed. The witch told him that she did not want to destroy his son Joseph's marriage. She did not even want to see Joseph again. It was only his seed she sought. When Chief Harlan asked 'why', the witch explained that it was providence."

"The witch then told Chief Harlan of how she was the last of her kind. She told of an ancient clan of people who conspired with the demons below to cheat death. There was one woman in the clan who ran away and pleaded with the spirits above to undo what her clan leader had done, for he had been changed into a beast that feasted upon their people. The witch explained to Chief Harlan that the leader of the clan was transformed into the Master Vampire, who soon created an army through his blood."

Amy took a deep breath. "The spirits loved the people and listened to the woman. When she was done they sought counsel amongst themselves. The spirits decided that they would grant the woman her request, for if demons bestowed immortal evil that feasted upon and killed their precious humans, then they would bestow immortal goodness to protect them. The spirits asked the woman to carry the burden, to be the protector of all humans, to be the Mother Witch.

"They told her she would be as strong as the vampires and live an immortal life using the elements of the earth. And that she too could create another through her blood. But because there was goodness in her heart, she was not to be confined as the vampires were, only to roam at night and feast on human blood. She would live a life amongst the humans she would protect.

"The woman agreed and she created an army as well. She went to clans and asked for warriors to help her, because neither she nor the Master Vampire could change anyone by force. Those changed had to accept their fate.

"Both the Master Vampire and the Mother Witch were limited in the number of warriors they could create, but they had armies in the hundreds. The vampires and witches warred for thousands of years, killing one another. The witch's kind was winning because they had the advantage to hunt during the day and burn the vampires with the sun. Also, it was found that the witches' blood was poison to the vampires."

Again a long pause while Amy took a sip. I felt like I was going to leap out of my skin. I had never wanted to know the ending of a story so badly.

Amy finally started, "After centuries, the vampire's numbers had dwindled and the witches became arrogant. They flaunted their abilities. The witch explained to Chief Harlan that the vampires were able to find a vulnerability that easily killed them. Soon the war had turned to the vampire's favor. Chief Harlan asked her what the vulnerability was, but she refused to tell.

"The witch told Chief Harlan how she has watched the vampires kill her kind. And that in the last battle, when she was the only one left, she went into hiding until the time would come for her to show herself. Chief Harlan asked her how many vampires exist. The witch explained that the vampire numbers have remained steady around two hundred.

"The witch told of how easily the two creatures could track each other from their scents. However, she was able to keep hidden from the vampires for the past decade, but she would not reveal how or where. She told him that the vampires have thought her kind to be exterminated."

Amy stopped only to take a deep breath and continued, "Chief Harlan asked the witch what this had to do with his son Joseph. The witch explained that her kind had never given birth, that they couldn't make life. Only the Mother Witch could transform it. But neither she nor the Master Vampire had the ability to make the change anymore."

Amy leaned forward, her expression intense and her voice severe. "The witch told Chief Harlan about a vision she had had recently. She was to give birth to a baby that would be the end of her life, finishing off her kind completely. But the child was the only chance to kill the vampires. That even shapeshifters would eventually succumb to the vampires without this child.

"The witch explained how her vision and a force pulled her to Joseph. He was the only one who could bear her *the* child. And so long as she carried this child, she was safe and that the child could not be tracked by the vampires.

"Chief Harlan pleaded with her to tell him the child's destiny, begged the witch to reveal his grandchild's fate, but she would not. She only knew that the child had to be conceived and given life no matter the cost. She would kill and die to make sure she gave birth to this child."

Amy sat back and in a lighter tone continued, "Then the witch left but no one knows to where. As soon as she was gone, Joseph's spell was lifted. It was as if she'd never existed. He only remembered her as a dream. Neither Joseph's wife nor anyone else could recall the affair. Only Chief Harlan remembered the truth."

With that Amy stopped and sipped from her mug. I wasn't ready for the story to end. I wanted to know what happened to the witch and what happened to the baby. I wanted to ask Amy to continue. But I didn't.

The small group was quiet. I could hear the crickets and

katydids over the crackle of the fire. I looked over to Derrick. He was glaring at Amy. I could tell he was livid. Then suddenly Derrick said through a snarl sending alarms through my body, "FINISH THE STORY."

"Derrick," his mother scolded.

I was totally confused. What did I miss? Why was Derrick so angry? I wanted to hear more too, but I wasn't pissed about it.

He jumped from his seat sending his chair crashing behind him as he demanded in a voice of fury, "I said, *finish* the story."

Worried, I scanned the group. Karen was nervously looking back and forth from Derrick, to me, and then to the Council members. Amy seemed completely oblivious to the scene that just unfolded, and the demand, as she sipped from her mug. Bill didn't look bothered much either.

Jack leaned forward with his pipe hanging from his mouth. Not looking at anyone in particular, mostly staring at the fire, he began speaking in a deep and raspy voice. "Chief Harlan was very reluctant to tell us this story, and only agreed to do so with me and Amy in private. He wonders at great lengths what happened to the witch and his grandchild. As Amy said, the witch had made him promise not to tell her story, or mention the baby until the time was right. If he revealed the truth too soon, his grandchild would surely be killed. It has been difficult for him all these years. When we arrived to his reservation, he knew the time had come."

I noticed Derrick's breathing increasing, his shoulders moving with every breath, his fists clenched. I didn't know if I should try to do something to calm him or not. So I just sat there.

Jack took a deep puff from his pipe. The white smoke snaked around his head as he continued. "This took place nineteen years ago. There was no picture of the witch, but the Chief remembered her as if he'd just seen her. As Amy said, she had smooth pale skin. She had a small thin frame. She had..." Jack's expressionless face looked straight into Derrick's, "startling green eyes, long dark hair, deep dimples in both her cheeks...and a five pointed star on the inside of her right forearm."

My full mug of hot chocolate slipped though my hands landing hard on the ground. The liquid spilled between my feet. "Oh, I'm s-s-sorry," I stuttered as I bent to pick up the mug.

I understood where this story was leading. I began to tremble. They had me confused with someone else and this was all a mistake. But then I remembered what Frederick had said, "You look just like her". No, this was a mistake. My mom was a redhead with a face full of freckles, definitely not a witch. My dad was a normal, boring guy.

I looked up and met Derrick's gaze. I felt all eyes on me, waiting.

"There...there must be some m-mistake," I said to him, "I'm not...not that person."

Somewhere off in the distance, I could hear Bill's quick deep voice. "We don't know for sure. But now that we've all seen you, you fit the description pretty well."

"Derrick," I squeaked. I wanted to leave. I wanted to go

home right then. I wanted my mom and my dad. I wanted this *not* to be happening. I knew the news was going to be bad, but not this. I didn't know what to expect, but I sure the heck didn't consider this. Not even in my wildest imagination would I have even come close to this.

"Derrick, I think you should take Erica to your room. We've had enough for tonight," Karen declared glaring at the Council. I had a feeling she wasn't very happy with the situation that was unfolding.

Derrick started pacing before finally coming to my side. I had tears in my eyes quivering to let loose. Derrick helped me up. I almost fell, my legs were so weak, but his strong arms caught me. He half carried me through the house. I thought I caught movement from the second floor balcony and wondered if Miya was still up. He led me down the stairs to his bedroom. The light was already on. He sat me on a hard chair next to a computer desk.

"I'm sorry Erica. I had no idea. DAMNIT," he yelled slamming his fist on the desk breaking the corner off. I flinched, staring at him.

He knelt in front of me, between my knees. "I'm so sorry, Erica. Will you be okay for a minute? I'm going to have a word with..."

"No. Please Derrick. Don't leave me," I cried as I reached for him, "They're wrong. They have the wrong person. It's just a story...right?" I pleaded, willing him to agree with me.

I watched as he paced back and forth in his room before he

came back to me, a little calmer.

"I hate to see you hurting like this," he cupped the side of my face in his hand. "They didn't need to tell us like this. I'm sure there was a better way."

"It's a story, RIGHT?" I pleaded again.

He had to agree with me, I was really losing it. He picked me up from the chair. I was shaking and my skin was ice cold.

"I don't know," he said setting me on his huge bed.

Without a word he took off my shoes and then asked, "How about you just wear one of my shirts to bed? I'll get your stuff in the morning. I don't want to chance running into one of them right now. I don't know if I could control myself."

I nodded, still in disbelief. He helped me out of Miya's jacket, my shorts and shirt. And I slid into one of his white tee-shirts. He undid my hair clip so that my hair hung loose. Then he guided me onto his bed and under the covers. He lay next to me on top of the comforter propping himself above me on an elbow. With his other hand he gently stroked my hair away from my face.

I was lost in thought and couldn't speak. I didn't want to even consider the possibility of what the story would mean if it was remotely true. My life with my parents would have been a complete lie. I just accepted the existence of vampires and shapeshifters. Are there, or were there, witches too? Derrick lay next to me not saying anything, just watching me drift off to sleep which eventually did come.

CHAPTER 11

I opened my eyes. My nightmares were true, confirmed by the strange room I was in. I inhaled deep, smelling a familiar scent. I was laying on my left side, with a familiar arm draped over my waist, a familiar body behind me. His hand rested on the bed in front of me, so thick and strong. I could see the calluses on his fingers. When he touched me though, they were soft and gentle. We were in a spooning position. Derrick was still above the comforter while I was beneath it.

I felt Derrick's deep even breathing on the back of my head. He was close. I didn't want to move for fear of waking him. I remembered back to last night, to the story. The story that played over and over in my nightmares mixed with Frederick and mountain lions. Everything was trying to hurt me one way or another. More than once Derrick gently shook me awake from my thrashing and crying. Then he would hold me until I fell back asleep. I doubted he got much sleep. I was determined not to disturb him.

My arms were in front of me. I tuned my right arm so I could look at my birthmark, the pinkish star shaped mark. It wasn't until Jack mentioned the mark that I understood what the Council was getting at, that they thought I was that witch's baby.

I began to wonder, hope, that Jack, Amy, and Bill were old jerks that didn't want me to be with Derrick. But how would they have known about my birthmark? Miya's jacket had it covered. My mom a witch? But my parents were in Hawaii. *This can't be happening! I'm in a nightmare,* I told myself. But then Derrick wouldn't be real. I couldn't think about it anymore. My sanity couldn't take it.

I looked around and noticed Derrick's room was huge. The bright sun streamed into the room through two high windows. He had a corner room in the basement. Straight across from where I lay was a long dresser with nine drawers, three sets of three, with a large rectangular mirror on top. I could see myself in the reflection and part of Derrick's body. I saw his shoulder, the arm that was over me, and the bottoms of his legs which stuck out past mine. His feet hung over the bottom of the bed.

I stared at my reflection, into my green eyes. I smiled revealing my dimples. My hair was a matted mess. I looked in the mirror past me to the wall behind us. There was a large bookshelf that had a lot of books, easily over a hundred. I also noticed a really nice stereo and a ton of CD's. I looked away from the mirror to the broken computer desk against a different wall, the one past the foot of the bed, and remembered Derrick's anger...his strength. He had a temper.

His room was clean. He had a weight bench with a bunch of free weights in one of the corners, and his walls were decorated with various family pictures and Native décor. I noticed three doors. One was the door leading out of his room. I assumed one was a closet and hoped the other door led to a bathroom, which I needed to use. But I'd wait until I was about to explode before taking the chance of waking Derrick.

I loved Derrick. I loved him so much, but part of me wondered if I had gone absolutely insane. Maybe I was living out this fantasy in a mental hospital, or in a coma in some hospital. Vampires, shapeshifters, witches and baby switching or whatever...Seriously, it all sounded like a bad horror movie.

But I loved Derrick and wanted this all to be real, because that meant Derrick was real. I knew it deep down in my soul that I loved him and wanted to marry him. I wanted to spend the rest of my life making him happy, right? But he was so angry last night. I'd never seen him act like that before. What if he had changed his mind? Sadness slowly filled my body as I thought about it. What if he didn't want to be with me anymore? What if the Council's plan was to tear us apart and it worked? Derrick not loving me anymore would be my worst nightmare come true. I couldn't help it. My eyes began to tear. What if he didn't like the idea of being married to a...a witch? I tried to hold it in. I tried not to cry and held my breath, but it didn't work. As silently as I could, I let it out.

I felt Derrick's arm pull me tighter, hugging our bodies close. I felt him kiss my head just above my ear. He whispered, "What can I do?"

I lay on my back to face him, quiet tears streaming from my

eyes, flowing around my ears into my hair.

"Tell me it's all just a story," I whispered back.

"I wish that I could" he said softly, brushing away my tears.

Slowly he bent to kiss me but I turned my head. "I can't Derrick. I'm too upset...I don't want you to..." He moved quickly and found my lips with his and kissed me before I could turn my head completely.

At first I pursed my lips together, a little pissed. But after a moment, I couldn't resist. I loved him too much and I needed him. As I began to let myself kiss him back, I felt his love for me.

"I'm so sorry," he said gently pulling away. "I hate to see you hurting, to see you in so much pain."

"Thanks for the kiss...I feel a little better." I let out a long sigh and moved from under his arm and asked, "Do you have a bathroom down here?"

"Yeah, right through that door," he pointed to one of the doors I noticed earlier.

"I'll go grab your stuff out of the truck...Be right back," he said getting up and leaving the room.

"Thanks," I said after him.

His bathroom was nice. It was as big as our main floor bathroom. His had a sink, shower, toilet, and linen closet. As soon as I looked in the mirror, I wished I hadn't. My eyes were swollen and red, my cheeks were puffy, and my hair looked like a good place for a rat to live. I washed my face with cold water, but still felt swollen and dirty. I decided to take a shower, a long, hot shower.

Once I was in the water, I figured I'd better not take as long of a one as I'd have liked, not knowing the hot water situation in this house. At my house, the three of us couldn't take back to back showers because the third person would end up with no hot water. I didn't want one of my first impressions with his mom to be that I ran her out of hot water, although nothing could be worse than what happened last night.

The spray hitting my back felt good. I washed and tried to visualize rinsing my anguish away as I watched the suds disappear down the drain, a tidbit I'd picked up from one of my mom's woman magazines. I was happy to see that Derrick used conditioner because without it, I'd never get a brush through my mop, clean or not.

I turned the water off and stood for a moment, letting the water roll down my body. I opened the shower door and took a deep breath readying myself for the day ahead, as I stepped out. Grabbing a towel, I noticed my suitcase on the counter next to the sink. I didn't even hear the door. It had to have been Derrick. I smiled to myself thinking again how lucky I was to have such a great boyfriend. No, not boyfriend, fiancé.

I dressed in khaki shorts and a white tank top. I folded my hair into a French braid. I brushed and flossed my teeth. I didn't even bother with makeup. It wouldn't help. My eyes were still red and swollen.

Finished, I went back into Derrick's room but found it empty. I made the bed and sat in front of his computer. I turned it on and got online to check my email. I had a bunch more emails from Gonzaga which I deleted without opening, an email from Sarah and one from my mom.

I opened Sarah's first. **Dimples, So, so sorry for the other night. I didn't mean to upset you guys. You're not returning my calls to let me explain. Hopefully you'll return my email. We need to talk. Hugs, Sarah.** I hit the delete button.

Then I opened the email from my mom. She and Dad had received my e-card and they got my message that I was at Derrick's. They were having a good time and hoped I was too. It took me a while to figure out whether I wanted to respond and decided a quick, "Got your message. I'm fine. Have fun," was enough. They had to be my real parents. They would never lie to me like this.

I turned off the computer and went back to the bed. Derrick had a really soft comforter. I guessed it was down with a simple black duvet cover. I searched for the end of the comforter at the bottom of his bed. I found it and was right. I could feel the down comforter between the several buttons from the duvet cover's opening. I was laying on my front, leaning over the end of the bed with my butt in the air when Derrick opened his door. I must have looked ridiculous in that position, with my hands hidden between the duvet cover opening, because his face lit with a smile.

"Do you need some help?" he asked as I backed myself onto the bed.

"No, I was...I thought the comforter was down," I tried to explain, a little flustered.

"I made you some breakfast...eggs, bacon, and toast. I didn't know if you'd want to eat upstairs or not. So I just brought it down here," he said placing two plates of food on top of his computer desk.

I wasn't hungry. But I smiled and said, "Thank you," as I walked over to the desk chair.

This was the first time Derrick cooked for me, so I didn't want to hurt his feelings. But once I started eating it wasn't hard. I actually began to feel kind of hungry and the food was good. I smiled thinking about how no one in our families would ever go hungry, or live off of Hamburger Helper. We all could cook. Well, except for my dad. He could only barbeque.

"That's nice to see," Derrick said from the bed where he'd taken his plate.

"What's nice?" I asked.

"Your smile. It is nice to see you smile," he said quietly.

"Oh," I knew he was worried. I needed to change my mood to help ease his.

"This is great. You have your mom's talent for cooking," I said trying to be more cheerful and giving him a bigger smile. It was fake, but a smile nevertheless.

"Nice try," he said with a frown.

"What? This is great. How did you know I liked my eggs medium?"

"No, the smile, Erica. You don't need to pretend around me."

"I'm sorry, Derrick. It's just that I am very confused."

"I know," he said getting up and setting his plate on his dresser.

He began to pace the room. "I talked to Mom while you were in the shower, before she had to go to work. There's more to the story."

"More?" I gasped.

"I guess they didn't get to tell us the part about the vampires wanting to find and kill you," he said sarcastically.

"Oh. Is that all?" I said matching his sarcasm, even though I didn't find that information funny at all.

"No, no, you took it wrong," he said quickly trying to explain. "What I mean is that they basically turned your world upside down in twenty minutes. The part they didn't get to was just the cherry on top. I'm sorry. This is new territory for me, Erica. I'm not sure what to do."

"That makes two of us," I said walking over and hugging him tight.

We held each other for a while before I asked, "Derrick, what is the difference between a legend and a history?"

After a pause he answered, "Well, legends are like a story passed down from generation to generation. They tell where we come from, who we are, and help to explain some of the mysteries of the world. Even though science has been able to answer a lot of questions there are still some that have no explanation. Like me for example." He smiled leading me over the bed. "But obviously we keep our abilities a secret. I can just imagine what kind of experiments the government would do. Plus, some say once you stop believing, and need proof, the magic leaves. Then we'd never be able to protect our people."

We sat down and he began again. "A history is more factual, I guess. Either someone has witnessed, documented, or researched an event. Not all tribes differentiate between the two. Some argue there is no difference. But we have the two categories. We haven't always, and I don't know when we started."

"So why did the story last night get called a history and the story of Sikyahonaw get called a legend?"

"Sikyahonaw is a legend because his story has been passed down through stories. I suppose last night's explanation was considered a history because the Council felt they witnessed an important account. I'm sure they will write it all down. Our people don't have to be afraid to document our beliefs and stories. Not like we used to. When the government forced us onto reservations, anything they found that was considered blasphemy, they burned, and then the heathen who was found with it in their possession was punished," Derrick said.

There was anger in his voice as he finished. "Maybe we would have more information about what's going on. A better understanding if things wouldn't have happened the way they did...if we had some sort of record."

I didn't know what to say. I took history in school. I learned about settlers and land grabbing, treaties and reservations, forced assimilation, but I didn't have any personal experience. "I wish things would have been different too," I said honestly

"So, you think what Jack, Amy, and Bill said last night is true?" I asked already knowing his answer.

"I know them pretty well. They wouldn't lie." I could tell he was being sincere. "Mom was mad. She's protective and gave them an ear full after we left. Mom didn't think all the drama was necessary. But apparently the Council thought it was best to tell us what they knew as soon as possible. They didn't want to wait. And to the Council's credit, they were telling us what they learned. But they're old, so I guess it's in their nature to make a performance."

He had just made a joke, but I couldn't laugh, not even crack a smile.

"They think I am the daughter of a witch and some guy named Joseph. That doesn't make sense, Derrick. I'm sure I would have figured something out before now...if I wasn't Mom's and Dad's," I argued.

I tried to think back to pictures, family events, anything that would give hints to my belonging to someone else. I couldn't remember ever seeing pictures of my mom being pregnant. But our family was so small, we didn't have many pictures. My mom was an only child. My dad had a brother who lived in China who was married, but they didn't have any kids. I'd never met them. I was the only grandchild. I had no cousins. We were a very small family, but full of love. I always looked forward to the summers I got to spend with my grandparents.

"What's running through your head?" Derrick asked curious.

"I was thinking...I just don't think I'm that person. Yes, maybe I look like her, with my wonderful dimples," I said sarcastically. I never did like them. "And maybe I have a star shaped birthmark," I turned my arm displaying the pink mark, "but I am not that baby."

Derrick took my arm and softly traced my birthmark with his finger. Then he very gently tickled the inside of my arm by barely touching my skin. I shivered from the sensation. Derrick kissed my star shaped mark. I leaned back on his bed, silently inviting him to lay with me. He took the bait and was on me, kissing my neck with soft lips and nuzzling my ear. I was eager for him to find my lips, but he was teasing me.

"I need to take a shower," he whispered in my ear between kisses, his warm breath on my neck sending shivers of desire through my body.

"No," I whined. Then I realized he was in the same outfit from last night. But he smelled so good, his heady scent and warm body, heavy on mine, was calling to me.

"Erica, I haven't showered in two days, and I worked yesterday. I feel grimy," he said getting up.

"You should have joined me earlier," I teased.

"I figured you needed some time to yourself," he said while grabbing some clothes from his dresser.

He was right. I did need the time by myself.

"Well, I could join you?" I flirted, walking to him and running my hands up under his shirt lightly tracing the muscles on his stomach with my fingers. He quivered from my touch, which encouraged me. I moved to his front and lifted his shirt so I could kiss his stomach and chest. His breathing began to quicken as my hands began to explore.

Then he said, "Maybe next time," as he gently pushed my shoulders back.

I wasn't offended. He hadn't seen me naked yet, and I really didn't think I could go through with it. I was actually relieved he didn't take my offer. I would have felt really dumb if he'd called my bluff.

"You can hang your stuff up in my closet if you want. There's plenty of room. And I made a spot for you in the left drawers if you need dresser space," Derrick said as he left for the bathroom. Soon I heard the shower turn on.

I unpacked my things, most of which I was able to put in the dresser. I did have a few shirts I wanted to hang up, so I went to the closet. Derrick was right. There was plenty of room. He had a walk-in closet which was pretty much empty. I noticed some boxes stacked atop one another on a high shelf. He had some camouflaged hunting outfits and dress shirts that took up about a quarter of the closet rod. There were some boots and shoes on shelves closer to the floor, but that was about it. I found some hangers and hung my shirts next to Derrick's clothes. I felt kind of silly, but I didn't want my shirts to feel lonely.

By the time I was done, so was Derrick. He came out of the steamy bathroom with a grin a mile wide.

"So, what should we do today?" he asked slyly.

It didn't matter how many times I'd seen him. His beauty was stunning and fresh. His jeans hung from his hips, the indents of muscle and hip bone visible. He shook his shirt out, before pulling it over his head and slipping his arms through the sleeves. I couldn't remember what he had asked. My vision tunneled. I had to have him right then and there.

Without giving him an answer, I met him at the bathroom door and kissed him with a fierce desire that took us both by surprise. He grabbed me, lifting me to him, kissing me back with just as much passion. I wrapped my legs around his waist and pulled him closer, wanting him. He carried me to the bed, laying me down with him on top of me in one gentle movement. My fingers tangled in his wet hair, as my body ached for more. I could feel his body wanting more. I wanted this. I felt ready.

Derrick pushed his torso up, looking down at me he said, "That wasn't exactly what I was thinking, but...WOW."

"I love you Derrick," I said pulling him back down to me. I guided him with my body to roll over onto his back. I straddled his hips. His jeans were pressing against me making me wish there were no barrier of clothing between us. He cupped the side of my head and sat up, kissing my neck, my ear, making his way to my mouth. I moaned in pleasure, unable to keep my breathing steady.

His hands were in my shirt, hot against my skin. He slipped off my shirt. My bra quickly followed. In a swift move he had me on my back and was on top of me kissing my chest, his tongue and mouth finding my nipples, the sensation sending spikes of need deep down in my hips. My hands grasped the comforter, not sure what to do as he moved his kisses to my stomach, then to the top of my pants. His hair was painting wet trails along my hot and sensitive skin as he moved. I felt his hand on the button of my khaki's where mine instinctively stopped him from going further. Without hesitating, his mouth was back on mine, his body heavy and hard. I kissed him back, and whispered, "I'm sorry, Derrick," against his lips.

He lifted himself up and rolled over next to me. "Don't be sorry, Erica. Its fine," he said as we lay on our backs looking at the ceiling letting our hearts slow.

"I want to, but then I just...can't," I said feeling the need to explain. I was such a chicken.

"It's okay," he said propping himself up on an elbow looking down at me. He began tracing invisible design on my stomach with his fingers.

"Do you want to wait until we're married?" he asked.

"Well, that depends," I said sitting up and putting back on my bra and shirt. "Can we get married this afternoon?" I gave him a smile that he returned. He made me feel so comfortable. He wasn't at all angry or accusing.

"But seriously, I think we will know when the time is right," I said. "Maybe it will be on our wedding night, maybe it won't. I don't think we should purposely wait, do you?"

"No. We will know when we're both ready. But when do you

want to get married?" he asked taking me by surprise. I hadn't really thought of a date yet.

"When do you?" I threw back at him before giving an answer.

"Well, I thought it over. What about before fall, or next spring? I don't think we should while you're in school."

I realized I forgot to tell him about my change of plans. "Derrick, I'm not going back to Gonzaga. I won't let you leave your home, especially now, and there is no way I am leaving you."

His mood changed immediately.

"What are you talking about? I am not going to be the reason for you to quit college." His temper rose as he sat up. I watched his face as the crease between his eyes wrinkled with tension. I knew he was angry but I never felt threatened, not even a little.

I stood and started to pace. I felt his eyes watching me. I refused to look at him as I tried to explain. "Derrick, I'm not quitting school, just not going to Gonzaga. I did some searching and I have decided to register at one of the community colleges..."

"Community college," Derrick interrupted. "You'd quit Gonzaga to go to a community college?" He was not happy.

"It's my decision...Derrick," I was getting defensive. "I don't know what I want to study yet. Besides, I did some calculations and it would be cheaper."

"I have money, Erica," he said, "enough for you to go to college."

"What about your family, Derrick? Can you really leave

them with what is going on right now?" I argued. "In fact, maybe I should wait a year or two until things settle down. How can you protect your family and me when there is only one of you?" I could win this argument without it being about money. I saw it in his eyes. Protecting everyone was a problem he thought about before.

"I don't want you to make a huge mistake," he said.

"I have made up my mind. I'm going to get my Liberal Arts Degree at the community college, do great, figure out what I want to study, and hopefully get a scholarship to one of the universities around here." I walked over to him and sat in his lap. "I don't want to pay more money than I have to. And, I think my parents will be okay with my decision...once I explain," I said seriously.

"They will think you're changing your mind because of me, and they'd be right to blame me," he argued.

"They'd only be half right. I wouldn't have looked into my options if I hadn't met you, fallen in love with you. Trust me. I've thought long and hard about this. It's the right thing to do...for us, and for me." I felt him relax a little as he wrapped his strong arms around me.

"It's your decision," he said.

"What about you?" I asked trying to get the conversation off of me. "Are you going to go to college?"

It took him a minute to answer, "My mom really wants me to. And I can. It just hasn't been the right time. But, since you're going to try the community college thing, maybe I'll take some classes too. I think the community college in Spokane has an extended learning school in Newport."

"Where's Newport?" I asked, more interested.

"Um, just about twenty minutes south of here," he said.

I was getting excited. "What if we went together?" I couldn't hide the hope in my face or my voice. "We could get married, find an apartment, and go to school together."

"Well, that's an idea." I felt the stress leave the room.

I knew he'd think about it, but I didn't want to push. I stood and walked over to my plate. The food was cold, but I kind of felt a little hungry. I nibbled at my eggs.

"Um...so...what did you want to do today?" Derrick asked again, changing the subject as he got up.

"I don't know," I answered.

I watched him pull his hair into a band at the base of his skull. I looked at my reflection and saw my hair had come loose from its braid. I removed the band and combed my hair with my fingers. My hair felt soft and was wavy from the braid. I decided to wear it loose.

"How about we go to one of my favorite places? We can grab some food and hang out for as long as you want," he suggested.

"What about the Council, and that whole business?" I asked, dreading anything to do with them.

"Let's forget about it for a couple hours. I think you've learned too much too fast. But I do want to show you something you've never seen before. Something good. I think it'll help cheer you up."

His smile made me curious. "Where is this place?" I asked.

"Just wait...It'll be a surprise," he winked handing me my shoes.

Soon we were heading up the stairs, each with our half empty plates. I noticed that the basement had a game room with a pool table, dartboard and foosball table.

"I like foosball," I said once we reached the top.

"Great. I'll kick your butt when we get back."

"Oh really...bring it on," I dared.

"It's a date," he smiled grabbing my hand. I followed him into the kitchen and put our plates in the dishwasher while he grabbed a couple of water bottles and filled them from the faucet at the sink.

"Our well water beats any of those bottled waters you buy at the store," he said handing me the first filled bottle. "Most of those are just filtered tap water with a fancy label anyway."

I nodded in agreement. I remembered watching a program that exposed the whole bottled water scandal.

"Where's your sister?" I asked as he began putting food into a bag from the fridge.

"She's at my aunt's. Mom thought it would be better for us to take some time to digest what we learned without Miya pestering us. Mom wants us all to have dinner tonight though, around eight, if that's cool with you," he said closing the door to the fridge.

"Sure," I answered not really knowing how I felt.

"Great. I'll leave her a message."

I watched as he jotted a quick note on a yellow Post-It and stuck the bright square on the fridge. It stood out like an eye-sore against the polished surface. Karen would never miss it.

Once outside, I observed a lot more of their house in the daylight. It was all logs with a dark brown metal roof. The front yard was small and lined with colorful flower beds. The house sat in a meadow surrounded by old pine and cedar trees. I loved the porch. I thought of how nice and relaxing it would be to sit on the rocking chair in the fresh air.

I followed Derrick towards the truck and waited while he went to grab something from the garage. To my surprise he came back with two fishing poles.

"I don't know how to fish," I informed him as he set the poles in the bed of his truck.

"That's fine. I'll teach you," he said with one of his heart stopping grins.

He opened the passenger door for me and waited while I climbed in before shutting the door behind me. I watched as he crossed in front of his tuck which reminded me of the first time I rode in his truck, not really all that long ago. I smiled to myself remembering how ridiculously nervous I was. I never in a million years would have thought I'd be here with him like this.

CHAPTER 12

The driveway was not nearly as long as it seemed last night, and I could barely feel the bumps in Derrick's huge truck. Once we were on the paved road headed north, my cell phone rang from within my purse. I grabbed it and saw that it was my mom. I hesitated. Sending an email was a lot easier than speaking, and I wasn't ready to talk to her yet. The nightmares were still too fresh in my head. I didn't want to think about it so I sent her to voice mail. Derrick gave my hand a comforting squeeze, not asking any questions.

We stopped at a service station.

"Why don't you grab your fishing license," Derrick said. "You don't really need it where we're going, but if we go somewhere else, you might want to have one with you. You can get it while I fill up."

"What license?" I had absolutely no idea what he was talking about.

He laughed and teased, "You really don't know much about fishing do you? And I thought you were the outdoorsy type."

"I like to hike and stuff, You know that. It's just that I never had anyone to teach me how to fish. My dad isn't really into it, I guess."

"Okay, just go in and tell Frank you need a fishing license," Derrick instructed as he handed me a twenty dollar bill. "This should cover it."

"I can buy my own license," I argued pushing his hand away.

The service station was old, smelled musty, and needed to be dusted. A buzzer had gone off once I opened the door, letting the attendant know there was a customer. A huge man, who looked to be in his forties with a full beard and startling blue eyes entered from a door in the back. He was wiping his greasy hands off on a rag as he greeted me, *Frank* was embroidered on his blue coveralls.

"Can I help you?" he said with a drawl.

"Can I get a fishing license?" I asked, fidgeting with my purse.

"Sure, L'il Lady," he said as he went behind the register counter. "I need you to fill out this'er paper and I'll need your driver license." He handed me an application looking form with a pen. As I began to fill it out, the attendant sat on a stool. He then began whistling the theme song to the Andy Griffith show and tapping the counter. I was out of my comfort zone.

"I'll be right back," I said turning to leave. I would finish the application outside. I made it to the door just as it swung open, making the buzzer go off. Derrick entered making me feel safer. Not that the attendant was threatening, but definitely weird.

Derrick put a hand on my waist and pulled me next to him. "Hey Frank," he said giving him nod.

"Knew that was you. Nice door. How's yer mom?" Frank asked.

"Doing good. What are you working on?" Derrick asked looking toward the rear of the station guiding me back to the counter. Derrick handed him some cash.

"Oh, I'm doin' a head gasket on a 76 Camaro," Frank said counting out Derrick's change. "It's a beaut. Wanna take a look?"

"Sure. Erica, you want to come?" Derrick asked.

"No, I'll finish filling this out. Go ahead."

Frank walked from behind the counter and Derrick followed him to the back of the building, both chatting about engines and horse power.

The form was about as generic as a credit card application. I had just signed and dated it when Frank and Derrick walked back into the store. "Finished," I said to Frank handing him the paperwork and my driver's license.

"This'll just be a minute," he said as he began entering the data into an old computer next to the cash register.

Derrick stood next to me, flipping through a hunting magazine, while I waited patiently. Five minutes later, my fishing license was printed out on what looked like a store receipt.

"How much?" I asked as Frank handed me my license.

"Already taken care of L'il Lady," he said nodding toward Derrick.

"Thanks," I gave Derrick a smile. "I would have paid for it."

"I know, but what kind of gentleman would I be if I made

you pay for my idea?"

"See ya, Frank," Derrick said as I slipped my hand into his.

"Have fun. Good luck," Frank said after us as we made our way out of the store.

"Frank's the best mechanic in the area. People will drive miles just to have him work on their rig," Derrick said as we walked to his truck. "He can fix anything."

"That's great." I wasn't really all that interested in cars, but I guess it was good information to know.

"He's a real good guy. Was friends with my dad. Since Dad died, he's helped do things for my mom." He started the engine and asked, "All set?" The roar of the engine echoed under the awning.

"Sure," I answered and we were off again.

After driving a few miles listening to the local country music station, my mind wondering relentlessly, I said, "Derrick...I was thinking. How could I be this 'chosen one' if I can get hurt and sick? The more I think about it, I just can't be who they think I am."

"I got hurt and sick. In fact I broke my arm a couple years ago. But since this shapeshifting thing has happened, I hardly get a headache...I feel great," he stated.

I was looking for contradictions to last night's story when Derrick interrupted my train of thought. "Let's make a deal, no thinking about vampires, witches, or any of what was discussed last night...We can do that later. Let's take a break and just have some fun together, okay?"

That sounded great to me. "Deal," I smiled.

"How much further?" I asked noticing it was almost two o'clock. We'd been on the road climbing a mountain for over an hour. My ears had popped twice.

"Actually, we're almost there," Derrick answered as he turned off the loose gravel road into the forest, no longer driving on any type of road.

Derrick drove his truck over small trees, dodging large rocks and other debris that were too big to run over. I held on tight to the armrest and dash, wondering how he knew where to go without some sort of trail or other type of markers. I heard him chuckle and glanced his way. I was pretty sure he was getting a kick out of my reaction to our "off-road adventure". Several minutes later he stopped.

"We're here," he said turning off the engine in a thick part of the forest. He couldn't drive any further even if he tried.

We got out of the truck and I stretched my legs while he grabbed stuff from the bed of the truck. "Follow me," Derrick said as he headed toward the wall of trees.

The woods were dense and dark. I made sure to place each step carefully as we traveled on a well worn game trail. As we walked in silence, I began to get a little nervous about fishing. I didn't know if I'd like fishing. It never looked very fun on TV, kind of boring and gross.

"Just around that bend," Derrick said pointing off ahead.

I carried my water bottle. Derrick had all the food and supplies in a dark green backpack on his back, and held both poles in one hand. With his free hand he picked a wildflower that grew in one of the few rays of light filtering through the dense canopy and handed it to me.

"Thank you," I smiled taking the flower from him. I smelled it as we started walking again, the scent was strongly cinnamon. "What kind of flower is this?" I asked.

"It's called a Shooting Star," he answered not turning around.

I liked the unique flower as I admired its maroon and yellow center. The stamen and pistils were grouped together pointing out like a beak, and the flower's dainty purple petals were curled back. I was focused on the flower when I tripped. Stumbling I lost balance and fell forward. I landed on my knees, but was able to keep the flower safe.

"You okay?" Derrick turned to help me up.

"Yes," I grumbled brushing myself off. My knees and shins weren't too bad, no bleeding just scratches.

"Good thing I'm carrying the poles," he teased with a smile.

"Oh, just keep going," I said, pushing him forward. I was embarrassed. It seemed like I was getting clumsier every day.

The forest was quiet. The only noise being my feet on dry branches. Derrick moved without making any noise. After a while I began to hear a faint, but constant noise. It grew louder the deeper into the forest we went.

"Is that water?" I thought the noise might be a river. I wasn't dressed right for hiking and was getting tired. I hoped we were close because I didn't want to complain, especially knowing how excited

Derrick was to show me this place.

"You'll have to wait and see," he teased.

We left the trail and weaved between some trees to a wall of dense brush that was over Derrick's head, and stopped. For a moment I wondered if he was lost. But after examining the brush for a few moments, like he was looking for something, he held back a section of a bush.

"After you," he said motioning me through.

Being deliberate where I stepped so I wouldn't get scratched or trip, I passed through. Once I crossed the barrier and looked up, I gasped from surprise. I'd entered the most breathtaking, amazing place ever. A setting I'd only seen through the special effects of movies or on a canvas through an artist's eye.

"Beautiful, isn't it?" Derrick asked watching my face.

I was too stunned to answer. We went from a dense dark medieval forest to a large open meadow. I smelled fresh water, the forest, and a pleasant mixture of honeysuckle, wild rose, and mock orange bushes. The meadow's smells mixed with Derrick's heady scent was amazing.

There were white, pink and yellow blooming bushes scattered along a large stream, which flowed from a waterfall farther up the mountain, a few hundred yards from where I stood. The stream was angry at the base of the waterfall, as it crashed over large rocks and miniature rapids, but it gradually softened until it moved lazily past us. The grass was tall, up to my knees, but soft and green. Hundreds of colorful butterflies fluttered everywhere. A doe and her twin fawns with spots were grazing in the distance. She looked at us, flared her nose and flicked her ears back and forth before deciding we were no threat. I watched a pair of bluebirds flying from one bush to another.

The water raged in the distance with a mixture of gentle trickling noises closer. There were song birds, the fast pecking of a woodpecker, and the buzzing of bees. And I heard before saw, a hummingbird investigate the Shooting Star I held in my hand before zipping away.

Derrick took my hand and led me to the edge of the stream. The sunlight reflected off gentle waves, making the surface look as though it were covered with silver glitter. We followed the stream a few yards when I saw our destination. Next to where the stream made a small pool sat a large flat bluish rock, a natural bench. Derrick set down the poles and shrugged off his pack while I went to the edge of the pool. I reached down to feel the water. It was ice cold though it looked like it should be warm as bath water.

Derrick sat down beside me. "This place...it's very special. You are the only one I've ever brought here," he said while making swirls in the water with his hand. "My grandmother used to take me here. This was our place and this," he gestured toward the meadow, "is where she explained to me that there is so much life all around us. That we need to slow down and notice the miracles that surround us. Stuff I guess I forgot for a while. She died when I was fourteen. I've only been back here a couple times since then."

"I'm sorry," I said.

"Don't be. She lived a long life. She was older when she had my dad, and was in her mid nineties when she passed."

I heard sadness in his voice. He missed her, like I missed my grandparents. I felt the sudden urge to call my only living grandma. I made a conscious note in my head to call her when we got back.

We sat for a while gazing at the beauty of the meadow. I especially liked watching the fawns, which were now playing with each other in little hops.

"So...you ready to do some fishing?" Derrick asked getting the fishing poles.

"Sure," I answered not really looking forward to the experience, but determined to try.

I watched Derrick put the poles together. "This lure is called a spoon," he said tying on an oval shaped paper thin piece of metal about the size of a nickel, then biting off the excess line. Derrick cast the hook into the center of the little pool. I watched the silver metal twinkle as it sunk in the clear water. Derrick handed me the pole.

It was almost instantaneous. Once I took hold of the pole a fish darted toward the silver metal and my line was uncoiling.

"Oh crap. Derrick, what do I do?" I squeaked.

"Flip your bail," he said calmly showing me how on his reel.

I copied his movements. Then I felt the fish tugging on the line, bending my pole forward.

"Okay, now reel," he said demonstrating how to hold the rod and spin the reel.

It was a total rush. I had never done anything like this before.

Once I had the fish to the bank, Derrick bent down and picked it up.

"Good job," he said taking the hook out of the fish's mouth as it flopped its body back and forth.

"What kind is it?" I asked moving in to get a closer look.

"It's a Brook Trout and a pretty big one at that."

"Really?" I felt proud that I'd just caught my first fish, but it was only about eight inches long. I didn't think that was very big. But it sure put up a fight, or at least I thought it did. I watched Derrick put the fish back into the water with his hand underneath it, waiting for it to go on its own. I noticed the fish's colorful scales though the water before it darted out of sight.

"Aren't we going to eat it?" I asked, realizing that the question was a little too late.

"No, not out of here. Maybe later we can go fish Pend Oreille River. We can eat those fish."

"Why not these fish?" I asked while he tossed my spoon back into the pool.

"It was a deal my grandma made with me. She'd bring me here and share its secrets, but didn't want anything killed from this meadow."

It happened just like before. I watched silver spoon sink, the darting fish, and then the fight was on. I was having a blast. And after about the fifth catch, I was casting and releasing my own fish. Derrick grabbed his pole and was having fun too. Once the fishing slowed, we took a break to eat.

Handing me an apple he said, "I think we caught most of

them. Their mouths are sore so they won't bite for a while."

We sat on the flat rock and ate the apples along with some of the trail mix he packed. I ended up drinking most of my water. Derrick was right, his well water was tasty, kind of sweet.

The sun was high in the sky and its warmth felt wonderful on my skin. I noticed my pale arms and wondered again why I never tanned or burnt. I knew it was odd I didn't have to wear sunscreen, even though my mom insisted I did until I was eleven. Eleven was the age she started letting me make my own decisions. I remember the 105 degree sunny day when I rebelled and went without any SPF. I was out all day and didn't even get a tan. Mom thought for sure I'd burn and learn a valuable lesson. Boy, was she shocked.

Derrick had taken off his shirt, and was just wearing jeans. I looked at his skin, tight over his muscles, a smooth dark golden brown. I envied him. Without thinking I reached over and touched his arm, comparing the contrast of our skin tones.

"What?" he asked.

"Does it bother you that we're different?"

"Different?" he didn't understand.

I didn't know how to ask without sounding like a racist, "Does it bother you...that I'm so white?"

He got it. His face told me he understood. "No, not at all...Does it bother you?"

"No. I wish I wasn't so pale, but I don't care at all that we're ethnically different."

"Well," he said, "if what Amy said is true, you might just

have some Native blood in you after all."

I know he didn't mean to offend me, but I couldn't help but frown. I didn't want to think of Joseph as my biological father. Not because of any other reason than I loved *my* dad very much. The dad who taught me to ride my bike even though it took a lot longer than it should have.

"Sorry," Derrick said immediately. "I wasn't thinking." He turned to look me in the eyes. "We have plenty of time to talk about that stuff later," he said giving me a gentle kiss.

"Right," I agreed, "but don't be sorry. I don't want you to be afraid to talk to me. But, let's stick to the deal...no witch talk."

I wasn't ready to drop the previous subject.

"Does it bother your family, me being white?" His mother had beautiful bronzed skin like Derrick's, but just a shade or two lighter. So did Miya.

"No, my mom and sister are cool. Our tribe is small. If we tried to keep to our own, well let's just say it wouldn't take very long before there'd be an influx of one eyed babies with three legs," he smiled, "The elders want our blood as pure as it can be, but unless the marriages are arranged, which some tribes do, we marry who we want...who we love."

He paused for a moment and said, "I want to show you something."

I took his hand as he led me through the tall grass. It was soft against my legs, like walking through a field of green feathers. A different pair of birds sang somewhere out of view. As we walked towards the other end of the meadow, where the water flowed faster, he stopped in a cluster of butterflies next to a pink wild-rose bush. There were hundreds of them, all different colors and sizes fluttering around. They landed in our hair, on our bodies, everywhere they could. I looked at Derrick and laughed. He was covered in butterflies.

To my surprise Derrick sat down in the grass under them. He gently pulled me onto his lap.

"Remember when I told you science can't explain everything?" Derrick asked quietly. "That you can't find everything in books."

"Yes," I said watching a very large black and white butterfly that had landed on his shoulder, moving its delicate wings up and down very slowly.

"Well..." I noticed he was struggling to tell me something which drew my full attention to his face, "I wouldn't have taken you to this place if I didn't think you were ready. You've learned so much the past couple weeks that contradict...well, your version of reality. And it's been so negative, but real, Erica. Just because something isn't explained in a laboratory, doesn't mean it can't exist."

"I know," I said concerned by the strain in his voice. "What is it you're trying to say?" Derrick looked away. I took his face in my hands and looked him in the eyes. "You can tell me anything."

"Okay, I'm not breaking any deals here. This is something good, something beautiful. So how about I just show you, because it's too hard to explain," he said.

I watched as he held out his hand, palm up with his elbow bent, in front of me.

"Watch carefully," he said before letting out a soft high pitch whistle.

"Be very still and don't make any sudden moves," he warned through a whisper.

Before long I saw a butterfly land on his palm, a little smaller than a monarch. I noticed how beautiful its wings were. They had multiple contrasting colors of greens, yellows, reds, purples, and black circles that were larger at the bottom and gradually got smaller towards the top. The wings were rough on the edges where they looked frayed. Once my eyes moved to the body of the insect, I gasped in shock.

"Shhh," Derrick said, "be very still. They spook easily."

I blinked my eyes to make sure what I was seeing was real. I had been in the sun for a few hours. My eyes refocused and I saw the same thing as before. This was no butterfly, at least not like the butterflies I had to collect in middle school. The body was all wrong. Its yellow head was an upside down teardrop shape with two large round black eyes at the top with what looked like a very small thin mouth at the pointy bottom. It reminded me of an alien's head with two fuzzy antennae sticking out of it. It had a long hourglass shaped green body and stood on four little black legs with two other legs where you'd think arms should go. Maybe they were arms, but I didn't see any hands or feet like you'd think of, just little black ovals.

It was fascinating. Soon another landed on Derrick's palm next to the first. The body had the same shape, the same alien look, but the wings were a completely different mixture of colors and the edges were smooth. I had never seen anything so delicate and beautiful. Before long Derrick had a handful of them.

"Move your arm like mine," Derrick instructed in a very quiet, slow whisper.

I did as he said and soon I had three on my palm. They didn't weigh anything at all, but I could feel a slight tickle as they moved around on my palm. I think the black ovals were suction cups. I noticed they were looking at me. Soon a bird flew overhead scattering the mutated butterflies, or whatever they were. But it wasn't long before the swarm was back.

"What are they?" I asked amazed.

"Grandma called them forest fairies."

"Fairies?"

"Yep. They live in this meadow. This is the only one I know of. Grandma said there used to be several meadows, but they're being wiped out." He was so frank about it.

"That's awful." I felt bad for the fairies.

"It sucks, but what can you do? These little guys should be safe though. They're on protected lands so as long as no one cuts a road through here, they should be okay."

"Can they talk?" I asked, which must have been funny because Derrick busted out laughing.

"No, no, no," he said shaking his head. "You're thinking about Tinkerbelle. These little guys just flutter around," he snickered a little more. "They do help keep this place beautiful though. They eat whatever is dead...grass, bugs, birds."

I looked around and didn't see anything dead, not even a dry leaf.

"And science doesn't know about these forest fairies?" I asked.

"I don't think so. I haven't heard about anyone discovering them. I do know that if you catch one, they'll die. Once when I was ten I think, I didn't listen to my grandma's warning and I caught one like this," he cupped both of his hands together. "It's really easy if you're still. The little guy died instantly. I dropped it, horrified, and then I watched as others landed on it and, well...I guess they're kind of like cannibals."

"Gross." That little tidbit took away some of their cuteness.

"This place is a secret. I think just my grandma knew of it. I might bring Miya here someday, but I haven't decided yet."

I felt honored he'd share such a special secret with me. I leaned toward him, my eyes locked on his. Soon our lips touched and I pulled myself closer to him. How could this moment be any more perfect? I was in the most beautiful place in the world, not only beautiful but magical, with my soul mate. We were in each other's arms, our lips gently caressing. Nothing else mattered at that moment.

"Um, can I ask you to do something?" Derrick asked pulling

away slightly.

"Sure," I mumbled leaving soft kisses along his jaw line, working my way to his ear.

"Can you...sing for me? Please."

I sat up straight. "What was that?" I asked, afraid I'd heard right the first time.

"You have no idea what your voice does to me," he explained. "I could listen to you all day, it is the most intoxicating sound in the world, Erica. If you would sing, just a little, it would make this moment so perfect, so beautiful." He softly held the side of my face with one of his huge hands, lifting my head so that I would look him in the eyes. I began to wonder if my voice had the same effect on him as his scent did on me.

"Please?" he asked again.

How could I say no? I would do anything he asked me to.

"Okay," I agreed reluctantly. "Give me a minute to think of something."

Last time I just sang a melody I'd made up. I thought that I should try something with words this time, but I didn't know many songs. Then I remembered a song that was popular back in high school called *I Wanna Love You Forever*. I had the words memorized, and it seemed to fit the moment.

"Um...do you like Jessica Simpson?"

"Who?" Derrick asked oblivious.

"Never mind," I said and cleared my throat. I focused on a tree far off in the distance and reminded myself that no one besides

Derrick could hear me. I was really nervous and started the song off weak. Once I was through the first verse I began to relax. And as I became more comfortable, I was able to really ease into the song. It was a tender song and I wanted to do a good job. I wanted to let Derrick know that I was singing this song not only for him, but to him. Halfway through, I started testing myself, seeing how far my range would go, how long I could carry a note, it felt great. I was no longer embarrassed, as long as it was only Derrick. I knew I'd never be able to sing in front of anyone else this way. When I finished the song, I turned to look at Derrick. He was just watching me.

"Was that all right?" I couldn't read his reaction, and worried I wasn't as good as I thought.

"Beautiful," he said in a husky voice as he pulled me to him. His lips were hard on mine. I sensed his need as I kissed him back.

I pulled away and whispered, "I guess you liked it," before his lips were on mine again.

It didn't take long before I was on my back. His bare skin was hot from the sun, his smell and touch sending a strong desire deep inside me. He rolled to his back, with me laying on him as our lips explored and caressed. I could feel him hard beneath me, making my need more urgent.

I pulled away and sat up, straddling him beneath me, unable to keep my ragged breathing even as I slowly rocked my hips back and forth. His hands were on my waist pulling me against him, his breathing heavy. One of his hands slipped beneath my shirt, under my bra. I moaned in pleasure.

"You should take this off," he said, his voice husky.

I pulled my tank-top off. Before I dropped the piece of clothing, he sat up and his lips were on my neck moving to my shoulder.

I pulled him close, feeling his hot body against mine. I felt his hand unclasp my bra. He pulled his lips from mine and looked at me, making sure it was okay. I kissed him hard encouraging him to continue. Slowly he slid one strap down at a time, delicately kissing my shoulders as he did. My body trembled with need, his soft caresses were steadily flaming the fire within.

He slid off my bra and leaned back to look at me. I blushed and tried to cover myself but he caught my hands and sighed. "You are beyond amazing," he whispered before kissing me again.

His strong warm arms were around me, his hard smooth chest against mine. I felt so small, yet so safe. I was lost in passion. It felt wonderful, and it felt right. He kissed my neck and gradually made his way down my chest with his soft lips and slowly continued to my breasts. His tongue and lips on my nipples made the yearning stronger. I quivered in anticipation, letting out sighs and moans. My body was hot and ripe, I wanted him. I was ready. I moved my hands to the button of his shorts. But he met my hand with his, stopping me.

"We can't," he whispered in my ear, followed by his soft lips and warm tongue.

"What?" I asked a little shocked and hurt.

"Not that I don't want to," he said quickly. "I don't have

anything with me."

"Oh," I said understanding what he meant, feeling stupid. A baby was not what either of us needed.

"But we don't have to stop," he said gently laying me on my back. "We can still have some fun."

He was on top of me, his hips between my thighs gently pressing into me. I was crazy with desire, and if this was all he'd give me, I'd take it. He began rocking against me, moaning against my lips. My hands were on his butt, pulling him to me.

"Erica," he breathed heavy as I felt him shudder. Quickly his mouth found mine as he slipped to the side a little, so his hand was free to roam. I felt him unbutton my shorts. I grabbed his thick forearm, as I had before, but this time I pushed his arm down, encouraging him to go further.

My heart was racing, my breathing ragged, as he gently found my depth. My hands were back on his shoulders, pulling him to me. What he was doing felt so good, my hips automatically moved to him wanting more. His lips were on my neck, my mouth, my breasts. I felt something building deep inside.

"Oh Derrick," I moaned as the feeling began to build. "Don't stop." I closed my eyes riding the ride until I reached the peak and cried out as my body exploded from pleasure.

The feeling faded like waves from throwing a stone in water. I opened my eyes and looked up at Derrick. He bent down and kissed me before rolling onto his back next to me.

We laid there for a while, letting our hearts slow and

breathing return to normal. I couldn't believe what just happened. I felt great, but tired and thirsty. I could only imagine what the real thing would feel like.

I moved to rest my head on his shoulder, my hand in his. The sun was hot on my skin, it felt nice. I decided I liked having my shirt off, the sensation was free. Now I understood why men liked to go shirtless so much.

Together we watched the butterflies and forest fairies above us, picking out ones that caught our eye. They liked to be together and fluttered in what made me think of ballet. And now that I knew what to look for, I could easily tell them apart.

"We should probably get going," Derrick said sitting up.

Once we had our clothes on and the grass out of our hair, I followed him back to our rock and helped pack up the fishing gear. He slipped on his shirt. We ate the rest of the trail mix before we started towards the truck. I had stored my Shooting Star in my water bottle out of the sun, and was glad it still looked fresh. I took the flower out to carry while Derrick slipped the bottle into his backpack.

"I'm so happy you brought me here," I told Derrick, following him.

"Me too," he said turning and sweeping me up into his arms. "I love you," he said before kissing me.

He set me down and we began walking again. I looked back over the meadow, and noticed the animals were gone, the butterflies and fairies as well. I realized the sun was dropping. It was getting late.

At the edge of the meadow he helped me back through the thick brush and soon we were back on the game trail. It was much darker than before. Barely any light filtered through the canopy of branches above. I shivered. It was cold compared to the warm meadow we left. I looked into the forest. The thin skeleton like trees were packed so tightly together, I couldn't see much farther than a few yards. I focused my eyes on the trail, being careful not to trip again.

We walked a few minutes when Derrick stopped in the trail. I was several feet behind him and figured he was waiting for me to catch up. When I got to him I could tell something was wrong. He was looking around, searching for something. I began to look as well. Maybe it was the setting or just the cold, but I was more alert.

Derrick turned to me, and in one swift move had me over his shoulder. He held onto my legs as I hung over his back, his backpack digging into my side. I realized I dropped my flower as I watched it hit the trail.

"Derrick, what's...," I tried to ask.

"Vampire," was all he had to say and I shut up, the backpack not so noticeable anymore.

Then he ran.

His speed was amazing. The weight he carried didn't slow him down at all. Derrick's feet were a blur and so was the ground. I couldn't make out a rock or a branch or anything. He ran quietly. I didn't hear a thing but the gentle jostling of the backpack and poles.

Nor did I feel any jarring motion. It was like I was flying, but in a very odd position.

We were at Derrick's truck within moments. A trip that had taken at least a half hour took us less than five. He chucked the poles and backpack into the bed of his truck and gently tossed me through the driver side door as he jumped in behind me. He had the truck in reverse, flying backward before I even had a chance to slide over and buckle myself into the passenger seat.

Once I'd pulled the seatbelt as tight as it would go, I sat there very quietly. I stared at him in utter shock. He was concentrating, looking over his arm through the back window. I remembered all of the obstacles that were blocking the way up here, and wondered how he was avoiding them. He had the pedal to the metal, in reverse. I thought for sure the truck was going to flip, but it never did, even when it was only on two wheels.

Soon we were back on the gravel road and going forward. Showers of gravel sprayed behind us as he hit the gas. I relaxed a little. At least we were traveling in the right direction.

I hesitated. I didn't know if I should talk, but I had to say something. "Vampire?" I whispered.

Derrick gave me a quick glance and then focused back on the road. "I could smell it. It was a long way off, but still, I needed to get you out of there," he said in an angry tone as his truck skidded around a curve.

I got the feeling he wasn't in the mood to talk right then. I pulled my eyes away from his face and looked out my side window, and instantly wished I hadn't. I was frightened for a different reason, one that seemed much more likely to kill us at the moment. Past the two feet shoulder was a very steep drop off. It would take a long, long time before the trees below would stop the truck from rolling.

"Derrick," I squeaked full of fear. My body was stiff with fright, my mouth dry. I was holding the dash with my left hand and the door with my right. I didn't want to disturb him, and I was certain he had control over the rig, but I was scared.

"Oh," Derrick said once he saw the horror on my face, and slowed the truck down, but just a little. "I'm sorry but you don't need to worry. I'm in control," he said as he patted the dash and gave me a reassuring smile.

Finally we made it to pavement. I glanced at his speedometer, the needle quivered around a 110 mph. We rode in silence. I watched the trees whiz by in a blur. I didn't know where we were. Every road we passed looked like the one we were on. There were no road signs. I wondered how people were supposed to find their way around. Then, as we passed one road, I noticed a bright Mylar balloon with HAPPY BIRTHDAY printed in large bubble letters tied to the stop sign and a green arrow pointed down the road with JONES written on it.

We were back to Derrick's house by seven. The trip back took about forty-five minutes. One of the cars that had been missing from the garage earlier, a gray sedan, was back in its place. I assumed his mom must be home.

He was out of the truck and opening my door before I

unbuckled. My hands were shaking. Derrick lifted me out of the truck and towed me by the hand into the house through the side door. I stumbled a couple times, but he was quick to help me. The door led us through the mudroom and into the kitchen. I smelled a delicious aroma and saw his mom busy at the island. It looked like she was chopping vegetables for a salad.

Karen set down the knife when she saw Derrick, knowing something bad had happened. In a strong firm voice Karen asked, "What's wrong?"

"Vampire...I have to get back there, NOW," Derrick said in a growl.

"What? NO!" I shrieked in horror.

His mom nodded and gently moved to hold me by my shoulders. "Go," was all she said.

I couldn't believe my ears. Did I just hear Karen give him the okay to look for a *VAMPIRE*? He turned to me and gently took my face in his large strong hands.

"It will be okay," he said looking me in the eyes. I realized he wasn't afraid at all. He was excited. "I will be fine," he reassured. "It's that thing that should be afraid."

Derrick let go and hurried towards the front door, the one that led to the porch with the swing. Once he was out the door, I shrugged loose from Karen's hands and ran to stop him. I made it to the open door but was too late. I watched as he leapt from the top of the steps. His clothes were torn from his body as he transformed into the mountain lion with the black tail. Then he was gone. It all happened so fast. I stood unable to move.

Karen quietly walked past me. I watched as she started picking up the rags from the yard. Without a word I went to help her. I followed her as we silently took the once fairly new outfit to the garbage can next to the garage, and then we went back into the house. I sat on one of the stools at the island and looked out the window above the sink as she picked up the knife and continued chopping, as if nothing had happened.

CHAPTER 13

I was out of shock before Karen finished the salad, and helped her chop some very strong onions. As the fumes stung my eyes and automatic tears began to flow, I let some of my own worried tears sneak in. I was scared. I knew Derrick could take care of himself. I watched him easily kill Frederick, but still I was afraid. I didn't want this to be actually happening, to be real.

The phone rang and Karen answered a cordless receiver that was on the counter next to the sink. I overheard Karen speaking to Miya, then to someone else. "Miya's staying the night at Julie's," Karen said hanging up. "That's my sister."

"Oh, okay," I said. I was uncomfortable in this house without Derrick. I'd never even had a conversation with his mom, and now dinner was just us.

"Do you mind eating in here?" Karen asked.

"That's fine," I answered. The island had stools and a bar area to eat on.

"You want to set some plates. They are in that cupboard." She pointed to a cupboard next to fridge, "and the silverware is in here." She pointed to a drawer next to the sink with her foot.

I set the island while she dished our plates. Then we were both sitting, ready to eat. I waited for her to take the first bite before I started on my plate, a formality I remembered from an etiquette class.

"This is really great," I complimented Karen. The steak had a distinct taste, one I couldn't place.

"Thank you," she said, "it's venison. I make my own marinade out of red wine and vinegar that takes out the game taste while enhancing the meat's delicate flavors."

"Deer meat?" I asked thinking of the doe and twin fawns I saw earlier in the meadow.

"Yep. This is Derrick's deer from last year. It's probably the best red meat for you," she said.

I'd never had venison before. I liked it. And I supposed all meat has a face. I thought of the cute pigs that I guess I liked to have for breakfast.

I wasn't hungry but I was able to eat almost the entire plate of food, only a bit of the fresh salad and dinner roll remained. We ate in silence. When we were done, I helped Karen clean up.

When I finished wiping down the island I stood there for a moment, wondering what to do. I was about to head down to Derrick's room when Karen closed the door to the dishwasher. She said in a soft voice, "Derrick probably won't be back for several hours. He'll search until he's either found the monster or until he's sure it left."

"Okay," I muttered.

"Let's have some tea," she said turning on the teapot. "Pick one." She opened a cupboard with several flavors of tea. I chose a green tea. She picked a passion berry, and after we steeped the tea in our mugs, I followed Karen to the living room.

We sat across from each other on the dark leather furniture. I sat on the love seat while she took the sofa. I wasn't sure what to say. I couldn't stop worrying, stop replaying that horrible scene of Derrick ripping apart Frederick. Or imagining Derrick attacking another vampire, or worse, Derrick being attacked. After an awkward moment of silence, Karen began to speak.

"Derrick's father, Robert, and I married right out of high school. We loved each other very much. He had a great job at the mill. I was a fry cook at a burger joint in town. People said we were too young, that it was a mistake. But we knew better. We could feel it in here," she said placing her hand over her heart.

"Did you know Derrick's dad built this house?" she asked me.

"Wow," I was impressed. "I think this house is fantastic."

"He was able to get a deal on the lumber from the mill. It took him almost two years to finish." It looked like she was reminiscing as she smiled to herself.

"Soon, I was pregnant with Derrick. Then Robert's dad died and he became the Chief. We had a lot of responsibility, but we were happy. Once Derrick was born, I quit the restaurant and stayed at home. We had some bumps along the way. Things were really tough when I became pregnant with Miya. It was a difficult pregnancy, and the delivery almost killed us both. After Miya and I were out-of-the-woods, my and Robert's love for one another was...rekindled."

Karen looked at me, her eyes glossy. "It's sad how it takes something so terrible to remind us how fragile life is, and to make you realize what a gift love is. After that, we lived each day to its fullest, as if it was our last. We still had our fights, but boy, did we make-up. Sometimes I think we'd fight just so we would make-up."

She gave me a soft sad smile before continuing. "We had a very loving home and did things as a family." I sensed she was getting to the bad part. Her voice took on a sad tone as she finished. "One night Robert worked late at the mill and was on his way home when a seventeen year old high on dope and drunk on booze decided to take a drive. He ran head-on into my husband. They were both killed at the scene."

"I'm so sorry," I said wondering what to do. Should I sit by her? Should I ask her questions? Should I share a sad story, but how could I come close? I decided to just sit there and say nothing.

"My husband loved his people. He loved being Chief. He did great things for the Washtucnas. He knew he was a descendant of Sikyahonaw, but never did experience the change. But there were differences after he turned nineteen. He never got sick. He was stronger than anyone, and his vitality stayed that of a young man...I was a very lucky woman," she said smiling one of Derrick's smiles and giving me wink. I blushed. I knew what she meant.

"Derrick had a hard time after Robert was killed. Then his grandmother died. He took it all very hard." Karen was looking at me when she said, "Derrick has always been a good son and big brother. He's done a wonderful job being the man-of-the-house, but he hasn't been happy for a very long time."

Karen moved to sit by me. She took my hand in hers and said seriously, "Derrick loves you...I've never seen him like this. I think I knew you were the one for him before he did, the visions he had were powerful. Ultimately all a good mother wants is for her children to be happy," she softly smiled, "and you make him very happy. I welcome you into our family, Erica. I welcome you as my daughter."

I was touched. Tears began to flow. "Thank you. Thank you so much," I said giving her a hug.

She returned my hug and patted my back while saying, "He'll be okay."

"Would you like to watch a movie?" she asked once our moment was over.

"Sure," I answered giving her one of my fake smiles. I didn't really want to watch TV, but it would be better than sitting in silence letting my mind wander.

"How about a quick tour of the house first?" Karen asked.

"Sure," I answered.

From the living room, which was to the left of the front door as you entered you could see the dining room behind it. Immediately to the right of the front door was a set of stairs that went up and down. About a quarter of the second floor was open to the living room.

Karen led me down a narrow hallway past the stairs on the main floor. Heading down the hall, to my left on the other side of the divider wall would be the kitchen and mudroom. The hallway wall was full of family pictures. I briefly caught a glimpse of a younger Derrick in a family photo taken with his dad. I saw the resemblance in the shape of their faces. To my right was a small bathroom with only a toilet and sink. We passed a TV room and then at the end of the hall was the master bedroom. Karen's room had a beautiful queen sized log bed that had to be at least three feet off the ground, with a matching dresser and rocking chair. She had a white patchwork comforter set and white curtains on both windows. The master bathroom resembled Derrick's, except there was a garden tub as well as a shower stall.

Next she led me up the stairs. There was a small loft to my left with a black metal guardrail that overlooked the living room. The loft had a couple lounge chairs, a computer desk and a bookshelf full of books. To my right was a narrow hall with two rooms, Miya's and a spare room that looked more like a storage room for Karen's catering business. It was packed full of silver dishware, tablecloths, and various platters and utensils.

"I think you're already familiar with the rest of the house," Karen said leading me back down the stairs to the TV room. There was a large soft couch and a couple beanbag chairs facing a flat screen TV that hung on the wall.

Karen turned on the TV and asked, "Anything in particular?"

"Not really, just nothing with vampires," I answered walking over to take a seat on the couch.

"What about this," she asked flipping the channel to the Food Network station. It was a reality cooking competition show. A contest to win the chance to prepare a three course meal for a celebrity event.

I didn't really care what I watched. So I nodded and answered, "Looks good to me," as Karen sat down next to me and patted my leg.

We watched the show. Well actually I just stared at the screen while my mind raced. It felt wrong that I was here watching TV while Derrick was out hunting a vampire, or worse, vampires.

The show finally ended. The triumphant chef made a great meal that won praises from the rich and famous. It was close to midnight.

"Goodnight Erica," Karen said through a yawn. "Make yourself at home."

"Thanks...and goodnight," I replied getting up as well. I figured I should try to get some sleep too.

As I made my way down the stairs toward Derrick's room, I passed the foosball table. I remembered Derrick and I had a game to play. I guess it would have to wait.

I wasn't tired at all. I looked through Derrick's books and music, but didn't find anything I wanted to read or listen to. I flipped on his TV, but nothing was on worth watching. So I decided to take a shower, a very long and hot shower. Since it was so late, I doubted anyone would care if I used up all the hot water.

I was undressed and about to hop through the shower door when I caught my reflection in the mirror. I moved closer and stared at myself. I looked for any trace of my parents, a freckle or a mark, anything that would connect me to either one of them. There was nothing. I let the possibility that my biological parents might be someone else slowly creep into my brain, but stopped when my chest hurt and I felt sick. I wasn't ready to go there quite yet.

I stepped into the pre-warmed shower and turned the water as hot as I could stand it. I let the pressure and heat from the spray relax me as much as possible. When I finished, my skin was red from the heat and toes wrinkly from the water. I brushed my teeth and hair and slipped into a comfy pair of pajamas. I quickly checked my email. There was nothing new.

It was almost two in the morning when I decided lie down.

When the lights were off, Derrick's room was too dark. I left the small desk lamp turned on telling myself it was so Derrick could see when he got home, even though I knew he had night vision. I took comfort in his smell on the blankets and must have fallen asleep because I woke to the hum of the bathroom fan and the shower.

Derrick was back.

I jumped out of bed and raced into the bathroom.

"Derrick?" I said quietly.

"The one and only," I heard him say from behind the shower door. I could barely make out a dark figure through the tempered glass.

"Are you okay?"

"Of course."

"Did you find anything?" I asked, knowing I wouldn't like either answer.

"No, I followed the scent through the Idaho panhandle and into Montana, where I decided that maybe I'd better stop and come back home." There was disappointment in his voice.

"I'm glad you're back...safe," I said softly.

I didn't think he could hear me, but he must have because he opened the shower door and poked his head out. "I'll always come back to you baby," he said with a huge grin.

I smiled back. Water dripped from his face to the floor. He winked at me then shut the door.

I went back to bed and waited for him under the warm black comforter. The desk lamp cast a soft glow in the dark room as if it were a candle. I was arguing with myself whether I wanted to hear more about his excursion or not. I did because I was curious, but I didn't because the thought frightened me.

Before I arrived to a decision, my attention was directed to the bathroom door as it opened. I watched steam escape and quickly evaporate. I felt the humidity and smelled his intoxicating scent in combo with soap and shampoo. The aroma sent an irresistible craving through my body.

My heart rate tripled. He was magnificent. I watched him move through the steam, which parted around him like smoke. He only wore pull on shorts. His long black hair was combed straight back. His body glistened briefly before he turned off the bathroom light, then he faded into the background of the dimly lit room.

I barely made out his shape as he walked to the end of the bed. I struggled to keep my breathing normal. I felt the bed moving under me, shifting from his weight as he crawled slowly onto the bed, my excitement building with each movement that brought him closer. Soon he was snuggling up to me, nuzzling my neck.

"Still awake?" he whispered, his lips close to my ear.

That did it, I couldn't hold still any longer. Softy I moaned and pressed against him. I turned to face him. His lips found mine. But I could tell something wasn't right.

"What's wrong?" I asked taking his face in my hands, waiting for a reply. When he didn't answer, I figured he must have been upset about not finding the vampire.

"You did your best. I'm kind of glad you didn't find it," I said quietly, unable to say the word "vampire".

He moved to sit cross-legged, his elbows resting on his knees, looking down at me. "It's still out there. That means it's still hunting...still looking for you," he said.

I sat up, taking a long moment before saying, "We don't know that for sure...that it's me they want. So let's not talk about it right now." He didn't respond, and I couldn't read his face.

"Your mom and I had an interesting talk tonight," I said trying to change the subject.

"Really?" he sounded curious.

"She told me about her and your dad," I said softly.

"Oh, yeah?"

"She told me about how much love they shared, that their life was very happy." I hesitated. "She welcomed me into your family. She told me she welcomed me as her daughter."

"I never had a doubt," he said a little cocky. I thought I could make out a smile.

"You know what else she said?" I asked, waiting for him to take the bait.

"What?"

"She said that her and your dad learned to live life to its fullest. And after she almost died from having Miya, they lived each day like it was their last...that they learned what a gift love was."

After a moment Derrick said, "I think that's a good philosophy."

"I'm glad you think so, because..., Derrick?"

"Yeah?"

"I want to do that. I want to live our days together as if they were our last as much as possible."

I paused briefly before asking softly, "Derrick?"

"Hmm?"

"I love you," I whispered as I lay down pulling him with me.

I decided to show him what I wanted instead of asking. I didn't want to think about anything else but that moment. As soon as our lips met and we could savor each other, I sensed he felt the same way. We focused on each other. We focused on our love, our passion, and the excitement of new experiences.

We felt our way to each other. He quickly had my shirt off

and didn't need to worry about a bra. Gently he pressed against me, his hot chest on mine. It felt perfect having him in my arms with his weight on me.

Soon Derrick was under the comforter with me. Our bodies together while our hands explored and aroused in the dark. I wanted him closer. I yearned for his touch. I arched my back wrapping my leg around his, pressing myself to him.

Derrick's mouth explored my body with soft caresses. His tongue drove me insane when it found my breasts and slowly moved down to my hip. Ever so gradually he removed my pajama bottoms, leaving a tender trail of kisses from the inside of my thigh up to my hip to below my navel. The anticipation was torture. I wanted him. My body throbbed for him. But first I wanted to drive him crazy with soft teases of pleasure.

Gently I guided his lips to mine and slowly rolled over so that my weight was on him. I kissed him long and deep. My lips found his ear and slowly traveled down his neck savoring the salty flavor of his skin. His breathing and soft moans encouraged me as I made my way to his chest. I softly teethed and played with his hard nipples. He moaned and his hands clenched the bedding as I made my way to his stomach. I copied his moves as I left my own moist trail of kisses from his hip to below his navel. I tried to be seductive as I slowly removed his shorts, but was a little shocked he didn't have on any undershorts. I'd seen his nude backside, but I'd never seen any man's frontside naked in real life before. I sat up gazing at his entire body, the faint light highlighting his contours. He was hard and ready. Slowly I bent to kiss his chest, laying on him at an angle, while my hand softly stroked. My kisses made their way to his mouth.

"Oh Erica, what you do to me," Derrick breathed heavily pulling me tight against his chest. Our kissing was frantic and deep, our yearning fierce. He arched and moved so that I was under him, our breathing heavy as our bodies moved rhythmically in response to our desire. I felt his need. He felt mine. We were going to make love. There was no doubt about it.

We were wild with passion, the delay torture to our hunger. Slowly he slid off my cotton bikinis and we were naked, tightly embraced, but nervous, hesitating to cross that line.

"Are you sure?" Derrick whispered in a gasp, struggling to find his breath, to control the ache.

I moaned in pleasure as he pressed against me. We were prepared and I was ready.

"I love you Derrick," I whispered as I guided him to me. And then we were together as one. Derrick's kisses found tears gently falling from my eyes. He stopped abruptly.

"You okay?" he asked, full of concern.

"Happy tears," I said pulling him to me. And we made love, exploding in ecstasy over and over until daylight broke through the windows.

As we lay together, letting our hearts relax and our breathing slow, I asked, "Derrick, have you ever felt so, so whole?"

"Never," he whispered in my ear.

"I'm so happy I'm afraid to sleep. I'm afraid this will all have been a dream. A good dream...but still, just a dream."

"I love you. We're meant to be together," he whispered pulling me tighter. "Try to get some sleep. When you wake up, I'm sure you'll remember it wasn't a dream when I'm naked in bed with you."

"You're right," I said through a tired giggle drifting to sleep in the comfort of his strong arms.

CHAPTER 14

I woke slowly, my eyes slightly faster than my brain. I felt sluggish. My mind began to clear and a large smile materialized on my face. I remembered every wonderful thing that happened between me and Derrick.

He was behind me. We were still snuggled close in the spooning position I loved so much, his arm draped across my bare waist under the comforter. I wondered if he was sleeping. I listened but couldn't tell. Slowly I turned, being careful not to disturb him. He was awake, his head resting on his hand propped up on an elbow.

"Good morning," he whispered leaning down to kiss me.

"How long have you been up?" I asked before his lips met mine.

We enjoyed a long soft kiss, before he answered, "Not long, maybe twenty minutes."

"Oh, you should have waked me," I yawned deep and wide.

"No, I was watching you sleep. I can see you through the mirror." He pointed toward the mirror over his dresser, the one I had looked in yesterday.

"Was I entertaining?"

He smiled, "Actually you were. I could watch you all day long," he said. I felt his eyes tenderly caressing my face.

I would have loved to chat some more, but I had to go to the bathroom. "Um, I'd better get up," I said reluctantly, a frown of urgency on my face.

"Nature?" he asked giving me a crooked smile. I nodded.

With the arm he still had around my waist, he flung the covers back in one long sweep. The cool air was jolting as it displayed my nakedness. The sun's rays filtered through the windows lighting the room. He could see all of me. I pulled the blankets back over us, which made Derrick laugh.

"I didn't know your whole body could blush. Please don't tell me you're going modest on me, not now," he said pulling me next to his warm hard body, which provoked a sudden desire that I had to ignore, because I had to GO.

"Well, it wasn't so light before, it was easier..." I tried to be flirty. Then I did feel kind of silly being so bashful after remembering some of the things we'd done. I let out a soft laugh which made my need for the bathroom worse.

"You have nothing to be embarrassed about, Erica. You are exquisite in every way. Your beauty inside and out drives me crazy, and your body is perfect," Derrick reassured as he slid a warm hand softly down my side then resting it on my hip, sending shivers of excitement through me.

I took a deep breath and decided to get up before I made a really embarrassing mess. I threw back the covers but not nearly as gracefully as Derrick had. It took me twice just to get myself uncovered. I got up slowly and walked to the bathroom. I wasn't going to give him any reason to laugh by my hurrying. I felt my hair brushing against the middle of my back and his eyes on my backside, as I deliberately made my way into the bathroom.

I caught a glimpse of my reflection in the mirror and saw that my hair was in its rat's nest style. A brush would never make it through without taking a lot of time. Since I was already naked, I decided to go ahead and take a quick shower using lots of conditioner. I made the mistake of stepping into the shower too soon and was forced wide awake when the cold water hit me. But once the water warmed, it felt good and relaxing. I wished my shower back home had half the pressure of Derrick's.

While I lathered I reminisced about how perfect our lovemaking had been. I wondered if Derrick felt the same way. I was definitely looking forward to the next time. Maybe once I was out of the shower, I could seduce him. The thought made me hurry.

I combed my hair, brushed my teeth, wrapped a towel around myself, and went to find Derrick, hoping he was still in bed. Unfortunately he wasn't. His room was empty. I took as long as I could to dress, at least ten minutes before I chose a pair of blue jeans and white tank top, then finally decided to give up on my seduction idea.

I turned on his computer to check my email. The Gonzaga emails reminded me that soon I'd have to withdraw from there and apply at the community college. I'd get all the necessary paperwork ready next week. That would be my job while Derrick went back to work. I planned to have everything ready for my parents when they got back.

I had an email message from my mom. They were having a great time but missed me. I smiled to myself. They loved me and I loved them. I would wait until they had a chance to explain before I jumped to any conclusions. I replied and told them what a great time I was having with Derrick and how wonderful his mom, sister, and home was. I told them I learned to fish, which I figured would shock them both.

Mentally, I chose not to acknowledge the possibility that they weren't my biological parents, not yet anyway. I'd been able to accept the incredible mysteries that were popping up around me so long as it wasn't happening to me specifically. So far I was able to digest that my fiancé was a shapeshifter/werewolf, and I even accepted the idea of witches versus vampires. But I was not ready to fathom the possibility that I was included in that circle of wonders.

Mom mentioned not to forget about checking the mail because "it was an invitation to thieves if the mailbox was overflowing" which meant I'd have to go home. I was sure there'd be mail and couldn't remember the Johnson's phone number to ask them to grab it for me. I figured I should probably check on the house anyway since I left in such a rush.

I started towards the door when Derrick walked into the room with a great big grin on his face. He looked great. He had on a pair of jeans, his feet and torso bare. I noticed his hair was wet.

Derrick picked me up in one big scoop and gave me a long luscious kiss. I hugged him tight and kissed him back.

"Hi," I said breathless as he still held me.

"Hi," he echoed softly against my lips. "I made you breakfast, French toast with strawberries."

My easily manipulated stomach made a noise, revealing how hungry I suddenly was.

"That sounds great," I said as he slowly set me down.

"You took a shower and made breakfast?" I asked following him up the stairs.

"It was a quick shower and it's not like French toast takes long," he winked back at me.

"The hot water tank in this house must be great. I never felt a change in pressure or temperature," I said remembering that no one in our house could run the sink or even flush the toilet without scalding or freezing whoever was taking a shower.

"I guess," he answered, clearly not realizing what a luxury it was to be able to take two showers at the same time.

The house seemed very quiet and empty. "Where's your mom?" I asked walking into the kitchen after him.

"She just took off to work. Someone called in sick," he said handing me two glasses of orange juice.

Derrick grabbed our plates and led me to the backyard patio where we sat at a simple black metal patio set. The sun was out so the cream colored cushions were warm beneath us. He slid my plate down in front of me and I set his glass next to his plate. As I ate, I admired their small back yard. The green grass was bordered with Thimbleberry bushes in full bloom with an old forest behind them. The yard was one of the nicest I'd ever been in. All they needed was a little fountain with a cherub.

"This place is so great," I smiled.

"Really," he asked, "you like it here?"

"Sure, it's beautiful."

"Well, I was thinking," he said, brushing a piece of hair from my face to get me to look at him, "What do you think about staying here with me?"

"What?" I coughed to loosen a piece of food I just choked on.

"Actually, Mom suggested it this morning. But it makes sense. This house is huge and we'd have tons of privacy. My little sister can be annoying, but you'd get used to her..."

"You want me to live here with you?" I interrupted as the idea sank into my brain.

"Erica," he said moving closer, "I can't be away from you. Just the thought makes me anxious. I have to be near you. And it's not a psychotic obsession like you'd think. It's like I have to protect you, to know you're safe. We live so far apart. So much could happen before I could get to you. And, I don't think your parents would like the idea of me moving in with them."

I smiled, "You're right. They wouldn't be keen to the idea. But I know what you mean. I feel it too, that I need to be with you. It hurts right here," I said pointing to my chest "if I even think about being away from you for longer than a few hours." More softly I asked, "Do you think it's normal?"

Derrick let out a deep sigh and shook his head. "No, no I don't. But honestly I don't think anything about us is normal. We're meant to be together and there is some force making sure that happens...We're destiny." He leaned closer to my face and softly said, "I feel like the luckiest person in the world. I'd never make it without you."

"Me too," I leaned in and softly kissed him.

"So what do you think?" he asked. "Or do you want some time to mull it over?"

"I don't need to think about it, Derrick. Of course I'll move in with you. My parents are going to have a friggin' breakdown when they get home though." I laughed nervously. "Maybe I should wait until after my birthday, and then spring the whole moving in together and the getting married information on them."

"That's right...your birthday's coming up," he said with a smile. "Next week, June 21st, right?"

"Yep, and if I stay with you until they come home, it would only be a day or two we'd have to be apart. Think you can handle that?" I asked seriously, because I didn't know if I could.

"I'll try," he said turning his attention to his plate.

I took a bite. "Thanks for breakfast, Derrick. This is really great," I complimented before shoveling another forkful into my mouth. I noticed he didn't have any strawberries, just syrup. "Don't like strawberries?" I asked.

"They're okay, just not my favorite on egg soaked bread," he said showing me a bowl filled with fresh strawberries. "I'll have mine on the side."

I'd have to remember he liked strawberries alone. I smiled to myself realizing that that's probably why he took such a puny piece of my mom's angel food cake the other day. It was topped with strawberries.

We watched and listened to birds while we ate. I had to swat away a few yellow jackets that wanted my food. I'd miss my parents but I'd like living here. To be able to enjoy this every day and be with Derrick, but I'd live in the ghetto just to be with him, if that's what it took.

"This place is so quiet and pretty," I said leaning back in my chair, "and fresh. I can't smell exhaust or any nasty city smells."

"It's nice, especially since none of us has to do much. Mom will plant the flowers she buys at the school's spring plant sale. I mow once a week. Miya will weed every now and then, but really that's about it," he said.

"Really? My parents go crazy at our house. When we first moved here, it was the first time either of them had to take care of a green yard. I think they bought everything the sales guy told them they'd need." I rolled my eyes remembering the greasy creepy guy wearing a red apron that helped us at the nursery. I had a feeling he was taking my parents for a ride. They bought over a grand worth of tools, fertilizers, pesticides, this and that's for the yard, most of which were still unopened in the garage.

"Back in Albuquerque," I continued sitting forward, "it doesn't take a lot of effort to keep a gravel yard. But we did have a rock and cactus garden, way too much work there," I said sarcastically "Eventually they figured it out here, and keep the grass nice."

"Did you like Albuquerque?" he asked.

I thought about his question before answering. It was a while ago. "Yes, I suppose. I like the dry heat and I had friends down there. Sarah was really my only friend up here." Thinking about Sarah made me sad, but I hoped she was happy.

I took his hands in mine, holding them tight I stared deep into his eyes. "But I love it here. I couldn't imagine being anywhere else. And since we've been together, it's like you're my home. I want to be wherever you are."

"That's good," he said with a sly smile.

"So much is going on. I'm having a hard time keeping up. But I do know I love you and you love me and we are going to get through all of this together. Whatever that is," I moved to sit on his lap. "That's the deal."

Nodding and wrapping his arms around me he said, "Yes, but speaking of deals," I felt him tense beneath me, "we need to talk about something I put off yesterday."

I sensed I wasn't going to like what he was about to say.

"Erica, I have to tell you something," he repeated rather abruptly.

"Okay," I said, feeling nervous.

In a deep voice full of stress he said, "Tonight is a full moon, and that means...werewolf."

I watched his face waiting for him to go on. More slowly he continued, "Well, this will only be my second time. I just don't want you to freak out."

"I won't," or at least I hoped I wouldn't.

"It'll be okay. Jack, Amy, and Bill will be here with you guys."

"Great," I said under my breath. They were the last people I wanted to see. He must have heard me because he was quick to defend them.

"They're here to help me," he tried to explain, "and they're sorry they upset you. But they really thought it'd be for the best." He took a breath. "You know, telling you what they knew and all. I still think it could have been done differently, and trust me, they know that."

Derrick took a few more deep breaths before continuing. "Well, I don't expect you to watch or anything, but the need to hunt is very strong. And since there's been a vampire around, I probably will be gone all night. And that would be a good time to...get to know them if you want."

"Oh," I said, understanding his subtle meaning without directly telling me to talk to the Council, which I had no intention of doing.

I wanted to change the subject.

"Well, I'll be waiting for you in bed, naked," I said shooting him a flirty smile, letting him know I was okay with the werewolf thing, which didn't bother me near as much as hanging out with the Council.

"I'll be sure to hurry then," he said giving me one of his sexy smiles.

We enjoyed the late morning sun a while before cleaning up and eventually found ourselves on the front porch. I sat on the swing and he followed me. We gently rocked back and forth holding hands. It was a beautiful day, warm with just a slight breeze. I watched a small squirrel dart across the yard.

I was lost in my own thoughts arguing with myself. I wasn't sure if I should talk about the love we made or not. I was nervous to mention anything, but I wanted to let him know how special it was for me. I couldn't have imagined in my wildest dreams that my first time would be so perfect. I was curious if he had a good time too.

Derrick interrupted my internal quarrel making me jump a little. "Umm, I'm glad we didn't wait last night, well...early this morning I guess."

I grinned, relieved he brought the subject up. "Oh Derrick, it was the best, most perfect, most magical thing that has ever happened to me. I love you and couldn't have imagined us being any more perfect. Well, until we made love," I blurted making it pretty obvious that that was what I'd been thinking about. "Was...was it okay for you?" I asked in a whisper dropping my eyes to my hands so he couldn't see the warmth in my face.

Gently he lifted my chin, and with a crooked grin said,

"Perfect."

I sat quietly smiling at him, lost in his features, in his deep dark eyes.

"You are so breathtaking. I'm amazed no one has scooped you up before now," he said caressing my face with one of his hands.

My smile faded. I didn't like to talk about me very much. I'd much rather talk about him, the weather, or even politics.

"I told you why I haven't had a girlfriend. Now it's your turn," he insisted.

"I'm just not that into women," I teased.

"No, really. Why no boyfriends?"

It's a boring story," I said. "I just was never very interested in anyone, and guess no one in me. Sarah set me up on a few blind dates, but it was like I had some kind of repellant. And I didn't care."

"Really?" He didn't seem to believe me.

"Yes. Really," I said. "I'd rather be outside hiking, than bored in some club. I've always felt relaxed in the woods, and could totally spend hours doing nothing. I've never *wanted* to spend time with any guy before you." I had eyes and noticed a hot guy, but nothing ever came close to impacting me the way Derrick did.

"So," I said changing our conversation back to the more interesting topic. "I thought you said you were a virgin. How did you know so much?"

"I've had a lot of time to think about it," he said with a grin.

He leaned in as if to kiss me but instead whispered softly in my ear making me shiver, "Erica, we are soul mates. We're meant to be together. That is the only thing that makes sense out of all this."

I felt his lips on my neck. A soft moan escaped me before his lips found mine. I shifted my body so that my legs straddled his thighs, my arms were tight around his neck and his around my back. He was kissing my neck, my chest, when his phone rang.

"Bad timing," he said breathlessly. "I'll be right back."

I moved so he could get up, and watched as he hurried for the phone. I could tell by the ring tone it was Karen calling.

While he was in the house I spotted another squirrel, or maybe the same squirrel I'd seen earlier, on the rail of the porch. I stayed still as it moved closer, watching closely as it bound a few times then pause eyeing me to make sure I wasn't a threat, until it was right next to me. I saw clearly its beady black eyes and little nose. The squirrel sat on its hind legs with a bushy tail curled up along its back. I watched as it picked something up, a seed I think, and with little hands holding the seed began eating it, staring at me the whole time. From out of nowhere, I mumbled a word and held out my hand. The squirrel moved to my palm and sat there, staring at me. It was only for a second that something took control of me, before the feeling vanished and the squirrel jumped from my hand to the ground and bound into the brush.

Before I had to time to acknowledge something beyond my control just happened, Derrick opened the screen door.

"That was Mom. She wants me to pick up Miya in a bit," I

heard him say as he was slipping on a t-shirt.

I was trying to remember what it was I said to make the squirrel sit on my hand. I had given him a command, but didn't know how I knew that. How did I know it was a him?

"Want to go for a little walk?" Derrick asked.

"Sure."

"You okay?" he asked looking concerned.

"Um, yeah," I answered, starting to wonder if I daydreamed the whole squirrel thing.

I followed him, my hand in his, as we walked a narrow trail through the woods behind his house. The sun was high and warm, sending rays of light to the ground which was covered with green ferns, bushes, and patches of wildflowers. My eyes spotted a flower I recognized. I stopped to pick and smell the familiar cinnamon scent of the Shooting Star.

"Do these grow all over?" I asked looking at the flower.

"Not really," he answered, "mostly down here, not so much up on the mountain. I think the one I picked for you yesterday was a loner. I didn't see any others."

"How'd it get up there?"

Derrick let out a deep chuckle, "Probably crap."

"Oh," I looked back at my flower. That made sense I guess.

The trail narrowed and I had to follow behind Derrick. I didn't trust my footing, so I slipped the flower behind my ear. I didn't want to be distracted and fall like last time.

My ears caught the sound of a bird I recognized. I searched

for its location. Up high on a branch, I saw a white dove cooing. I stopped to admire the bird, glowing like a lantern in the sun's rays. Next thing I knew, two strong arms were around my waist. I leaned back against him and we watched the dove until it flew away.

"We're almost there," Derrick said leading me up the trail.

Soon we crested a little hill and I stared in curiosity. "Is that a lake?" I asked marveling at the large deep-blue mass at the bottom of an open valley. It didn't look right to be water. There were no waves or a bank.

Derrick smiled and led me down the trail. As I got closer, I realized the blue mass wasn't water, but a field of flowers. I stumbled and fell into the back of Derrick. He helped me catch my footing and handed me the Shooting Star that fell from my ear.

"What are these?" I asked as we began walking through the thick patch of knee-high blue lily-like flowers.

"Camas," he said pulling me down to sit beside him. "This field blooms late, and is one of the few original fields from a long, long time ago."

I picked a blue flower and held it to my nose, but didn't smell anything. I looked at Derrick with curious eyes. He dug up a plant and held the root for me to see. It had the creamy flesh and shape of a small lily bulb.

"Our people used to eat these," he said brushing away the dirt from the dangly roots. "We still harvest them for special dishes at gatherings. But only a few people know about this field, only people in my family." His brow furrowed with stress.

"Why?" I asked as he handed me the small bulb so I could look at it closer.

He let out a long sigh before starting to explain. "Many people have died because of this plant. It was an extremely important staple for the Washtucnas and other tribes in this area. It was stored away and fed the people through hard winters. When the government forced Natives to the reservations, many people refused to leave because of this plant. And before that, many tribes fought over lands that grew these," he said taking the bulb from me. "Now it seems this root might make great pulp for paper. It's a money maker I guess, but we've decided to keep this field like it is, a place close to our ancestors." I could see in his eyes how much he cared about his heritage, and the future of his people.

Derrick leaned in closer and took my hands, his face softened with one of his dazzling smiles, his teeth so perfect behind those lips. We were sitting in a lake of blue flowers, his black hair gently blowing in the slight breeze. His eyes deep and dark. I was so plain next to him. I looked down at my hands wondering why he would want to be with me. I knew that he did. I felt it in my heart, but I didn't understand why.

He took my hand and held it to his soft warm lips caressing the top of each knuckle, sending bolts of electricity up my arm. My focus was back on him and this place he'd taken me to.

"Erica," he said shifting from beside me to in front of me. He was on his knees sitting on his heels. I heard love in his voice. I felt ashamed to have questioned his devotion.

"Yeah?" My sixth sense was beginning to ring, he was about to tell me something important. I crossed my fingers mentally hoping it would be good news. That's when he reached into his pocket and brought out a ring. My heart began pounding in my chest and my breathing quickened as I watched him. I knew what was coming and my eyes filled with tears.

"I know you already said you'd marry me. But I want to ask again. With a ring this time." He took my hand. "Erica, I love you and you will make me the luckiest man on earth if you'll be my wife. Will you marry me?" he asked softly, his eyes deep and dark staring into mine, waiting for an answer.

"Yes," I said, my voice cracking. I was swallowing fast to force the lump in my throat to my stomach. Slowly he slid the ring on my left ring finger and took my hands in his. Then Derrick leaned in and kissed me. I was overwhelmed by the passion of his kiss, the yearning, but quickly I matched his desire with my own.

I lifted my arms straight as he pulled off my shirt. He knelt, resting on his knees and began kissing my stomach. I pulled his shirt over his head, excitement building within me. He undressed me slowly as I stood in front of him. He remained on his knees, kissing and exciting with every touch.

My body quivered with desire. I couldn't stand it anymore. I wanted him. I pushed him gently to his back, my hungry mouth on his as I fumbled with the button of his pants. I got them unzipped and found him hard waiting for me. "Take them off," I whispered in his ear between kisses.

Quickly he kicked off his shoes and slipped out of his pants and boxers. I straddled him, kissing him hard, not sure what to do next. It didn't take long before Derrick moved himself into position, and slowly I filled myself with all of him. He grabbed my hips as I began to move. My eyes were locked onto his, our breathing ragged. I moved faster as the pressure within me built, as if my body were climbing a mountain of pure pleasure. I reached the peak, unable to control the cry that escaped my mouth exploded in ecstasy the same time as Derrick. I collapsed on his chest, listening and feeling his heart hammering against his chest.

Enjoying the closeness of being one, I took a moment before sliding off him.

"Wow," he said breathlessly.

I laid next to him, letting my heart rate return to normal. We both were naked enjoying the warm sun on our skin. He propped himself up on an elbow, looking down at me. "How are you feeling?" he asked.

"Fine...and you?" I wasn't quite sure what he meant.

"I'm fantastic," he said. "I just don't want to do too much too soon."

I saw the smile on his face, and looked down and saw he was ready for more. I pulled him to me, kissing him hard to let him know I could handle it. And we made love again in the lake of blue flowers.

After the third time, we lay next to each other holding hands. I decided I liked not wearing a shirt, but was a little uncomfortable without my undies. As I slid them on I noticed my ring was gone. Frantically I began searching the ground.

"What's wrong?" Derrick asked in alarm.

"My ring," I cried in panic. "It fell off."

Derrick slipped on his pants and helped me search. Before the tears spilled from my eyes, he found the ring beneath my shirt.

"Thank god," I said taking the ring from him. That was when I noticed how elegant it was. The silver band had beautiful turquoise and opal stones within it, and there were little wolves, cougars, and eagles etched between the stones. You had to really look to notice them.

"I love it, Derrick. It's so beautiful." I'd never seen a more perfect ring.

"It was my grandmother's wedding ring," he explained as we dressed. "She gave it to me and made me promise not to give it to anyone but the one I wanted to spend the rest of my life with. It's supposed to bring us good luck."

"We will have to get you a similar ring," I said combing the flowers from my hair with my fingers, noticing Derrick didn't have any in his hair.

"We can do that," he said looking at this watch then taking my hand, "We should get going. I need to get Miya."

I followed him on the trail back through the woods to his house lost in thought about how rich his history and culture was. I kind of wished I knew something about my parent's history, but quickly dropped that thought from my brain when I remembered

Amy's story. I'd rather have *no* history than *that* one.

"Want to go with?" Derrick asked walking me to the front porch.

I sat on the swing and shook my head. "No, I'll wait here." I didn't want to meet anyone and I had a feeling Derrick would want to introduce me to his Aunt Julie.

"Okay, I'll be back in a few," he said after going into the house to grab his keys. He gave me a quick kiss before vaulting over the porch railing to the ground several yards away.

"Show off," I yelled after him. He smiled and waved to me from his truck as he drove down the driveway. I sat there listening to the fading noise of the engine when I realized I'd forgotten to tell Derrick about my plans to run home. In fact I spaced my plans altogether. I grabbed the phone from the kitchen wall and called his cell phone. When I heard the familiar ring tone from the living room, I realized he'd left it. I thought about waiting for him to get back, but changed my mind because that would just take longer...and he had big plans for tonight.

I decided to make a quick trip into town and hurry back. I'd just check the mail and make sure the house was okay. I jotted a quick note on a yellow Post-It by the phone.

Derrick,

I had to run home real quick to check the mail.

Be back ASAP.   Love, Erica

And stuck it to the fridge where Derrick had put the one for his mom yesterday.

I ran downstairs and figured I'd better look at a map before I left, especially since I'd followed Derrick in the dark. I highly doubted I'd find my way back to the highway without help. I flipped on his computer and Google mapped my address from his. I jotted the turns on a piece of paper, turned his computer off, grabbed my purse and ran upstairs. I didn't lock the door behind me. Derrick would be back soon and I doubted there was a serious threat of thievery out here.

I was in my car and on the road within minutes. I was grateful I'd looked at a map. Once I left Derrick's driveway, there was no way I'd have found my way back to Spokane if I hadn't. I relaxed more when I passed the lumber mill, a sign I was going in the right direction. I found the highway, making sure to pay close attention to landmarks. It would be really embarrassing having Derrick come find me because I got lost on my way back to his house.

The drive was nice. It was almost four in the afternoon and traffic was smooth. I turned off the radio and fantasized about what was going to happen tonight. I'd watched him transform into a mountain lion twice. I wondered how different it would be for him to change into a werewolf.

I wondered what he'd look like. Was he going to look like the werewolves I'd seen in movies? A huge wolf, or a human hybrid all nasty and vicious, or something completely different? I felt kind of excited about the whole thing, the anticipation of what was to come. Suddenly I was shocked by my acceptance of the idea. Not long ago I'd have thought someone insane for thinking such things even existed.

I realized I was starting to be more comfortable with my new reality. I was accepting the fact that everything I'd been told was make believe, might not be so fictitious after all. I wondered what else might exist besides vampires, witches, shapeshifters, and forest fairies. I shuddered at the thought of a boogeyman and smiled at the idea of mermaids. I still doubted Amy's story. I was sure she and Frederick had me confused with someone else.

I was less than 15 minutes from home when my cell phone rang. It was Derrick so I answered it.

"You should have waited for me," he was upset.

"Well 'hi' to you too," I said.

"Erica," he said before repeating, "you should have waited for me."

"It's just a quick trip, Derrick. I forgot to mention it earlier." I knew that if this was a normal relationship, the temper and controlling thing would be a huge red-flag.

"Come back," he said.

"I'm almost there," I said. "Derrick, I'm just getting the mail and making sure the house is still standing. It'll be quick."

"Okay, but call me when you're on your way back. I just...I have a bad feeling about something."

"Sure," I was starting to get a little nervous.

"Be careful," he said.

"Don't worry, I will."

"I love you."

"I love you too," I said before hanging up.

I was a little uneasy about the concern in his voice. He was really worried. I thought about turning around. I could always check the mail tomorrow. But I was so close and it was daylight. No vampires would be out in the daylight. I'd take less than a minute in the house.

The idea that Mom and Dad weren't my biological parents popped into my head. The thought made my stomach hurt and the back of my throat tightened as tears filled my eyes, but at least I was able to think about it, a little anyway. I guess somewhere in the back of my mind I always knew I was different from them. But I never considered I wasn't theirs.

First I figured I'd tell them about my change of plans with college. I really didn't think that issue would be such a big deal so long as I stayed in school. And after my nineteenth birthday, I would tell them about my engagement and plans to move in with Derrick. I'd considered just moving while they were away, but decided I owed them more than that. They would be disappointed about the news, but more accepting of my choices if I was up front with them and didn't sneak around. Besides, dishonesty wasn't my nature.

Depending on how well they took my engagement news, I'd confront them with the whole "whose baby am I?" question. There was always the possibility I'd been switched at birth, so they might not even know. I was surprised that I was able to have the thought without the hurt in my stomach. Maybe I just needed some time to absorb it all. Maybe tonight I would take Derrick's advice and talk to the Council, to see what else they know about the witch and Joseph.

I was less than a few turns from home when my phone rang again. Figuring it was Derrick I answered not bothering to see who was calling.

"Hi," I said a little cautious.

"Dimples?"

I thought about hanging up. But it sounded like she was crying.

"What's wrong, Sarah?" I asked.

"Dimples, I need to see you," she cried. "Where are you?"

"What's wrong," I repeated. She was definitely crying.

"Larry is liar," she sobbed. "I'm so sorry for everything."

"What do you mean?" I wasn't sure what she was talking about. It was too late for us to be BFF's, but I didn't like hearing her so upset.

She wouldn't stop crying, and I couldn't understand what she was saying.

"Sarah, I'm almost home. Let me call you back in five. Okay?" I could talk to her on my way back to Derrick's house.

"Okay," she whimpered. "Call me back."

I hung up the phone just in time. A cop passed me going the opposite direction.

Soon I was pulling into the driveway. I parked my little Escort and went to the mail box, which was empty. I thought that was kind of strange. Maybe Mom had called the neighbors and they were getting the mail. But she asked me to do it. If she asked someone else I thought for sure she would have told me.

I grabbed my purse and headed toward the house. I'd make sure everything was okay, go to the bathroom and then leave. Maybe I'd take two minutes.

I set my purse on the bottom step and hurried upstairs. I always used my bathroom, no matter how bad I had to go.

Everything looked fine, but I wanted to leave. Maybe it was the serious tone of Derrick's call, but I didn't feel safe. I ran to the kitchen to grab a soda for the ride home when my peripheral vision caught a stack of mail on the kitchen counter. It was a stack of mail I didn't put there set next to our only spare key with the neon green smiley face. I stopped dead center in the kitchen, all my senses screaming danger. Then the smell hit me. I turned, and there standing at the end of the kitchen, where I'd just been, was a vampire.

CHAPTER 15

The vampire had the same translucent skin, the same Jedi cloak, and the same rotten egg smell as Frederick. But this one was female. Her full lips, large eyes, and arching brows reminded me of Cindy Crawford. She'd be pretty if not for the spider veins all over her face. We stared at each other for a moment, her eyes red and fierce.

In a velvety voice of evil she said, "I'm not going to kill you."

I wasn't convinced. The sun was outside. She was at the opposite end of the kitchen from the backdoor. I had to try. I darted for the backdoor which was only a few feet away. But she was between me and the door before my second step.

"What do you want?" I whispered, my knees weak.

Her lips curled into a smile as she hissed, "You."

She slammed me to the ground with such force the wind was knocked from my lungs. She was strong and cold. It was as if she were a metal robot with smooth flesh. As I struggled to breathe, she bound my hands and feet.

"Please don't do this," I begged when I had enough air to speak. She promptly gagged me. I recoiled from her touch...it was cold as ice.

"I will join you tonight," she whispered next to my ear, and then she was gone.

I was on my stomach. My knees were bent and my arms stretched straight behind me. My wrists and ankles were bound together. I was hog tied. The rope she used was cutting off circulation to my hands and feet, which began to go numb. The gag was digging into the sides of my mouth, slowly cutting my skin.

I couldn't believe it. Everything happened so fast, within seconds. I had to escape, but every time I tried to move, it made the pain worse.

I heard my cell phone ringing from the foyer. Then the house phone rang. The answering machine clicked on and I heard Derrick's voice, "Erica, I'm on my way. Leave the house NOW." Then he hung up. I heard the pain in his voice. He already knew I was in trouble.

My eyes filled with tears. My sobs were muffled by the gag. The physical pain was pacified by the emotions running through me. I was so stupid. All this was my fault. I should have waited until tomorrow to come to town. Or at least waited until Derrick got home from getting Miya. It would have only taken a few extra minutes. The happy future I'd been planning just disappeared.

I heard a noise outside, two loud slams and then the front door opening. I listened to the shuffle of feet coming towards me and smelled the horrible stench as they drew near. I tried to look up to see my abductors, but the counter obscured my view.

Unexpectedly I was lifted from the rope that held my ankles and wrists together. Stabs of pain shot through my shoulders and lower back. It felt like I was breaking in two. I screamed in agony, but to no avail. No one was going to help me.

Briefly I noticed two pairs of black military lace-up boots, and saw the vampire's reflection on the oven door. They were dressed in chemical suits covered head to toe. I saw a large black bin with white letters that read, TOXIC: KILLING AGENTS and a few Mr. Yuck stickers before I was tossed into it. My ribs slammed against the bottom.

"Hurry," I heard a man hiss as I was encased in blackness when the lid was snapped on top.

I felt the bin being lifted and was carried out of my house and down the steps. I heard a rolling door, as if from a delivery truck, and felt the bin sliding along a flat surface. I heard the rolling door sound again followed by a loud clank and a lock. Soon another two slams, the roar of a diesel engine, and then we were moving.

The plastic bin I'd been put in was barely large enough for me. My knees touched one end and the top of my head the other. Both of my elbows rubbed the bin's sides and my hands and feet pressed against the lid. Any movement was excruciating. The container had a couple small air holes but not enough. The air inside was thick and hot.

I was terrified. I imagined the various ways the vampires would feast on me. How they would kill me in slow torturous ways. But mostly I was worried that Derrick would try to find me.

The ride began to get rough. Every bump sent a new wave of agony through me. I bit into the gag, through the pain. My mind raced with thoughts of Derrick. I prayed he wouldn't follow me, but I knew he would. I hoped he couldn't find me. I felt sad for him when he would discover my mangled body. I prayed there would be nothing left for him to find. Our lives together had just begun and now it was ending. My tears of physical pain turned to tears of sorrow.

I must have passed out, because I woke to my plastic coffin sliding forward before slamming into something. My knees took the impact but I barely felt anything. My body was numb. I heard the doors again and felt my bin being slid, lifted and carried. I listened for any noise but heard nothing except my own racing heart. My face was soaked from salty tears and blood. My hair was matted to my face. Then I was descending, and by the rhythm of the rocking, I guessed my captors were carrying me down stairs. We stopped. Finally I heard a voice.

"Is that her?" came the same velvety voice that I'd heard in my house.

"Yes, Serena," I heard a man hiss back.

"Take her to the lighted cell," Serena ordered.

Again I was being moved.

Soon the bin was set down hard, slamming my head and ribs against the floor. The lid was removed and I bit into the gag, determined not to scream as I prepared for the pain which came instantly as I was lifted out of the bin the same way I had been tossed in. I felt for sure my arms were dislocated and my back broken. I was able to bite through the pain tasting blood, but I didn't make any noise. I was dropped to the cement ground. My already bruised ribs screamed in pain. I struggled to breathe. I was sure one or two ribs were broken.

My bindings were cut loose and all at once and my limbs flopped to the floor. The sensation was excruciating, forcing a hoarse scream from my empty lungs. I couldn't feel my hands or feet. I heard footsteps leave and a loud clank of a door being shut. I couldn't breathe without pain. I laid there for a while in the dark, waiting for the numbness to fade. Soon I felt the weird tingling as the feeling came back to my arms and legs, then down to my finger and toes.

When I was able, I pushed myself up and sat. I blinked hard and long, trying to help my eyes adjust to the dim lighting. The floor was cold and hard. I smelled dirt, sewage, mildew, and other foul odors through the stagnant air. The damp atmosphere reminded me of a root cellar. I fumbled with the gag but was unable to take it off. My fingers were not cooperating. I could barely move them.

I was alone in a small cell, confined by three walls of large cement blocks and one wall of thinly spaced rusty iron bars, which I realized was one of smells I couldn't place before. There was one light bulb screwed into the center of the low ceiling. A large metal bucket covered in slime and goop was placed in one of the cement corners. I heard the squeaking of mice from within a pile of moldy hay in the other corner.

I rubbed my shoulders and circled my arms, suffering through the pain. I balled my fists and opened them several times trying to get the blood to flow. Soon everything began to loosen up, and I was able to move and breathe easier. I found the knot to the gag and struggled to get it untied. Eventually I was peeling the crusty fabric from my face. My eyes watered as the gag fell to the floor and my mouth took its normal position.

I stood, suffering through the crippling pain in my lower back and staggered toward the bars. I looked down the dimly lit passageway, but neither saw nor heard a thing.

I didn't have my watch. I had no idea what time it was or how much time passed. It felt like forever. All I could do was wait and wonder what they wanted, what they were going to do to me. Frederick had wanted to kill me, so I doubted these vampires kidnapped me to play Scrabble.

I tried to remember all the weaknesses movies and books revealed about vampires. I knew not all supposed myths were true, like turning into a vampire with just a bite, but the sunlight thing was right-on. So what about garlic, stakes, holy water, and crosses, not that any of those items would help me now. I didn't have any of them with me. I searched my memory for some thread of information that might be useful.

My eyes caught movement between the bucket and wall. I stepped closer to get a look. It was a dead rat covered in maggots. I threw up.

Wiping my mouth, a new wave of fear raced through my

body when I heard soft footsteps echoing from the corridor. The noise was getting louder. Someone was coming. I moved to the corner with the hay. Mice squealed and squished beneath my feet. I pressed my back against the slimy corner. I wasn't going to go easily.

A cloaked figure with their face hidden in the shadows of the hood fronted the iron bars. I watched a white veiny hand withdraw a skeleton key from a fold within the waist of its cloak and unlock the door. The figure stepped back holding the door ajar.

"Follow me," ordered a velvety evil voice. It was Serena.

I didn't move, except for trying to press myself into the corner. I felt mice crawling over my sneakers, up my jeans.

Without any warning, I was being dragged from the cell by my hair. I didn't see her move at all. But I felt the pain on my scalp as a fistful of hair bore my weight. I screamed in shock and pain. My feet found purchase and she released me.

"Follow me," Serena said again, in the same tone as if nothing transpired.

I decided to drop my rebel façade and followed her down the long dim corridor. Blood trickled down my head and neck. I felt my scalp where she had pulled expecting to find a bloody bald spot, but my hair was still there, or at least most of it. It was almost the same spot where Fredrick had pulled out my hair.

The passageway was longer than I expected, and the sounds of my footsteps resonated loudly off the cement walls compared to Serena's. Dim, evenly spaced light bulbs cast hazy cones of light from the ceiling to reveal the existence of the corridor. But I had to walk through several large gaps of pure blackness before the next cone of light. As I walked through the dark spots, cold chills went up and down my spine. It felt like something was watching me, grabbing for me. I kept my focus on the lights trying to ignore the phantoms in the dark.

We came to a thick metal door which Serena easily pushed open. I followed her silently through the large door. She closed it behind me and we ascended rough cement stairs that wound their way upward. At the top of the stairs was another heavy door, but this one was made of wood. She led me through the door and we entered a very large hollow chamber. The ceiling was made of glass. As I looked up, I saw the large full moon behind wispy black clouds. I realized a lot of time had passed.

The large center of the room was circular, which lay below the circular glass ceiling, matching in size and shape. The cement floor was patterned with speckled dark granite tiles that glittered in the moonlight. The tiles formed a large six pointed star. And where the tips of the star met with the perimeter of the circular floor, stood a large column with a horned satanic beast head holding a lit torch in its smiling mouth.

The room was empty except for a large wooden post in the middle of one of the stars outer triangles, the one closest to where I stood. The post had a set of chains hanging from its top, and another set coiled around its bottom. As my eyes adjusted, I observed five other cloaked figures. They were hooded with their faces hidden and a rope belt around their waist. Each had their place in the shadows centered between the columns.

I searched for an escape, for another door. But the walls were decorated with arched protruding molding and wild eyed beasts, which made it impossible for me to differentiate a door from just wall. Even the door I'd just come through now matched the wall's pattern, making it look as if there was no door.

Serena walked to the lone post in the room and turned to face me as I stood shaking in terror by the closed door that I knew existed. "Come," Serena ordered.

Quickly I realized what it was she intended to do. She was going to chain me to the post. I turned and ran. I made it the few feet to door behind me, but I couldn't find a handle. I didn't stop searching until Serena had me in her metal clutches. I knew the attempt would be futile, but I had to try. She was very tall and easily lifted me off of the ground. She carried me by my hair again, her grip like the freezing iron bars of the cell I'd just left. I struggled and kicked her, only to hurt my feet. She threw me against the wooden post. I sank to the floor, pulling my knees to my chest, terrified of what was to come.

I didn't struggle while she propped me against the post, shackling my wrists to the chains above, then my ankles to the chains below. My arms were almost fully extended, I had very little slack. Once she finished, she moved to the only empty space between two of the columns, making a total of six cloaked figures barely noticeable in the shadows.

I searched the room. The moon cast a bright silver light over me, making it difficult for my eyes to focus. It was just moments when I heard a noise in front of me. I watched a hidden door open. It was straight across from the door I entered the room from. I made a mental note just in case I could escape.

A male vampire entered and glided toward me. He was the first vampire I'd seen not wearing a cloak. Instead, he wore a flowing black robe that trailed behind him on the ground. The edges of the robe were trimmed in gold thread and beads interwoven in elegant complex designs. He had a deep widow's peak with long straight blond hair that reached his shoulders. He was flanked by two men in dark cloaks and rope belts, just like the others, but I recognized their black lace-up boots as they approached.

The three vampires moved fluidly toward me. They had the same translucent skin with dark veins mapping their faces. The blond vampire in the black robe had the same red eyes as Serena's. The other two had black eyes.

"I am Lamont," the vampire in the robe said introducing himself as he stopped in front of me. I noticed he wasn't much taller than me, his guards towered over him.

Lamont glared at me. I turned my head to look away from him. His eyes were pure evil and his rotten egg smell disgusting. Firmly he took my chin in his hand, and with a freezing cold metal grip forced my face to meet his stare.

"And you are?" he asked. His voice was nothing like the other vampires I'd heard. His reminded me that of a child's.

I didn't answer. I remembered Frederick attempting to extend pleasant introductions and wondered if they got some sort of sick pleasure from it. At least Serena's demeanor was sincere.

"Erica Mathews. I know your name already," he said with an evil smile that revealed his fangs, both white and sharp. "In fact, I know much about you." He stared at me a moment longer before releasing my face and dropping his hand.

Lamont hissed "I see you are frightened," his eyes piercing into mine, "and I suppose you should be." He began to pace from side to side. His guards stood still.

"You see, when Frederick did not report his arrival in Seattle, we became concerned. I was sent with a guard to investigate. Imagine our shock when his trail ended and his ashes found." He stopped in front of me. I felt his evil gaze on me even though I kept my focus on the ground. Lamont hissed, "Not that I was too disappointed. I had very little respect for Frederick. He was much too impetuous."

I swallowed my fear and listened as he continued, trying to remember every word, every detail...just in case.

"We began to search for his killer and soon discovered one of the reservations around here had a shapeshifter. 'Why?' We asked ourselves, why would this happen now, after all this time? We had not forcefully feasted upon their delicious blood in centuries. That is when our Master realized," Lamont spat with hatred, "she must have fulfilled her destiny. You look just like her and...you bear her mark." He grabbed my arm in a metal grip, turning it so that he could see my birthmark.

Lamont hissed, "I ordered her death myself, not so long ago. I was at my club in New Orleans. We all were to keep our eyes open and listen for warnings. But we believed all the witches to be dead. Suddenly I caught her nasty scent, the scent only a witch could leave." Lamont began to pace again.

I kept my eyes on the floor, refusing to look at him as he explained. "I couldn't believe she would enter my club knowing it would lead to her demise. Our slaves worship us...they eagerly do our bidding to earn favor. At first, I thought it might be a trap. So it was I who followed her through the oblivious crowd to the alley, where she quietly waited. In the darkest of night's shadows she stood there, only her eyes and stench revealing her existence. I smelled no others. She was alone. I called my subject and gave the order. I thoroughly enjoyed the show, praising those with the most imaginative ways of torture. When she could take no more, I carefully cut out her heart. She died watching it beat in my hand."

He stopped in front of me and forced me to look him in the eyes. "I found it odd that she didn't run. She just stood there, an easy target. I watched her writhe in pain." Lamont searched my face for a reaction, "I watched her suffer. How I wanted to hear her scream, to hear her pain...but she never did, although her jade eyes flamed in agony. Your screams, my dear, will have to satisfy both the then and now."

I began to shake. How he killed the woman that might be my mom was sickening. He recounted the event with such pleasure, and

I could see in his expression the excitement of killing me. Expressionless, tears began to fall from my eyes.

"I took her corpse to our Master. He wanted proof. He was so pleased with me. Instantly I went from a low standing club owner to one of high status. This corner of the country is mine to control...my prize. The rewards I shall reap from killing you," he fantasized, "shall be more than any vampire in our existence has ever had bestowed.

"Alone, our Master examined her. He had had a special connection to her from their mortal lives. You see, he was her father." Again Lamont paused and stared at me, waiting for a reaction. It seemed the less I gave in to what he wanted, the more he would talk to provoke me. I was determined not to give him what he wanted. But I felt sick about where my supposed family line was coming from.

Lamont continued his story in a hiss, "Master told only a few of us with the highest of status that he had a vision of a child, a hybrid. But he discredited the vision after the examination. There was no evidence of a pregnancy or childbirth. He assumed he had misread the signs, the thought of such an abomination was unfathomable." I wondered if maybe the body was too disfigured from being beaten and mutilated to reveal any signs. This woman, who may be my mother deserved vengeance.

"All these years you have been here, hidden from us." Lamont leaned in close to me inhaling deeply near my neck. The rotten egg smell coming from him turned my stomach. I debated throwing up on his face. "And still I cannot smell you, although you are right here in front of me," he said as he reached up and ran an ice cold hand down the length of my arm to my side.

I flinched from his touch. The hair on my arms stood straight. But for the most part I stayed still.

"It is strange. Witches' stench can be smelled miles away. But you, I cannot smell *anything*. It is as if you were not here at all," he said, sliding a cold finger across my forehead bringing it to his nose, before wiping the finger on his robe.

"Master wishes us to kill two birds with one stone, so to speak. He has sent me Serena, his most valued assassin." He hissed quietly in my ear, "Your werewolf will find us tonight, and he will be killed."

Once he mentioned Derrick, my heart began to pound. I tried to stay emotionless as more tears fell from my eyes. It was obvious Lamont was trying to trigger a response. He wanted to watch me suffer. I struggled not to satisfy him.

Lamont began to pace again as he spoke. "It seems as though you do not have the abilities of your mother. The Master wanted to kill you himself, and is in transit, but is not willing to risk the danger of your existence. You must be eliminated as soon as possible. He will not take any chances of you making it to your nineteenth birthday." He stopped and looked at me. "We shall see if you react the same way to death as your mother."

The thought of feeling my heart being cut from my body, and watching it beat while I died, was mortifying. Why wouldn't they just drink my blood? I knew I didn't have any abilities. They had me confused with someone else. I was certain of that. I had to concentrate and swallow fast and hard to keep the sob in my throat from erupting. I focused on the tile below me and tried not to think of what was going to happen. I was determined not to give Lamont what he wanted.

"I must kill you before you obtain your...other abilities," he said more to himself. What did he mean by "other abilities"? I didn't have any current abilities, besides finding ways to fall down. I kept my best poker face but my mind raced. Lamont looked to the moon then continued pacing. "You see, Erica, in his human form your werewolf is weaker and more vulnerable."

They were using me as bait. I called out to Derrick with my mind. I begged for him to stay away, screamed to him it's a trap. He had some sort of magnetic pull that would lead him to me, not to mention the stench of the vampires, so he'd find this place. I was sure he would. I hoped his visions would show him the trap. I prayed our unique connection would let him hear me...somehow. He had to stay away.

As if on cue I heard a loud long howl. My heart sank to the pit of my stomach. Why would he announce his arrival? Then I noticed the shadows between the columns moving slightly. I felt the tension in the air increase. The vampires were nervous. I looked at Lamont's face. I saw fear cross his brow before he quickly regained his composure. Derrick's presence intimidated them.

"So the beast has come," I heard whispered somewhere

behind me.

And in a different more worried hiss, "He hasn't tested her yet."

I watched Serena leave her spot and glide to Lamont.

In a cold voice she scolded him, "Fool, you take too long with your stories. Now we have no time."

Lamont retorted back through a hiss, "He is still miles away. We can hurry. This will not take long. Take your place."

"Make haste," she hissed, but did not move.

Lamont drifted toward me and pulled out a small dagger. It was a beautiful piece of craftsmanship with elegant designs and jewels decorating the handle. The blade itself was only a couple inches long. The metal was a swirl of red and black.

"This," he informed as he held the dagger in front of my face, "is the same blade that I used to cut out your mother's heart."

"Bring me the slaves," Lamont ordered. Serena left through the door Lamont had entered. She returned almost instantly, being followed by three cloaked subjects. They were not nearly as graceful as the vampires as they neared me. Each was walking which made Serena look as though she floated.

"Take this," Lamont ordered to the closest and tallest slave as he handed over the knife. As the slave moved closer, immediately I recognized the features hidden behind the hood.

"Larry?" I gasped. I looked toward the other two, and as I did, my eyes met Sarah's before she looked back to her feet.

"Sarahhh," I screamed. "Sarah look at me." How could she?

It all made sense now. She knew where the spare key to my house was. She was obviously in on this.

"How could you? We were friends...best friends," I yelled.

Lamont began to laugh. "Now this is intriguing," he said. "I had no idea the connection was so personal." He took the knife from Larry and said, "Sarah, you shall do the honors."

"N-n-n-no thank you," Sarah stuttered still looking at the ground.

Serena backhanded her. "It is no request, Dog. You do as your master orders."

Sarah's hood slipped from her head as her hand went to her cheek. She had a black eye and the whole side of her face was bruised, her lip split. Trembling she took the knife from Lamont. Larry moved to where the other slave stood. Both were watching the scene unfold with smiles on their lips. I caught a glimpse of slave number three, and thought I recognized him, but couldn't quite place where.

"Cut her," Lamont ordered in his childlike voice.

Sarah walked a few steps and stood before me, her eyes refusing to meet mine. "Don't do this," I pleaded.

"I'm sorry, Dimples," she said. "He made me join. I have to what they say or they'll kill me."

"Cut her now," Lamont ordered in a more forceful tone.

Unable to watch, I closed my eyes and turned my head. The betrayal cut deeper than any knife.

I felt pressure on the underside of my right arm, just above my armpit. There was no pain. I wondered if she cut me at all. I looked and saw a slice about two inches long. I watched as blood began to bubble until it crested and spilled in one crimson stream down my armpit to where it was absorbed by my shirt.

"Sorry," Sarah cried tears streaming down her face. I saw the pain in her eyes, and part of me almost felt for her.

"So, you're not susceptible to its properties," Lamont smirked holding his hand out for the knife. Trembling Sarah placed the knife on his palm and walked back to stand between the two other slaves. I heard her quietly sobbing. Looking back to my wound I wondered what Lamont meant by "properties" as another bubble of blood grew until it too fell down my arm.

Lamont summoned one of his guards, pointed to me and whispered something too quiet for me to hear. In horror I watched the guard wearing one of the pairs of boots I recognized approach me. I was quickly losing my determination not to freak out. I began to squirm and tried to pull free from my restraints. Lamont was smiling, taking pleasure from my reaction.

As the guard closed in, terror filled my body. Slowly he slid back his hood revealing a bald head covered in horrific demon tattoos feasting on tortured women. He grabbed me, forcing me still with his icy grip, his evil black eyes glaring angrily into mine. I lost my nerve and screamed as loud and high as my vocal chords would go.

My terrifying scream echoed off the walls. The glass ceiling above shattered, showering us with glass. I looked down to protect my face as shards sliced through my skin and landed in my hair. Many crimson rivers of blood began flowing down my arms and face.

The vampires seemed oblivious to the glass, although they had covered their ears. The three slaves were looking down, protecting themselves with their hands over their ears. When I stopped to take a breath, the guard covered my mouth with his hand and forced my chin upward. Looking down from the corner of my eye I saw him hesitate a moment before revealing two fangs that he sank deep into my neck.

The pain was excruciating. It felt as though two pencil sized flaming dull pokers penetrated into my throat. Every suck was another stab of agony worse than the previous. The pain from being tossed around was nothing compared to this.

Suddenly he released me, the pain disappearing once his fangs were extracted from my flesh. The guard clasped his throat with both hands as he fell to the floor. Then it was him who began screaming in pain. He thrashed and convulsed briefly before going completely limp. I recoiled as far as I could when he burst into flames. I looked at Lamont and Serena who'd silently watched, their emotionless faces now frozen in place. Serena returned to her post between the columns as Lamont glided toward me, eyeing me curiously.

"Well, apparently your blood is the same as hers," he hissed. "Things are about to get interesting," he said, "but fighting is beneath me. I shall return for the fun."

Lamont and his remaining guard glided toward the hidden door from which he had entered with the human slaves following in line. The stench from the burning vampire was seriously triggering my gag reflexes. I had to struggle to keep the bile down as I watched the group get closer to the door. They had almost made it to the end of the room when a brief gust of wind brushed against my face. I felt the room vibrate from a heavy landing and heard the most vicious growl ever. Derrick had arrived.

CHAPTER 16

Derrick's werewolf body was horrifying. On all fours his head was higher than mine. His body resembled that of a giant hairy beast. His body was somewhat human, broad and thick with bulging muscles. He had hands and feet with razor sharp claws. His entire body was covered in thick black fur with silver highlights glistening in the moonlight.

As soon as Derrick hit the floor, he was fighting. I watched two vampires leave their shadowed positions and simultaneously attack him. They each had a wooden spear with the red and black blade attached to the tip. The vampires thrust the spears at Derrick. But both spears fell to the floor as if hitting stone. Immediately they were on Derrick, biting him with their teeth, clawing and tearing at him with their fingers, but to no avail. They screamed in frustration. Derrick was impenetrable to their efforts.

From the corner of my eye I saw Lamont hurry through the door followed by his guard and slave I vaguely recognized. As Sarah was about to pass through the frame, she instead closed the door and turned on Larry. At first it looked as if she embraced him, until I saw the silver tip of a knife protruding from Larry's back. Sarah stepped away and watched as he crumpled to the ground. Sarah looked at me and our eyes met briefly before Serena ripped off her head. I watched Sarah's beautiful blond curls matted in blood roll to a stop just in front of me. Her blue eyes now stared lifelessly into mine.

I heard a howl and saw Derrick tear into the vampires. They tried to fight, but he bit them off of his back ripping them apart in the process. Derrick's angry snarls were vicious and intimidating, a thousand times more horrifying than the vampires. In one effortless leap Derrick pounced on a third vampire who'd dropped his spear in an attempt to flee, and easily tore the loathsome creature to shreds.

Larry and Sarah's death, the killing of the vampires all happened within seconds. Derrick took down a fourth vampire and turned to attack the next, when I felt a blade at my throat.

"Werewolf," came the velvety voice from behind me resonating off the walls as if there were surround sound.

Derrick turned and stopped. He stared at me, his eyes full of hate and anger, and fear.

"Werewolf," Serena said, "if you value her life, you will stop."

"Don't listen..." I was able to get out before she pressed the blade deeper into my throat. I felt the warmth of fresh blood trickling down my neck.

Derrick didn't move, but I felt his growl vibrating the air.

"You will take your human form, NOW," Serena ordered.

I wondered if Derrick was able to change. I knew he had little control under the power of the moon, and this was only his second time as a werewolf. I willed him to defy her, sent him mental messages not to listen, while praying that he couldn't follow her command.

Derrick was still, except for the blood dripping from his claws and teeth. Gore was strewn about the room, pieces of vampire everywhere. I noticed some pieces gluing themselves back together, like two drops of water forming one. The smell of rotting eggs was overwhelming. Derrick's growl grew deeper, louder. I felt the vibration deep in my chest.

I screamed as my right side exploded in pain. I saw the end of a bloody blade sticking out of my stomach a few inches to the right of my belly button. It happened so fast, I was oblivious that the knife had moved from my throat. Serena had run me through. Any struggle made the pain worse, the cut bigger. I screamed again as she slowly withdrew the blade. I felt like I was going to pass out. Then she had the knife back to my neck. My clothes were covered in blood which was now oozing down my waist and legs and pooling at the base of my post.

A sad whine escaped from Derrick. I stared him straight in the eyes, pleading for him not to listen. His body trembled. A loud ear piercing howl tore through the room. Tears fell from my eyes as I watched him transform back into his perfect human body.

"Good boy," Serena chided behind me.

"Chain him," she ordered.

I watched the two vampires, Lamont's guard and the only other one left besides Serena, carry in two posts that resembled mine. They removed several tiles from the floor and inserted the posts into hidden frames. One of the vampires wrapped a white cloth around Derrick's waist which hung loose to his thighs.

Derrick didn't struggle as they shackled him to the posts. I was chained to a single post. He was stretched tight between two that formed a T. His hands were angled up and out from his body and his ankles chained to the floor like Leonardo da Vinci's Vitruvian Man. He was no more than fifteen feet in front of me. I smelled his musky scent through the rotten eggs.

"Deetra," said Serena, "take my place." Lamont's guard stayed while the other cloaked vampire came toward me. I noticed it too was female. She had the same striking features as Serena, arched eyebrows, thin nose and full lips, but her complexion was ruined by tracks of veins under paper thin skin. She stunk and her eyes were black. I felt the blade leave and return to my neck. Serena glided towards Derrick. My eyes were frozen on her back when she stopped in front of him, blocking his face from my view.

Lamont and his remaining slave entered the room and made their way around the body parts to me. "Check her," he ordered the slave.

The slave fronted me and lifted my shirt. He pressed on my wounds, which made me flinch and cry out in pain.

"She will not die," the slave said.

"Dusty?" I whispered in surprise. I recognized the voice, the touch. He was my nurse from St. Joseph's Hospital. "Dusty, is that you?"

He looked at me and a grin of evil spread across his face. "You will live, only to suffer a worse death," he sneered.

"Serena," Lamont said, visibly angry. "Had you killed her, you would pay dearly for such insubordination."

"I knew the wound was not fatal," she retorted not bothering to look at him. "Do not question my loyalty."

Lamont moved toward Serena, his guard with the boots now close behind him. Dusty stayed standing close to me. He kicked Sarah's head like a soccer ball to the other side of the room. It made a disgusting thwacking sound as it hit the marble column.

With repugnance I looked at him, questioning how I could not have sensed what a monster he was. Dusty gave me a wink and said, "My Master promised I get to have some fun with you before the night's over," and grabbed his crotch.

"Now," I heard Lamont order drawing my attention. With one quick fluid motion Serena swung her arm back. I saw the moon glisten off the silver six inch blade, and with the same knife she just impaled me with, she stabbed Derrick.

I thrashed against my chains, "Noooo," I screamed through sobs. The knife at my neck cut deeper, but I didn't care. Dusty was laughing, completely enjoying himself.

Serena, Lamont and his guard moved just to the side of Derrick to conference. My eyes searched through tears for Derrick. I didn't want to look, but forced myself. Expecting to find a gaping wound, I was overcome by a wave of astonishment. There was nothing. He gave me a little grin when our eyes met.

"I love you, Derrick. I love you so much. I'm so...so sorry," I cried.

"Erica," he said softly. "Be strong."

I found love and comfort in his eyes. I was tired, in pain, scared and weak, but if he asked me to be strong, I would try. I swallowed hard to stop crying. I stood straighter and locked my eyes into his. Our love was an invisible force only we could feel, a bond that would get us through this together.

Dusty was still laughing, as if the scenes before him were some great comedy. The group of vampires dispersed and Lamont drifted to front Derrick. I was able to clearly see Derrick's face over Lamont's head. Lamont withdrew his smaller rainbow blade, the one he had cut me with, and quickly sliced Derrick across his chest.

I watched a look of anguish appear on Derrick's face. Instinctively Derrick's right arm broke through its chain and grabbed Lamont's hand. Derrick tore Lamont's right hand and forearm from its elbow. Lamont's awful scream ricocheted through the chamber as he clutched his stump. Time seemed to slow as I watched the severed limb fall to the floor, the hand dropping the knife when it hit. There was very little blood.

Serena was on me instantaneously. I screamed as her blade penetrated my chest slightly, just over my heart.

"Werewolf, do you wish to see her killed?" she asked in a vile voice.

Derrick went still. And with a nod from Serena, Lamont's guard reshackled Derrick's free arm. Lamont grabbed his squirming limb from the floor and held it to his stump, letting the two pieces bond their way together. He and his guard stood a few feet from Derrick, their faces full of hate.

"Next time he makes a move like that," Serena commanded Deetra, "cut her throat."

Dusty looked at Serena. "Dead or alive, you will have your way," she said. He smiled like a mad man.

I kept my eyes locked into Derrick's, focusing on him for strength. Serena glided to where Lamont's knife lay and quickly had it in her hand. Once she stood, she blocked my view of Derrick's face again.

"So your skin is susceptible to this blade...but not the other metal," she hissed. Interesting that neither of you are poisoned by its properties like we are...but it cuts you just the same."

I heard what she said. The metal was poison, but the terror I witnessed as she sliced him much more deliberately than Lamont had was taking all my focus not to scream. She was testing Derrick's commitment. From what I could see, his body stayed rigid. He didn't express any discomfort as she cut him in one long slice diagonally down his torso. She moved so I could see.

Deetra still had her blade to my throat, but I barely noticed it as I wept uncontrollably from the sight. His blood flowed down his body from the two cuts, one small cut over his heart and one long deep cut from his right shoulder to his left hip. The top of his cloth cover was saturated in blood. Unable to absorb more, his blood rained to the floor from the cloth's ragged edges.

"Your will?" Serena asked Lamont.

"You may proceed," Lamont snapped.

Serena ordered to Lamont's guard through an eager icy hiss, "Bring me the whip."

She held the knife up so Derrick could see it, slowly swiveling it in the moonlight. "This metal is not from this world," she explained. "Master was able to smell its unique properties from across the Black Sea. The smell led to a meteor that had crashed to this planet centuries ago. Master had a vision to extract certain properties from the meteor, to melt and forge those properties into a metal to use as a weapon. It is very poisonous..." she stopped abruptly, then shook her head and cackled as if it didn't matter.

Before Serena could say more, Lamont's guard was back in the chamber with a whip. It was a hideous looking torture device, a thick black braided handle with a long leather strip. I shook violently when I noticed the same small red and black blade tied to the end of the leather strip.

This was it. We were about to die. "I love you," I said barely above a whisper.

"Forever," he said just as quietly.

Lamont's guard handed the whip to Serena and glided back to Lamont's side. Dusty was now rocking back and forth on his heels, an eager grin across his face.

"So, Werewolf, will you die in her stead?" Serena asked, her velvety voice full of excitement.

"Derrick, NO!" I screamed ignoring the pain at my neck.

"They're going to kill me anyway. Please save yourself. PLEASE!" I begged. "If you love me, you will GO!" I knew he could break free; he could easily escape. His eyes met mine and I read them. He'd never leave. He couldn't, just as I would never be able to leave him.

Gracefully Serena removed her cloak and let it fall to the floor, revealing a perfectly fit body. Long curly auburn hair hung to her waist. She wore a tight black leather unitard that covered her entire body but for her face and hands. She had black stiletto boots that went to her thighs. She looked like a sadist.

Serena rhythmically tapped the braided handle against her hand as she took position behind Derrick.

"Cut his hair," she commanded.

Lamont's guard unsheathed a dagger and walked behind Derrick. I couldn't see the vampire cut Derrick's hair, nor did Derrick move a muscle. But when the vampire glided back to his place, I saw Derrick's long black hair drag the ground before being tossed aside on the floor.

I cringed as the most horrible, evil smile spread across Serena's face. In revulsion I watched as she raised her right arm up and back as far as she could. And with sheer force, she cracked the whip striking Derrick's back. I heard the sickening slap of the blade hitting flesh. I felt the breeze from the whip on my skin and saw the agony on Derrick's face as he clenched his jaws tight, refusing to scream.

Derrick's eyes found mine. I saw the pain in them, and the love. He was going to suffer through it. He was going to die, die for me.

"Derrick, please don't do this," I begged through sobs ignoring the knife that was still at my throat. These loathsome creatures were going to force me to watch as they beat my love, my soul, my other half, to death before they killed me.

Serena struck him again. This time Derrick's eyes left mine. He wouldn't look at me anymore. She struck him again, and again. Still he refused to cry out, but not me.

Watching Derrick being tortured was so much worse than if it were me. I didn't care who saw me. All my arrogance vanished. I went hysterical and thrashed against the post like a wild animal. I was sweating, shaking, and screaming through tears, begging for her to stop. I pulled against my chains completely unaware of the shackles as they cut deep into my skin or the knife that cut into my throat. I only slightly noticed the sensation of blood flowing down the inside of my arms and down my neck. I was in total anguish watching Serena kill him.

After about the tenth strike, Derrick's body went limp. His head fell to his chest as he passed out. I cried out for him. No one cared. Serena looked my way and gave me another one of her wicked smiles as she continued the flagellation. Her red eyes flamed with pleasure.

Somewhere deep in my subconscious I heard a voice calling my name, *"Erica, Erica, Erica."* It was a soft, familiar female voice, but the pain before me was too intense. Watching Derrick's death had my complete attention. Then louder I heard, *"Erica...CHILD."* I stopped screaming for a moment and listened. As soon as I began to search for the voice I was suddenly floating above the scene before me. I saw my body still chained to the post, hanging as if I had passed out, covered in blood. The cloaked female vampire remained at her spot with the knife still at my neck. Dusty was eagerly watching as was Lamont and his guard. Lamont's face was gleaming with delight.

I watched as Serena pulled her arm back to release another lashing. And from this angle, I could see Derrick's back ripped apart. I threw up from the sight. I witnessed my hanging body puke on the female vampire's arm. She withdrew the blade momentarily to shake the vomit from her sleeve, only to move it back in place, just not as close as before.

I screamed but no one could hear me. I thought maybe I was dead, a silent relief telling me it would soon be over. Derrick and I would be together again, if not in flesh in spirit. But then I found myself lying on the soft grass of a meadow. I felt the breeze on my face and the warm sun on my skin. Deeply I inhaled, filling my lungs to their maximum capacity with fresh air and caught the fragrance of wildflowers and spring water. In the distance I heard a waterfall.

I sat up to look around, and soon realized I was in Derrick's secret meadow. I searched for the forest fairies, and found the swarm next to the wild rose bush, just where I remembered them being. In the distance I saw a half rainbow from the waterfall's spray and the doe with her twin fawns grazing below. Slowly I stood, looking towards the pool where we went fishing. On the flat blue rock I saw someone with long black hair sitting with their back to me.

"DERRICK!" I screamed running towards the rock.

We were dead, but we would be together forever. I ran to him. But as I closed the gap, I noticed the figure's shape didn't look right. I slowed to a walk, fear flooding me.

"Derrick?" I whispered reaching my hand out to touch the person's shoulder, already knowing it wasn't him. Before I made contact, the figure turned revealing my reflection. I screamed and stumbled backward. I fell hard but felt no pain.

The woman that stood before me looked exactly like me, only her hair was darker and straighter. Her eyes were like a thin jade stone held in front of the sun. She wore a flowing gown that matched the color of her eyes. The gown was sleeveless and billowed just above her ankles revealing small bare feet. The soft silk rippled slightly in the gentle breeze.

She smiled and instantly I felt calmer. I looked down at myself. I was clean, in a similar dress but a soft pink color. My body didn't hurt at all.

"Erica," she said in a very soothing angelic voice. "I am Natasha. I am your birth mother."

The fear was back. I began to tremble. I didn't want to hear this. I was about to close my eyes and shut my mind when she spoke quickly, but gently. "He will die, Erica. He will die if you do not help him."

"Derrick?" I asked, debating whether or not I was

hallucinating.

She nodded and offered her hand to help me up. I hesitated for a moment then took her hand in mine. It was soft, warm and felt real to the touch. I felt energy course through me from her, as if she were a source of energy and our touch the conduit. I stood, but she didn't let go of my hand. Instead she guided me to the flat rock where we sat next to each other. She faced me and continued in an intoxicatingly beautiful voice.

"We don't have much time, child. It was not supposed to happen this way." She frowned slightly. "The vampires are stronger and smarter than I thought."

Natasha looked deep into my eyes. Hers were like green emeralds sparkling in the sun as she spoke to me. "You have to accept what you are, inside," she said softy moving her hand from mine and placing it gently over my heart. "I cannot explain everything to you now, my child. Soon, though, very soon you will understand."

I was confused. What she was talking about? "What do you mean?" I begged, thinking I'd gone completely insane.

"Half of you came from me," she gently said, "half of you from your birth father. Half of you is witch, and the other half, shapeshifter."

"Is any of me human?" I asked aghast.

With a beautiful smile she nodded and softly continued. "Your father is human, child. Shapeshifting is a gift to Native peoples, a gift from the spirits when witches could no longer protect them."

So the Council had some of it right. Slowly I began to accept the possibility that I was really experiencing that moment, that perhaps I was living a nightmare.

Quickly I remembered the dire situation at hand, that my soul was being torn to shreds. "How can I save Derrick?" I pleaded, tears spilling from my eyes.

In a more serious, but still angelic voice she explained. "You have not known about this part of you. I feel your resistance of accepting what you are. But understand the choice is yours to recognize and accept me as your mother, this supernatural reality." Natasha took both of my hands in hers and looked even deeper into my eyes, as if she were talking past my body into my soul. "If you do, you will acknowledge the magic of our kind and be changed. It is in you, it has always been there, just dormant. Witches have been given great abilities to hunt and kill vampires, greater than that of werewolves. We exist only to kill vampires."

She pulled me closer. Her breath reminded me of the freshness a rainstorm leaves behind. "Child, if you choose not to accept me as your birth mother, then you will go back to where you just came from. You will die and go to the spirit world."

"And Derrick?" I asked.

"He too will surely die and join his ancestors."

"Would we be together?" I asked, seriously considering the "not accepting" option.

She nodded and gently moved one of her hands to stroke the

side of my face. Her touch was soft and warm. I noticed a black five pointed star on the inside of her right forearm, it was the same size and shape and in the same spot as my pink birthmark.

In a more serious, but gentle voice she explained. "Yes, child, we all go to the same spirit world. However, I am in a spiritual plane between the two continuums. I'm here to help you. But know humanity will end, and many will suffer terribly. You were solely created to be the final weapon to eradicate all vampires."

"Created?" I asked in disgust suddenly feeling like a science experiment.

Natasha nodded. "Created by the only two creatures who could produce a perfect being such as yourself." She smiled taking my hand.

"I don't understand...What am I supposed to do?" I cried.

"Child, there are many questions, but the time for answers is not now. You must save Derrick."

"I don't have any special abilities, Natasha. Even though I see you here, you've got the wrong person. I can barely bounce a ball," I blubbered. "How can I possibly save anyone?"

Natasha took both of my hands in hers. I could feel her energy. It gave me strength.

"Don't doubt yourself, child. You only had difficulty because the witch in you wanted to be recognized. Once you accept the witch, all will easily come to you...It is instinct." In a more hurried tone she continued, "I will be helping you as much as I can from here. You must accept that I am a part of who you are. You need not worry about ability," she said seriously, both in voice and expression which really freaked me out seeing my facial expressions look completely different than how I felt.

Natasha asserted, "We must hurry. Derrick will die within the minute."

"What?" I screamed.

"You must accept who you are and bear this burden." Natasha's angelic voice was urgent. "Erica, you must accept to bear The Burden of being a witch. Because with these abilities comes responsibilities, and immortality."

"Immortality?" I gasped.

"Your witch body will only be vulnerable to very few threats. Age and disease cannot hurt you, only human attacks. However, once you reach your nineteenth birthday, even humans cannot hurt you. Your only threat will then be the alien blade in your human form, as you witnessed with Derrick. You will not find peace until the last vampire is killed, and you will live in your prime until that time comes. Only after the last vampire is dead will you be able to live the rest of your years as a mortal. My child, it is not fair this position you are placed in, to decide so fast, but you must!"

"Will I be able to save Derrick?"

"Yes, if you hurry."

"Then, yes. Yes I accept this burden," I cried.

Instantly I was back in my body and in action. All my fear was replaced with anger on a scale tenfold.

I pulled my wrists free from their restraints grabbing the arm that held the blade to my throat and ripped it from the female vampire's torso. Before her arm hit the floor, I tore off her other arm. She didn't have time to scream as I twisted off her head.

Lamont's guard, the vampire with the boots, instantly leapt for me. The chains around my ankles broke free as I jumped meeting him in the air. We slammed together like two locomotives. While in the air I easily ripped him apart, ignoring his ghastly screams, before landing gracefully on my feet.

Above me wispy clouds became thicker. Thunder roared loud and close. Moonlight was replaced with lightning that tore open the sky. It was as if the atmosphere was mimicking my anger.

I stood in the middle of the star absorbing all the surrounding natural particle wave energy. My hair flew wildly about as I felt every wave enter my exposed skin fueling my strength and senses. I knew everything that was happening. I was able to focus on several things at the same time. I knew where Derrick hung lifeless. I knew where the remaining two vampires stood. I knew Dusty stood quaking in the pants he just soiled. I also knew where the weapons were on the ground, and the placement of every object in the room. I could even sense the mice and snakes from the chambers below.

Now it was my turn for an eager smile. I knew instantly my speed was at least as fast as the vampires if not faster, and that my strength easily exceeded theirs. Before Lamont made a single move I felt his intention to flee. I was a conduit and focused the energy I'd absorbed through me and out my palm, directing the three spears that still lay where they had fallen towards Lamont with such speed and force sonic booms toppled the six columns with the satanic beast heads. The flames on the torches were snuffed out by the debris.

The first spear impaled Lamont through his left eye pinning him to the wall several feet behind him. The next went through his left arm and stomach as he still held his limbs together. The third spear went through his right shoulder. The now semi-severed limb dangled briefly before falling to the floor. Lamont screamed in anger and pain.

I leapt for Serena. Briefly our eyes met. I saw her wicked face full of fear. But she was fast. Her shock instantly controlled as she dropped the whip and fled through the opening above. I fought the need to hunt and kill her, my concern for Derrick stronger than my instinct. I made it to Derrick in less than a few seconds, but I was too late.

I wrenched his chains loose and gently lowered his limp body to the cold floor. I rested his head on my lap. Desperately I listened for signs of life. I heard Dusty's whimpers, Lamont struggling to get free, pitter patter of mice, but nothing from Derrick...no breathing and no beating.

I remembered CPR from a health education class. I placed him flat on his mangled back and rhythmically blew shallow breaths into his lungs then pushed against his chest trying to restart his heart. Over and over I tried until I felt his ribs crack beneath my hands, but still...nothing.

"Derrick, NO. Don't leave me!" I screamed as thunder boomed overhead and lightning light the black sky. Heavy rain drops began to fall as tears streamed down my face.

"NATASHA," I screamed through the icy rain pelting my face. "Help me, PLEASE! I cannot live without him."

Through violent shaking I was able to pull Derrick onto my lap and hold his cold lifeless body. Gently I rocked him side to side, begging for him to wake up while making deals with gods, spirits, Native ancestors...anyone who I thought might be listening. "Anything, I will do anything you want, just don't take him from me...Don't let this happen," I cried thinking of scenarios that would have led to a different situation. His death was my fault, all my fault. If only I would have waited to come to town.

Deep in my subconscious, just as before, I heard Natasha's angelic voice. *"Child, feed him."*

Instinctively I knew what she meant. I bit myself deep beneath my star shaped birthmark, which had turned black, and quickly pried open Derrick's mouth with my other hand. Surprisingly there was no pain, only pressure from my teeth. I watched as the blood surfaced and spilled from the two crescent shaped cuts. I milked the surrounding tissue with my thumb increasing the flow to a thin stream that trickled into his mouth. Within moments the wound closed and I waited, pulling him close and stroking his damp cold forehead.

"Derrick, breathe," I begged through tears and sobs. "Please. Derrick...Don't die."

As I held him I noticed oozing on my legs. I turned him slightly to get a better look at his back. I was consumed with rage when I saw the butchery Serena laid upon him. His back was shredded. I could see his shoulder blades and ribs, white pieces of bone was scattered throughout the torn tissue.

Gently I moved from under Derrick and placed his head on the hard wet ground. I stood as thunder exploded in one continuous succession and lightning slashed through the night providing constant light. A bolt of lightning struck the center of the star, blasting granite and cement pieces into the air as I took my first step toward Lamont. The hair all over my body stood erect as I absorbed every particle wave around me. At that moment Lamont was the only one I could purge my wrath upon. Though I knew Dusty was running for the exit, I could not even think about harming him. I lifted my hands over my head breathing in deep as I filled my body to the core with pure energy.

I glared at Lamont. He had almost shimmied himself free. I saw fear through his hatred.

"DIE!" I screamed as I unleashed my fury on him. Energy flowed through my body as I directed it with both palms toward Lamont. The invisible force hit him hard slamming him back against the wall before he burst into flames.

I opened my arms wide releasing one large wave of energy, screaming the loudest I had yet, letting pain my ebb through my voice towards the sky. I ignited every piece of vampire that lay around me or within several miles of where I stood. Dusty had been stepping over a piece of vampire as it flamed which caught his robe on fire. Dusty's screams filled the night for a few moments before his demise. I didn't take pleasure in his death, but I didn't feel any sympathy.

I fell to the ground drained. I sobbed uncontrollably as rain showered heavily on me. "Derrick, oh, Derrick. I'm sorry," I cried, but no one could hear me. I felt alone. I was alone. I wanted to die too. I shouldn't have accepted Natasha's offer. I should have waited, been patient, then Derrick and I could have at least been together in spirit. Now I was destined to live without him. I wouldn't do it. I knew I couldn't do it. I was sure Natasha knew that as well, or why else would she have helped at that precise moment instead of waiting. Because she KNEW. She KNEW I needed him.

I lay in the fetal position holding my knees to my chest as rain poured down from the sky. The pain was an unbearable weight. I couldn't move. My soul had been ripped from my body. I sobbed in the rain wishing for death. I only stopped when I thought I heard a new sound.

I held my breath. It was a noise I needed to hear once more. I looked at Derrick and then...I heard it again.

Instantly I was next to him, gently placing his head back on my lap.

"Derrick?" I cried as I heard the noise again. It was his heart. It was trying to beat. I could hear it slowly push blood through his system.

I bit myself again but deeper. I wanted the wound to bleed heavy and long. I didn't need to milk my arm this time as a thick crimson stream flowed fast and free.

I placed my arm to his mouth which was still slightly open. I listened as hard as I possibly could for any signs of life. I easily heard the animals and reptiles below the chamber, but focused my hearing on any noise that resembled a human heart beat that wasn't mine. Then I heard it again. THUMP-thump.

"Derrick, Oh Derrick. I'm here. I'm here," I sobbed as hope replaced despair.

The rain stopped. Only the glow from the scattered vampire fires gave light.

"Drink it, Derrick," I insisted, not wanting to say the word "blood". I refused to even think about how gross and twisted I was being right then and there.

Very softly I felt his cold lips press against my arm.

"Yes, Derrick, drink it...It will help," I instructed, resting my check on his head, my anguish of sorrow turning into anguish of expectation.

Soon I felt his tongue and hard sharp teeth as he began to gently suck and swallow. He was drinking and immediately unexpected surges of pleasure raced through my body. Every section of my skin was soaking in energy. I could feel it flow through me into Derrick.

Derrick began to swallow faster and suck harder. He was able to move his hands to hold my arm to his mouth. His breathing began to deepen as he drank. The spasms of ecstasy coursed through me with every suck...every swallow. I moaned in pleasure as sweat poured from my brow. It took all my strength to stay still, not to move.

I heard Natasha deep in my head, "*Stop, child, you must stop. Too much will kill him.*"

I tried to focus through the euphoria. My new super senses were overwhelmed with pleasure, making it hard to concentrate.

"Derrick, you need to stop," I moaned.

Gently I tugged my arm away from his mouth. He responded by sucking harder, pulling my arm closer. I felt his tongue, his lips, his teeth. My body wanted to ride the wave longer, but I forced myself back to Derrick.

"Derrick, STOP," I said more sternly as I started to pry his fingers off my arm.

Suddenly his dark eyes flew open and met mine. I knew he'd stopped before he let go of my arm. The sensation that raptured my body stopped as abruptly as it started.

Slowly he let go, but he was still very weak.

"I love you," I repeated over and over holding him close.

"Your eyes..." he was able to say in a raspy whisper.

"You'll be okay, Derrick," I said.

The clouds above parted and silver moonlight lit the chamber. As soon as the beam hit Derrick, he arched stiffly, his eyes telling me to move.

Reluctantly, but quickly, I moved out of the way and watched his body morph into the werewolf, but at a much slower pace than I'd previously seen him transform. Before he made the change completely I noticed the wounds on his back were almost healed.

And what hadn't, I could see mending before my eyes.

I looked at my arm. The bite mark already closed. It had stayed open while Derrick drank, but as soon as he stopped, it healed. I looked at both my arms. None of my previous wounds existed.

Derrick sauntered to me in his werewolf body. He was on all fours. He moved easier in that position. I looked into his eyes and reached for him. He let me touch him. His hair was thick and coarse, but soft. I began to cry as I let myself fall onto his warm body. I held him tight, as tight as I could because I knew I couldn't hurt him.

"Derrick," I cried. "I thought I'd lost you."

He moved to stand and soon I was engulfed in his embrace, his thick furry arms were gentle as he picked me up and held me to his chest. He held me while I let it out, the feeling of losing him then having him was too much to handle.

After my cry, I stood and took a moment to look at the disaster that surrounded us. The vampire fires were still burning. Somehow I knew they would burn until every last piece was nothing but ash, even through the rain. The building was in ruins. I saw one of the satanic horned heads next to Sarah's. I was sad she was dead, but proud of her last act of heroism. In the end I think she tried to do what was right.

Then I looked at Derrick, my purpose, the reason I took on this burden. "Let's go," I said.

He looked at me with his beautiful dark eyes before he started towards the door Lamont used. As my eyes followed him they caught sight of the whip Serena dropped. Derrick's tissue and blood was caked to the once beautiful blade. I walked over and quickly yanked the blade from the leather strap. I ran to where the spears still held parts of the burning Lamont. I pulled them from the wall and broke off the red and black metal tips. Something told me to grab the metal. Derrick was watching as I wrapped the blades in a piece of bloody fabric I scavenged from the floor, and shoved them deep into my pocket.

Then I softly called to him. "Derrick...this way."

I ran and jumped, soaring through the air. The feeling was amazing as the air caressed my weightless body. Softly I landed on the edge of the roof. I looked down at Derrick through the broken glass ceiling, a huge grin on my face revealing the enjoyment of the experience. He hesitated a moment. It looked like he shook his head, as if to shake away the shock. Then he took a couple bounds using the debris as steps until he took one large leap and landed next to me.

"Where are we?" I asked glancing around.

We were on a steep grassy hill surrounded by miles of lush dark forest. The hill didn't resemble a building at all. I saw a cargo truck parked at its base in front of a lone door that led into the hillside. It must have been the truck I was kidnapped in. I read EXTERMINATOR SERVICE on the side panel in big black letters against the white background. I felt a knot of anger form in my stomach remembering the terrible ride.

We began to walk down the hill when I caught a scent. It was

Serena. The rotten egg smell was now much more complex. The smell was still putrid, but I could distinguish her unique scent of death and evil.

I turned toward the path she'd taken and started running. I wanted to kill her, to tear her apart...but slowly, so she would suffer the way she made Derrick suffer. I was lost in my thoughts of how to torture her when Derrick stopped in front of me. I hit him at a full run, the impact sent us flying several yards crashing and tearing through the forest until we skidded to a stop.

"Derrick?" I gasped in surprise.

His eyes were intense. He looked to the moon and let out a long wail. I heard his suffering.

"Okay Derrick...I'm sorry. I didn't.... Let's go," I said turning back the way we'd come.

The hill wasn't where I expected it to be, it was miles from where I stood. It took me a moment to realize that I'd just run *that* distance within a few seconds.

I fell to the ground trying to catch my sanity, telling myself this was really happening and repeating that everything was going to be okay because Derrick was alive, when I felt a huge fuzzy hand help me up. Once I was standing he dropped back down to all fours. I looked into his eyes.

"I'm sorry, Derrick...I think I'm about to have a breakdown," I tried to smile but couldn't. "How about I follow you?" I whispered.

Derrick started off in a direction perpendicular to the path I'd just run. He was headed south. I was able to tell the direction by reading the stars, a skill I'd learned from an astronomy class I'd taken during my senior year of high school. I guess my old teacher was right, knowing how to read the night sky would come in handy someday.

Soon he was trotting. I easily kept that pace. Then he was running and I followed. Derrick tested my speed with a full sprint that I matched. We raced through the woods.

I was amazed by my new agility. I easily wove between obstacles without slowing at all. I could jump over streams and deadfalls without any effort. At first it took me a while to trust myself. I had to fight learned behavior from my clumsy nature. But once I let go, my intuition guided me, letting me know what my body could do.

While running I was able to admire my surroundings, even though I was a blur of speed. I easily heard the animals of the forest and could even make out the faint sounds of dew drops dripping from leaves to the ground. And I could see miles ahead in the dark, everything had a silver glow.

I followed Derrick, watching as he gracefully bounded through the forest. I listened to his breathing and the beating of his heart. I smiled to myself. I decided that his heartbeat was the most precious sound in the world to me.

Suddenly anger and repugnance flashed through me as I thought of Serena. Her wicked smile and pleasure of torture was burned in my memory forever. I promised myself she would pay...They all would die. My fear of vampires had turned to loathing instantly. As we traveled I fantasized the various ways I was going to hunt and kill every last one of them.

I was brought back to reality when we arrived at Derrick's house. I slowed to a stop in his driveway. The purple hue of dawn was breaking on the horizon. I noticed the Council's cars parked in the same place as last time.

I hesitated on his driveway, not wanting to see anyone. The weight of what happened crushed me all at once. I was no longer Erica Mathews, the klutzy nerd, normal kid of Bill and Molly. I was the biological daughter of a witch and shapeshifter. There was no doubting that fact anymore. I had just accepted The Burden, which had changed the course of my life in a completely different direction. I'd just easily killed two vampires, and unintentionally a piece of crap human. I'd never killed anything before besides bugs. I had just run hundreds of miles within an hour, obviously not normal.

I began to feel dizzy. That's when I felt Derrick's strong arms around me. He was back in his beautiful human body. I turned and embraced him, crying into his chest as I held him tight.

"Derrick, I love you so much," I said looking up into his eyes.

"Erica, what happened?" he asked, confusion clouding his face.

"Do we have to talk about it now?" I begged through tears, "Can't it wait just a little bit, because Derrick...I just made a deal with my mother...the witch," I blubbered.

Gently he picked me up in his strong arms, one arm behind

my back the other under my knees. I hung on tight, my arms around his neck and my face buried against his neck. I took comfort in his aroma, the heady smell I knew so well. As he carried me, I refused to move my head or open my eyes. I knew when he reached the porch by the four steps he took. Next I heard the screen door open.

"Derrick. Oh my god...ERICA!" I heard Karen cry.

"Not now, Mom," Derrick said in a deep voice letting everyone know to back off.

I felt him descend the stairs and soon he was placing me on his soft black comforter on the bed we had made love on just the night before.

So much had happened since then.

I watched as he pulled on a pair of shorts and snuggled up behind me. He held me tight, and quickly we fell asleep, both of us physically and emotionally drained.

CHAPTER 17

My dreams were full of Natasha. I was struggling with an identity complex. I found myself so plain and ordinary, but her beautiful and mysterious. Yet we looked almost exactly the same. I heard her amazing voice in my head telling me that she was my birth mother. I heard Lamont claim she was the Master Vampire's mortal daughter. Natasha's voice telling me I was part witch and part shapeshifter. I was immortal but susceptible to human attacks? I was confused. Then I saw Serena, her vile grin and Derrick's mangled back.

I woke with a start, inhaling deeply as sweat poured from my face. Derrick's bedroom was bright from the sunlight streaming through the basement windows.

I watched Derrick as he slept. We were both on top of the comforter, I was on my back and he was on his stomach. I was covered in gore. He was naked. By the furrow in his brow and the small movements on his face, I figured he was having a bad dream. I didn't know if I should wake him. Gently I moved his arm from across my waist and sat up. His hair was cut so short. My eyes searched his back for any evidence of what happened. I was relieved to see that it was absolutely perfect, not a scratch left where Serena had torn him apart.

The memory of his shredded back hit me all of a sudden making me sick to my stomach. I needed to get to the bathroom fast. As soon as I saw the toilet, I threw up, but my stomach was empty. I suffered through many violent dry heave spasms.

I turned the shower on to let it warm and the bathroom quickly filled with steam. I brushed my teeth before peeling off my clothes, ignoring the dried blood. I stepped into the pre-warmed shower. Slowly I washed my hair and body, watching the pink rivers find their way down my skin and pool at the bottom of the shower before funneling down the drain. Once I felt clean I just stood there, letting the pressure of the water beat against my back.

I sensed the bathroom door open and then the shower door opened. I watched Derrick slide into the shower through the steam and move closer. Uncontrollable tears welled in my eyes. I loved him more than anything and when his gaze met mine, he had me in his arms.

I let Derrick know how much I needed him with my kisses and caressing hands. His body and desire responded eagerly to my touch. He lifted me so that our bodies would fit. Gently he held me while resting my back against the shower wall, my thighs tight on his hips. Tears rolled quietly down my cheeks as I relished in the moment. Our love had intensified beyond anything we'd experienced. His need was suddenly as fierce as mine as he thrust faster. He moaned my name and I cried out in pleasure as we exploded in harmony. He held me tight, still as one, kissing me tenderly as the waves subsided.

"I love you," he said softly as I nuzzled his neck.

I had to prove Derrick was alive and healthy, that we made it out of that hell alive and together. My need for Derrick was not over. I wanted to feel his love and show him mine. Soon we were on his bed making love again and again. That was until my stomach made a growl.

"Why doesn't your stomach ever make noise?" I asked after the second time mine complained in a rumbling, gurgling sound that lasted at least five seconds.

"I don't know," he said smiling down at me while his fingers softly caressed my stomach. "But yours is sure noisy."

I sat up and gave him a fake angry smile.

"Do you want me to bring you something, or do you want to go upstairs?" he asked.

"I don't know...is anyone up there?"

He nodded. "Yeah, Mom's up there. I think she's pretty worried. I should at least go upstairs so she knows we're okay."

"You're right...You should talk to her. I'll go take a shower, again," I said, "but I don't want to talk to anyone. I still need to figure things out." I watched his face. I saw the stress return. I knew he wanted explanations, but it was my turn to take my time.

I grabbed some clothes and headed towards the bathroom while Derrick slipped on some sweats. I took another shower and quickly dressed. I was in his bathroom brushing my hair when the steam began to evaporate. I dropped the brush and let out a blood curdling scream when I saw my reflection for the first time since I'd accepted The Burden.

Derrick was at my side within moments. "Erica, Erica," he repeated gently trying to shake me out of my sudden paralysis. But I couldn't move.

"My eyes..." I whispered not able to look away from the mirror. My eyes had changed color. They were no longer the green I knew. They were the jade color of Natasha's.

"It'll be okay," Derrick said lifting and carrying me to his room.

I wiggled free, and once my feet hit the ground I looked at my birthmark. I stared at where the once pinkish star shaped birthmark was now completely black.

I had become a witch. I was marked.

Derrick took my arm and kissed my mark. "Let's eat," was all he said.

Derrick ran back upstairs and came down with fresh fruit, toast, and orange juice. We ate in silence.

"That was good," I mumbled with a full mouth. I couldn't believe how hungry I was. I still felt like I could eat, but there was nothing left.

"Mom had it ready for us," he said.

"What time is it?" I asked.

"Almost four," Derrick said as he pointed to a little digital clock that sat atop a night stand next to his side of the bed.

"In the evening?" I was surprised. I had no idea so much time had passed.

He nodded and in a more serious tone said, "Mom's really worried about you. I was able to tell her what I remembered...She noticed the hair," he pointed to his head, "but Erica, when are you going to let *me* know what happened?"

I felt like I was punched in the stomach. I swallowed fast keeping the sob at bay when I thought of what happened to him, which was replaced with hatred when I thought of vampires. I suddenly wanted to hunt them. I needed to hunt them like I needed to eat. Serena had been heading east, which was where I was going to go. I figured I'd go back to where...

"Erica," Derrick interrupted. "What's going on?"

Seeing the confusion on his face, I supposed it was time to tell him what had happened, who I was, what I'd become.

"Do you want me to tell you alone, or should I tell everyone? I don't really want to talk to the Council," I complained. I wasn't even sure if I could speak to them, especially Amy.

"It's okay. They've already left. I guess seeing me in the buff carrying you covered in blood, they called it a night," he said with a smile trying to relieve some of the tension that filled the room, but I saw the worry on his face. "It's up to you. I know Mom wants to hear, but she understands if you'd rather not. I can tell her what you want her to know later."

"Where's Miya?" I asked.

"She's staying with Amy. I guess her granddaughter is in town from Seattle for a couple weeks," I flinched at her name.

Derrick continued ignoring me. "Amy's pretty cool. I'm sure you'll change your mind about them when you get a chance to actually know them," he tried to explain.

He was probably right but I couldn't help but blame them for some of my problems right then. They didn't really have anything to do with what happened, just the bearers of bad news. But still, I needed some time to absorb what was going on before revealing my personal baggage to strangers.

"I think I want to tell you both," I said. "I like your mom, and she deserves to know what happened...then she can decide if she still wants me to live here." My voice cracked on the last part. Then I had to let it out. I'd been holding the fear back. Derrick moved to take my plate from me. I let him hold me while I cried into his shirt. I was worried about what I'd become, and that Derrick wouldn't accept me.

"Erica," Derrick said after I calmed down a little. "You don't have to worry about that. There is nothing in this world that is going to make me leave you...not now, not ever. And my mom cares a lot about you too. She'd never keep us apart...okay?" he reassured, making me look into his eyes.

"Okay, Derrick. Let me freshen up a little first," I said walking to the bathroom. I washed my face, careful not to look in the mirror, and ran a brush through my hair.

"I'm ready," I said walking back into the bedroom. I noticed he was changing the bedding. I went to help him.

"What happened to my bloody clothes?" I asked following

him with an armful of sheets into the laundry room, which was next to his bedroom.

"I tossed them when you took your second shower. I didn't think you'd want them."

But I did. I remembered I had four very important blades in the pocket of my shorts. "Actually, Derrick, I do," I said concerned.

"Oh shit." He grabbed the dirty sheets from my arms and pitched them into the washer. "I set them on fire," he explained running up the stairs with me right behind his heels.

I followed him behind the garage, where we stopped next to a fire pit of smoldering ashes.

"Sorry," he said, moving the ashes around with a stick.

"Wait. Derrick... Give me that," I said taking the stick from him. I poked around where I thought I saw something. "Look," I said as I noticed a blackened piece of metal.

I bent down and grabbed it. It wasn't hot. "Here," I said handing the blade to Derrick. "There's more."

I sifted through the ashes until I found the remaining three pieces of charred metal. I took the fragments from Derrick and found an outside faucet. Quickly, but carefully, I began to clean them. The red and black metal slowly revealed itself as the ash washed away.

I stood and showed Derrick. "Look at these," I said moving my palm up to his face. The blades were shimmering in the sunlight. Derrick took one of them and examined it carefully.

"Remember what Serena said?" I asked.

"Who?"

"Serena, she's the one who cut you with the blade." His expression told me he knew who I meant. "I think these are important. But we shouldn't tell anyone about them Derrick. Not until we know exactly what this stuff can do. Serena's knife wouldn't even make a scratch on you...but the one made out of this did."

He nodded taking the rest of the blades from my hand. "I have a box in the garage. Just a minute," he said. I watched as he disappeared into the open garage and returned with a little wooden box. Then I followed him towards the house.

"I thought I saw you put something in your pocket last night," he said over his shoulder, "but didn't even think to check before I torched your clothes. Sorry," he apologized again.

"It's okay. The fire didn't ruin them," I said, meeting him at the door.

"Ready?" he asked.

I took a deep breath, and with a nod followed him into the house. We found Karen sitting at the dining picnic table. When she saw us she quickly met me with a hug.

"I'm glad you're up," she said trying to hide her emotions. "Just a minute..." she said before vanishing through the swinging door and returning with the door's inward swing. "Either of you hungry?" she asked placing a huge plate of chocolate chip cookies in the middle of the table.

Derrick grabbed a couple. So did I. I ate my two before Derrick finished half of his first, then ate two more. They were so good, the best I'd ever tasted. I was still hungry. I thought about eating more, but decided to take a seat at the other end of the table by the sliding glass door, far from the cookies. Derrick sat on the bench with me. He was to my right and Karen sat across from us.

"Erica is going to tell us both what happened," Derrick explained to his mom.

Karen nodded and waited patiently for me to start.

"Where should I begin?" I asked Derrick quietly.

He thought about it. "How about when I left you here."

"Okay," I said as my voice cracked a little.

Derrick took my hand and moved closer. His leg was touching mine.

"Well, I'd checked my email, and Mom reminded me to check the mail. So when Derrick left, I went home to get it...I wished I'd have waited for you, Derrick, then none of this would have happened. I almost turned around when you called me, but I was almost there. It's all my fault...I'm so sorry." I couldn't help the guilt that crushed me every time I thought about it.

"Erica, don't blame yourself," Karen said. "All things happen for a reason."

I smiled at her, but didn't think it'd be anytime soon, if ever, I'd forgive myself, and seriously doubted she'd be so understanding had she witnessed what happened to her only son.

"She's right," Derrick said giving me a reassuring grin, but I could tell he wanted me to get on with what happened.

I took a deep breath and started again, "So, I got to the house, but felt something was off. I was only there long enough to go to the bathroom but...Serena was there. Sarah called me just before I got to the house, and I'd told her I was on my way. I'm sure she let them in. Sarah set me up."

"Sarah was Erica's friend, and Serena is a vampire," Derrick explained to his mom. She nodded in understanding.

"Serena tied me up, and then I heard you on the answering machine," I looked at Derrick my eyes pleading for forgiveness, "but you already knew," I whispered.

"I'd been home for a while. Miya and I were playing UNO when I had a vision, just like the last time. I saw you in trouble. I called, but you're right...I knew it was too late. I ran toward your house in my spirit form. But I crossed their trail going the opposite direction before I made it very far. The magnetic pull between us helped to guide me. Then it was night, and when the moon came out I automatically changed into the werewolf. I followed your trail way past the Canadian border," he explained.

"Really? The ride didn't seem that long," I said more to myself, but then remembered I'd passed out.

"Ride?" Derrick asked.

"Oh yeah. At my house, two more vampires put me in a plastic box and then in the back of that truck, the one we saw at the bottom of the hill," I explained to Derrick.

"In the daylight?" Karen asked curiously.

"Um...yes, it was light. I think they were wearing body suits. The truck was disguised as an exterminator truck. All I could see clearly were their boots." I took a deep breath before continuing, trying to calm my nerves. "When we got there, they put me in cell down in the basement or dungeon...I'm not sure. It was dark and cold. Then Serena took me to a huge chamber with a glass ceiling and chained me to a post."

I began to tremble from the thought of what happened next. I debated skipping that part but decided not to. I think Karen could see my stress because she got up and came back with a glass of wine and water before I started again.

"Derrick tells me you're not a fan of wine," she said with a smile, "that you prefer it with water."

"Thanks," I said taking both glasses from her. I slammed the wine and chased it with the water like last time. Soon the warmth spread through my body and the shaking subsided.

"Well, they wanted to do some tests on me," I said quietly, sensing Derrick growing tense. "Apparently vampires have human slaves. There were three there. I knew all of them. Sarah and her boyfriend Larry, and a guy named Dusty."

"Dusty?" Derrick asked. "Who the hell is he?"

"Remember the first night we met, when you dropped me off at the hospital. Dusty was my nurse. I remember he seemed really interested in my birthmark" I looked at the mark on my arm, now all black like a tattoo. "I wonder if he started this whole thing."

"Lamont, the short vampire who was the leader made Sarah cut me," I looked at Derrick, "with the same blade that cut you." His eyes never left my face. "Something about seeing if I was affected by the blade's properties."

"Then..." I felt like I was going to puke, my eyes began to leak, "one of them bit me." My hand went to my throat where the vampire's teeth burned through my skin. I wondered if I had any marks. Derrick held his expression firm with his eyes on me. I noticed Karen flinch but quickly regained her composure. "I screamed as loud as I could...the glass ceiling crashed down on us but they didn't care. They wanted to see...to see if they could drink my blood." My eyes found Derrick's, "They were anxious because they heard you, Derrick. You made them scared."

In a deeply reserved, but quiet voice and hard eyes Derrick said, "I heard you scream. It helped lead me to you. Those things had the whole forest stunk up. I kept following false trails. I was having a hard time finding you. Now that I think about it. I bet it was because you were underground, it murked up the magnetic pull. But when I heard you, I knew your direction...and that you were in pain."

I looked at Derrick briefly, his eyes still hard on my face, before continuing. "They can't drink my blood, though. The one vampire died and then caught on fire," I said matter-of-factly. "And then, well, that's when you showed up."

I took another deep breath and looked at Derrick. "Lamont...," I paused briefly before continuing. "Well, he kept trying to make me upset, and the more I stayed straight, the more he'd talk. He said something about killing me before I turned nineteen, before I knew my other abilities, and that he had...cut out my birth mother's heart," I took another deep breath, working up the courage to finish. I looked down at my hands and whispered, "He told me that she was the daughter of the Master Vampire when they were mortals."

I waited for Derrick and Karen to make the connection.

"Oh my God," I heard Karen gasp.

"The Master Vampire is my grandfather. So I won't blame you if you don't want me here anymore," I blurted.

"Oh, Erica," Karen said gently taking my hand and giving it a squeeze. "You are a part of this family. You hear me. We stick together, and you're always welcome here...no matter what."

I looked at Derrick. He was just staring at me. I couldn't read his expression. Karen let go of my hand and I took that as a clue to keep going.

"Um, well, Derrick...he k-k-knows what happened after that," I stuttered hoping he'd take over.

"I told her my version of the story, Erica. We want to hear what happened to you," he said encouraging me to go on.

I hesitated briefly. "Well, when you showed up, Lamont was on his way to hide. I don't think Sarah wanted to be a slave because she turned on Larry and killed him. Then Serena, the redheaded vampire pulled off Sarah's head and threw it at me." I saw Karen cover her mouth, her eyes were wide, "Derrick killed four of the vampires before Serena blackmailed him into changing back into his human form. She stabbed me."

My hand went to where the wound had been. I lifted my shirt to see if I had a scar, there was nothing.

"How'd you do it?" I asked Derrick.

His face was clouded with frustration. He didn't want me to change the subject. But he answered my question anyway. "At first I couldn't. I tried when she first ordered me to. But after you were stabbed, I was able to control my anger and focus my energy. Once I made the change, it was easier to maintain my human form."

He took my hand in his and his face softened just slightly. "Erica, I know this is hard for you, but please finish telling me... us what happened."

I nodded and tried to pick up where I'd left off. "They chained Derrick up. He could have broken free but he wouldn't and...," I couldn't finish. There was no way I could talk about it, and I wouldn't. The memory was still too fresh, the pain too much as I remembered.

"Serena had my hair cut and then whipped the shit out of me until I blacked out," Derrick said quick and flat. "Then what happened?"

"Derrick, I can't..." I pleaded. I didn't want to talk anymore. The hurt was too much for me to handle.

"You can stop if you want," Derrick said but he didn't mean it. His eyes burned into me, willing me to finish. I knew he wanted to hear what happened after he'd passed out. It was eating at him that he didn't see...didn't know what had transpired.

I looked into his eyes and saw his love for me, despite the anger clouding his face. I remembered the strength he gave me through those eyes while we hung there. I was determined to finish.

It was the least I could do after what happened to him because of me.

"I can finish, Derrick," I said quietly. "After you passed out, I heard a voice in my head." I tried to explain the best I could. "Then I was floating above everything, but my body was still hanging from the post. It was really weird, like a dream but more real. When I saw your back," I looked at Derrick, "I felt myself puke, but I watched myself from above throw up on the vampire next to me."

I took a deep breath and another drink from what was left of my water. I was shaking hard and could barely hold the glass. The wine's calming effects had completely vanished. "Then I was in a very special meadow." I was careful not to say out loud that it was Derrick's secret meadow, "and...and...." I was having a hard time. "I saw her."

I watched Derrick's face. He was listening intently to every word I was saying.

"Natasha. She is my birth mother...and she looks just like me. But her hair is darker and straighter, her eyes are...well, like mine are now," I said. "She told me I needed to accept what I was. That I was half witch and half shapeshifter, but that shapeshifters are still human. She said that Natives were given the gift after witches couldn't protect them anymore." I was pretty sure that was what she said anyway. "She said that the vampires found a..."

Suddenly I was interrupted by the angelic voice deep in my head. *"Child, you must not tell. Not here, not now."* It was Natasha and I knew what she meant, but I couldn't understand why she'd want me to keep quiet.

"Erica, Erica," Derrick was shaking my arm bringing me back to the conversation at the table.

"Um...sorry, where was I?" I asked trying to refocus.

"You said that the vampires found something. What was it?" Karen asked.

"A weakness that killed the witches," I continued, skipping the part about being vulnerable to human attacks. "Then she told me that I had to make a choice of accepting what I was or not. That if I didn't, then Derrick and I'd die. She said if I accepted The Burden then I could hunt vampires. She said witches were created to kill vampires...and that I was created solely for that purpose. She told me I've been so clumsy all my life because that was the witch in me wanting to be recognized." I tried to smile.

I noticed both Derrick and Karen were listening, being patient with my stammering, but I couldn't help the nervousness. "She said that I'd remain immortal in my prime until the last vampire was killed and...that I'd not find peace until then. She said that it wasn't supposed to happen like this. That I wasn't supposed to find out and make the decision so fast. But I had to...to save Derrick. I accepted The Burden and then I was back in my body. I killed two of them quickly. Serena got away, but I stuck Lamont to the wall before he could escape."

I looked at Derrick silently suffering while I remembered the agony. "But I was too late. You were already dead. I'd only been away for a couple minutes but I was still too late. I tried to save you. I did CPR. I felt your ribs break." I looked down at my hands remembering the horrible feeling and sound. "Natasha told me to feed you, from inside my head." I couldn't look at him. I didn't want to tell him what I did. I was afraid he'd be so disgusted that he'd never touch me again.

Suddenly the extreme anguish from losing Derrick hit me hard and pulled me back to that moment. "Erica, your eyes," I heard Karen say just before I heard Derrick's concerned voice. "Erica, it's all right...," But the voices were far away and the dining room. Derrick, and Karen faded from my vision. Somehow I made my way to the backyard before I'd completely gone back to the circular chamber. In a monotone voice I told the story as I relived the experience.

"I bit my arm and let the blood spill into his mouth. But it did not work. He was dead. I was angry. I had made a deal. But the deal didn't work." I felt the misery and fury of the moment again, just as I had the night before.

"I called upon my strength," I narrated as I reached my hands to the sky absorbing the surrounding energy. Eagerly I soaked in the surrounding particle waves as my hair whipped across my face, the energy quenching my parched thirst. I heard thunder rumble in the sky. I could hear the crack of lightning close.

My voice was vicious as I started again. "Lamont was almost free. I could see him wiggling down the spears. Dusty tried to run away. I unleashed my fury, igniting Lamont and all those vile creatures that lay around me in pieces. Dusty caught fire and burned as well." And as if I were seeing Lamont in front of me, I shot the energy force though my palms imploding a large cedar tree.

Then I fell to the ground in the same fetal position, my knees to my chest, the pain of Derrick's death unbearable. Thunder boomed overhead and lightning tore apart the sky. A bolt of lightning hit the ground close to me as I screamed in agony over my loss.

Soon I was being pelted by cold rain as I sobbed. "He was dead, my love, my soul, he was dead. Because of ME! How was I to go on? I wouldn't. I'd find a way to die. I wouldn't live without him. If only I'd been patient, we'd both would have been dead, together, forever in spirit."

Somewhere, as if in a dream from within a dream, I thought I saw Derrick restraining Karen from their backyard patio, but it was a very distant blurry image that faded. Quickly I was back in agony, suffering again from the torture of Derrick's death.

"Then I heard it." I sat as I had then, tilting my head listening. "Then I heard it again." I jumped up and ran the short distance to where Derrick should have been. "I knew what to do," just as I had before I bit deep into my arm below my mark. "I fed him," I said as I moaned in pleasure reliving the elation. "Then she said to stop. Too much would kill him. But we didn't want to stop. It felt so good. But we had to," I said jerking my arm to my stomach. I heard a slight crack of lightning and a far off grumble of thunder. The rain had stopped. I looked lovingly at my imaginary Derrick and said, "He's alive. He'll live, my love, my reason for being."

I jumped at the sudden feeling of two large strong arms

around me that shouldn't have been there. I struggled not knowing what was happening. Thinking it might be Serena I started to fight back.

"Erica. Erica. It's me, Derrick. ERICA!" I heard from a familiar voice.

"Derrick?" I whispered coming out of my trance. "Where am I?" I asked, wondering why I was on the wet ground in the middle of his back yard.

"Erica...it's okay, you're here safe. Safe with me," I heard his soothing voice. I relaxed as he held me tight to his chest. "You're safe. It's okay," he said over and over holding my body close. I felt his cheek resting on my head.

My brain was starting to clear, but he wasn't about to let me go.

"Derrick...what's going on?" I asked in a muffled voice from under his arm.

Finally he released me when I pressed against his stomach with my hands. I looked up to his face. Alarm shot through my body. My heart began to pound. My throat tightened from the sight of tears in his eyes.

"Derrick," I was scared. "what happened?"

I smelled smoke. I looked for the source. I saw Karen hosing down a tree at the end of their yard, which was on fire. "Does she need help?" I asked in shock.

"No, she's got it taken care of," Derrick answered quietly as he grabbed my hand and led me into the house.

Derrick took me straight down to his room. I sat quietly on the edge of his bare mattress waiting for him to explain. I tried to remember what happened, but I'd blacked out. I remembered telling him and his mom about Natasha and killing the vampires, but after that...the next thing I could recall was Derrick shaking me awake in his back yard. No wonder he was so anxious to know what had happened. Blacking out is very unsettling.

I glanced down at my lap and jumped at the sight of blood. I was covered in it. I looked for a source, a cut or something, but found nothing. Derrick must have noticed my confusion because he finally came to sit by me.

"You went into a...trance or something," he explained, "and we watched you hallucinate."

I gasped in shock. My eyes went wide waiting for him to continue.

"You...you made clouds, thunder, and lightning. Somehow you blew up Mom's tree. Your eyes, Erica...They were glowing."

I started to shake, I felt dizzy.

He held me as he continued, "I had no idea...,"

"The blood?" I asked in a whisper.

"You bit your arm. It was like you saw me there. The blood from your bite pulsed out of you...like someone *was* drinking from you," his voice was in awe. "But when I went to shake you out of it, the cuts closed," he said softly rubbing the area below my black birthmark.

"It was awful, Derrick," I whispered. "I thought I'd lost you, but then...it was so gross, but it felt so good, and it worked. I knew it would," I tried to explain while changing into a clean outfit.

"I don't really remember drinking...your blood," he said, "but I do remember waking up in your arms. You were the first thing I saw. And your eyes were glowing then. I thought I'd imagined it, but I didn't. Now I know I saw them glowing just like I did tonight."

"What do you think it means?" I asked.

"Natasha is the Mother and you accepted The Burden?"

I nodded.

Derrick's voice was soft as he explained, "After we started home and I saw you jump, I knew something big had happened. And then when you took off after her scent, your speed was not human. I definitely wanted to know what the hell was going on. But I couldn't change back to my human form, I was too weak to fight the force of the moon. Your speed home was a surprise too, but not so much after what I'd just seen. When we got here, I could see it in your face...you were losing it...fast. I wanted to know what had happened to you. I was concerned for you. But I figured the best thing was for you to rest. But then when we got up, it was obvious you had other things on your mind than talking...which was fine with me," he attempted to give me smile. "I'm sorry I made you talk tonight, but I needed to know. And now that I do...," his voice cracked, a sound I'd never heard before, my heart broke instantly, "I wish I hadn't."

"I'm sorry Derrick. I promise I won't blow up any more trees...," I interrupted.

"No, that's not it. Erica, don't you understand what you've

agreed to?" he asked taking my face in his hands.

I couldn't help it. I started to cry. I didn't really understand what he was talking about. I just knew he was hurting and it was tearing me up inside.

"You have just devoted your life to hunting vampires. It'll never be the same again," he tried to explain.

"What...No...," I was almost hysterical. I started to understand where he was going with this.

"Erica you won't be the same. Trust me...I know," he said pulling me closer. "I can't even bear the thought of you fighting them," he said softly against the top of my head. "I'm supposed to protect you."

He held me for a long while before releasing me and softly kissing my forehead.

"We'll be able to get through this...right?" I asked taking his hand.

He only nodded, his eyes full of sorrow as he pulled me tighter to his chest.

CHAPTER 18

Our moment was interrupted from the sound of feet thundering down the stairs. Derrick jumped from the bed ready for a fight. I too felt ready to fight. I was instantly pumped.

"Where do you think you're going?" Karen yelled.

"Where she be?" came a strange female voice.

Derrick was at the door. "What the hell is going on?" he roared.

"Give her to me," came the strange voice again.

Derrick blocked the doorway. I could see long black arms past him.

"Ello.., Erica," the voice called to me. "I be Delia. Natasha sent me."

I ran to the door pushing Derrick aside, the fight instinct fading.

Delia entered the room in a rush. She was as tall as Derrick.

I stared curiously at the woman. I'd never seen anyone like her before. All I could think of was...Amazon. She wore a simple white cotton summer dress revealing her slender yet busty figure. Her skin was a soft ebony color, and her strong Egyptian facial features were dramatic with her very short hair style.

She spoke with a strong Cajun accent. "Dis be me girl. You look like her...yer momma," Delia said.

"Natasha sent you?" I asked in shock.

"Be that she did. And an expensive trip it be, to get a ticket to come all this way so fast. Now the tickets I bought for next week be for nothing," she spat.

"Next week?" I was confused and having a really hard time understanding what she was saying.

"Maybe we should all go upstairs?" I heard Karen from somewhere behind Dalia.

"Fine by me," Delia said turning towards the stairs, but not before grabbing my hand and pulling me with her. I looked in Derrick's eye as I passed him. He was as confused as me.

We went to the living room and sat on the leather furniture in front of the river rock fireplace. Karen brought us glasses of water while coffee brewed.

"How did you know where to find me?" I asked as soon as everyone was sitting.

Delia sat next to me on the love seat, while Derrick and Karen sat across from us on the sofa. Delia began, "Mmmm, Tasha showed me where 'bouts you be. Then all one had to do is follow where the only thunder and lightning storm be on such a clear night."

She took a deep breath and gently stroked the side of my face with her very long and soft fingers. She couldn't stop looking at me.

I think she was comparing my face to Natasha's.

"Me and Tasha lived together for many years. Seemed the Bayou kept them vamps from her. She taught me ways, showed me things that I'd need to know...to teach her child."

She took my face in her huge hand. "Cher," she called me. "Tasha be the best thing that ever happen to me. And I will do me best to make her proud." I sensed the love she had for Natasha in her voice as she spoke. After an awkward moment, she let her hand drop and stood abruptly.

"But we'd not much time. See them vamps already on their way. They coming for you girl. They goin' to do all they can to keep you from turning nineteen." Delia started to pace. "You be in great danger," Delia said pointing at Karen, "and the little one too."

"The hell they are," Derrick said standing. I saw his face shimmer and his features go feline briefly before he controlled it.

"Boy, if a hundred of them things came here right now, do ya really think you'd be able to get them all before they got to your mamma and sister?" she said looking him straight in the eye. It looked like Delia might even be a little taller than Derrick.

"What do I need to do?" Derrick asked, his voice deep and angry.

"We need to hide them."

"Hide?" Karen asked.

"Tasha smart. She fine a spell that can hide us humans from them vamps. If they can't smell, can't see, can't hear you, then it's like you're not there at all. She did that spell on your momma-ndaddy," Delia said taking her eyes from Derrick to me.

"My parents?" I asked, suddenly realizing the danger they'd be in.

"Yep, your parents be safe. They can't be hurt by them vamps...but, well, we'll talk about that later. Where the little one be?" Delia asked looking at Karen.

"I can go get her now... but first tell me what this is all about?" Karen demanded in distress.

"Me en her are gonna cast that same conja on you two, like the one on her parents." Delia pointed to me. "Those vamps are gonna cum looking for her." Delia's finger stayed pointed at me. "They can't smell her, but they already know about where she be. But they just have to smell him." Delia looked at Derrick, "to know where she be."

Fear and guilt filled me. I didn't even think about the danger I'd put those in by simply being around me.

"Should I leave?" I asked in a whisper.

"No!" yelled Derrick and Karen in unison.

"Go get the girl. Me and Erica need to get ready," said Delia.

Karen went to get Miya. I led Delia to the back yard while Derrick went to grab a brown bag with chicken feet tied to the handle, as directed, from the trunk of Delia's rental car.

"Ummm...that be a good place," Delia said pointing to the place where I had just been a couple hours before, feeding the imaginary Derrick.

"Why?" I asked nervously.

"It's already had some sacrifice," she answered.

My stomach hurt. How did she know that?

"I don't know anything," I blurted out, feeling overwhelmed.

"That be okay. I know enough. It be me brains and your body we're using tonight."

"My body?" That did not sound very enticing.

I watched Derrick. He hesitated a moment at the side of the house before walking to us. He remembered the spot too.

Delia nodded to Derrick as she took the bag from him.

I watched silently as she withdrew some salts and half burnt candles from her bag. She lit five candles and evenly spaced them in a small circle. She placed a wooden bowl in the middle of the circle. She sprinkled some of the salts in the bowl and tossed some around the yard. I watched nervously as she started to unbutton her dress.

"We need to be getting down to our drawz," she said to me.

I didn't move as she slipped off her dress, revealing a beautiful body that belonged on the cover of the swimming suit edition of Sports Illustrated. She was only wearing a lacey white thong, which was in stark contrast to her black body. I noticed Derrick was just as startled as I was. She sat with her legs crossed next to the candles, her amethyst eyes on me, waiting.

"Do you want me to undress?" I gasped.

"Down to your ste'pin, more if you'r willing," she said bluntly.

"What?" I had no idea what ste'pin was.

"Your underwear, Girl," she answered. "And you," she

looked at Derrick, "you keep still over there. And when your momma and sister come, you keep them in the house...understand?"

Derrick nodded.

"Why take off my clothes?" I asked Delia not taking my eyes away from Derrick.

"The more skin the easier it be for the energy. Girl, come now. It be getting late," Delia said impatiently.

Quickly I kicked off my shoes, slid out of my shorts, and took off my shirt. I left on my bra and undies. I sat across from Delia, my legs crossed like hers.

She gestured for my hands. I let her engulf my hands gruffly in hers. We sat there, me in my bra and underwear, her in her beautiful skin, holding hands over a circle of lit candles with a small wooden bowl holding some salts placed in the center.

She closed her eyes and looked up to the night sky. I watched curiously.

"You be fighting it girl," Delia said sternly. "I was to tell you about this stuff next week, help you make the choice. But we not the time now. I don't have the power that you do...Focus."

"What do you want me to do?" I cried.

"How'd you make the storm?" Delia asked.

"I don't know?"

Derrick explained loudly from the patio. "She went into a trance. I had to shake her out of it."

Delia nodded as if she understood something I completely missed. "Cher, you need to relax," she instructed, which was a lot easier said than done.

"Close your eyes," she said in a new softer tone. "Follow me breaths."

I listened to her breathe in and out very deeply. I followed, trying to match her rhythm the best I could, but her lungs were much larger than mine.

"Mmmm...Good," she said in almost a whisper.

Gently she began swaying side to side, guiding me with her hands that still held mine. I had to force my eyes to stay shut.

"Cher, I'll soon be calling to the spirits of earth, wind, fire and water. You must let the energy come into you. Don't let go of me hands, and when you feel it, you start the singing."

"Singing?" I asked aghast.

I couldn't help it. I stopped and stared at Delia waiting for an answer. With her eyes still closed, she yanked my hands to force me into the swaying motion again.

"You'll know. Tasha'll help," she answered.

I closed my eyes and tried to relax, tried to do what Delia wanted me to. Miya and Karen depended on me.

I focused on my breathing. Soon the swaying felt like I was rocking myself to sleep. The cool night air felt good on my skin. The heat from the candles was warm under my arms. The air smelled of smoke and rain. The chorus of crickets and katydids softly played.

Delia began to chant a soft, beautiful mixture of sounds. I suddenly felt very thirsty and hot. Then her chant took a more forceful direction and my skin began to feel dry. A gentle breeze started across the yard. She chanted in loud guttural syllables from a different language, but it was nice. The sounds and motion rocked me like a lullaby.

I felt the energy waves gently pushing against my skin, the sensation reminded me of being under water. Delia was calling to the energy and it wanted in me. Slowly I opened up to the force. I was able to find the switch in my mind that would let it in. As I flipped it open, the energy rushed through me into Delia. I trembled slightly from the current as raw energy entered me through every pore of my body. I knew when both our bodies were full. Then I flipped the switch off, ending the flow of energy.

The swaying stopped. I felt pulsing in my body, my chest heaving forward, then back. The energy inside our bodies now wanted out. Delia was still chanting. I felt her body jerking through my hands.

My body rhythmically rocked back and forth and my head swayed from side to side as my subconscious drifted to the meadow. I saw Natasha on the rock. She was reaching for me. Once I made it to her, she held both my hands with hers.

"*Child, we must call to the spirits with our song...Follow me,*" she said with her angelic voice as she began to sing in a very high continuous pitch.

It was like a dream, but I knew it wasn't. I tried to match Natasha's pitch. I started off weak but soon was up there and surprised by how long I could carry the note. I didn't need to breathe.

When she stopped, so did I. I stared into her eyes, confused by my feelings for her. I wanted to ask her questions. "Natasha...," I called, but before she could answer, I was back to the séance.

Before I was completely back to my body, while Delia and I were still sharing energy, Delia showed me a few impressions. I wasn't too surprised about the invasion into my subconscious, but the images she showed me...broke my heart.

The chanting and rocking stopped. I opened my eyes.

Delia let go of my left hand but held on tight to my right. A tiny stream of blood flowed from my black birthmark into the wooden bowl. I recoiled in horror, trying to pull my arm from her grip, but she held it firm. Finally she let go and I jumped back in disgust.

I searched for Derrick. He was still on the patio, watching intently. My eyes meet his briefly, but quickly I looked away afraid I'd lose my resolve.

"What was that...?" I asked Delia angrily as I put my clothes back on. My birthmark looked as if nothing had happened.

She ignored my question and said, "It be for the best," and began to mix my blood in with the salts.

I didn't want to watch anymore. She was done with me. I went to Derrick.

"You okay?" he asked when I reached the patio.

"No," I answered honestly, "That was freaking insane."

Derrick nodded and took my hand. I followed him into the house. I sat at the dining picnic table while he went to grab us something to drink. Soon I saw the lights from Karen's car flash through the huge living room window and dance across the walls as she pulled up the drive. Karen and Miya were walking in the house when Delia came through the sliding glass door of the dining room. To my relief she was fully dressed.

"Ahhh, there she be," Delia said to Miya. Miya looked like she just woke up. Her hair was coming loose from a ponytail, and she wore a Sponge Bob pajama set.

"What do we need to do?" Karen asked. I saw the worry in her eyes.

"Sit," Delia gestured toward the bench seat.

In a very serious voice and expression to match, she explained. "I'll burn this," she said revealing essence sticks, "an you two need to breathe it. Breathe it in deep until I tell you to stop."

My mouth dropped in disgust when Delia began using the blood and salt mixture to paint Miya and Karen's faces. I noticed Derrick enter the room through the swinging door. He moved to stand behind me. I took the glass from him and drank the cold water. It was the best tasting glass of water I'd ever had. We watched Delia in silence.

Miya and Karen sat next to each other. Miya was confused and scared, but she listened and followed her mother's lead.

Delia lit the essence. "Breathe now," she instructed placing the smoking sticks on the table between them. Slowly Karen leaned forward. She cupped her hands and began pulling the smoke to her face. Miya followed her mother's movements. And as they inhaled the smoke, Delia chanted above them with her hands resting on each of their heads.

The smell wasn't bad. It was an earthy smell. But it was all too much for me to handle at that moment. I felt sick and had to leave the room. I went to the little bathroom in the mudroom. As I passed Derrick, I saw his worried eyes focused on his mother and sister.

I took a long time in the bathroom. I was confused and scared about the danger I posed to his family, my family. I couldn't be the reason for harm to come to them. I wouldn't, not after what Derrick just went through. I knew he'd die for me, and I also knew I couldn't survive without him. Just before she let go of my hand, Delia showed me what could happen if I stayed. The vampire's would find and slowly kill Derrick's family, to try and force Derrick to give me to them. And when he wouldn't, they would torture him to death. I knew he could die. I already watched him die once...I wouldn't let it happen again. All their lives would be on my hands if I stayed. The thought of those I loved dying because of me, was enough to make me leave without even thinking twice.

I stared at my face in the mirror. I had changed, inside and out. My eyes sparkled like Natasha's, emeralds in sunlight. I searched my throat but didn't see any bite marks, which was good. I noticed my skin was softer and smoother. It was still the milky pale color, but different from before. My hair was shinier.

It was time to toughen up. When I was the catalyst for the witch, I was indisputably awesome. But when it was just me, I felt less confident. Yet with every minute that passed from when I accepted The Burden, the braver I was becoming...as just me. The witch and I were merging. We were becoming one person. I was feeling stronger and I definitely wanted to hunt vampires even though I'd never hunted for anything before. I'd had a taste of killing them and wanted more.

I had a lot of questions for Delia. I especially wanted to know how to talk to Natasha. But first I had to talk to Derrick. I knew what I had to do, and it wasn't going to be easy.

CHAPTER 19

By the time I made it back to the dining room, the spell was finished. Karen and Delia were in the dining room sitting across from each other, drinking a cup of something hot. Karen's face was clean.

"You two will be safe now. Them vamps can't find you now. But remember what I told you about strangers...Look for the tattoo," I overheard Delia telling Karen.

Once they noticed me, Delia gave me a stern glare. "You girl, you should've stayed," she scolded.

"I'm sorry. I just had to take a breather. Where are Derrick and Miya?" I asked.

"Derrick's putting her to bed," Karen answered.

"I'm sorry all this is happening," I apologized to Karen.

"Me too. But it will be okay," she said, but I could hear fear in her voice.

"Time for bed," Delia said to Karen. "You need to rest now and let the magic do its work."

"I do feel tired. Goodnight, Ladies," Karen said as she got up.

"Goodnight," I said. "Thank you Karen, for everything."

"Of course, Erica," she said giving me a hug. "I've already shown Delia the guest room. I'll see you two in the morning."

"'Night," Delia said as Karen turned towards her room.

"I'll be waiting in the car," Delia said to me once Karen was out of hearing distance. She already knew my decision.

"Okay. It'll be a minute," I said, my heart breaking. But a broken heart was much better than losing part of your soul.

"They already be on their way, Girl. Don't take too much time. It only be for a couple weeks," she said before disappearing out the sliding door.

I went downstairs to Derrick's room and started packing my things. If all I had to do was stay away to keep Derrick and his family safe, I had to do it. Plus, there was so much I needed to learn in the short time Delia planned to teach me. Being alone with her would make things easier. If I focused on those reasons, then leaving Derrick might just be tolerable.

Delia was going to teach me how to be a witch...an actual witch. Things were happening so fast, I hadn't really had time to fathom the idea that I'd have magical powers and supernatural abilities. I had a brief image of Samantha from the old sitcom Bewitched. But there wasn't a war between witches and vampires in that sitcom. Actually, in reality the war would be between one half witch, me, and several hundred vampires. I remembered the number from Amy's story and hoped the ambiguous number was much lower.

I walked out of the bathroom with my cosmetic bag of girly

stuff and found Derrick sitting next to my packed suitcase. His hands were folded resting on his lap. He was beautiful and I loved him more than anything, more than myself, more than saving the world. He was my sole motivation. I had to leave to keep him safe...to kill the vampires...to keep him alive.

"You leaving?" he asked, his voice barely a whisper.

"I have to, Derrick, just until after my birthday...I think," I answered.

"Where?" he asked.

"I don't know."

Slowly I walked to sit next to him, taking his hand in mine. "Vampires can't find Karen and Miya, but their slaves can," I said. Derrick looked at me confused. "I couldn't tell you before. Natasha wouldn't let me, but I think I can now. You can't say anything to anyone though. Okay?" Derrick nodded, still a look of confusion on his face.

"Witches can be hurt by humans, Derrick. That's their weakness. I can be killed by them. So the vampires would send humans to attack me, you, and your family. Their human slaves have a barcode tattooed to the inside of their wrist. So keep a look out. I know you'd be able to kill them, but not me. Even though I knew Dusty was a horrible person, I couldn't purposely hurt him. It was like my brain couldn't even go there. I can't hurt humans...,"

"I can," he interrupted.

"Derrick, killing people is different than vampires...You could get arrested," I explained quietly. "You need to stay here and protect your family from the vampire's slaves. They're more of a threat than vampires right now. If I'm gone, then hopefully there won't be a reason for anyone to come here. They'll be too busy trying to find me."

Derrick got up from the bed and went to his dresser. He opened and shut the top drawer before sitting back down next to me. "Take this," he said handing me a leather wallet. "There's over two grand in there."

"No, Derrick. I..."

"Don't argue with me, Erica," he said sternly. "How much money do you have right now?"

I didn't answer. My purse was at my house with my wallet and everything else in it.

"That's what I thought. Take this money, please," he said. I took the wallet from him. It was a simple leather billfold full of hundreds.

"Thank you," I whispered.

Derrick pulled me into his arms and held me tight. "How will I know you're safe?" he asked.

"I've got my phone...well actually I don't. It's at my house...in my purse," I answered sadly. It was probably best I didn't have my phone. If movies had any truth to them, my cell could be traced or bugged. "But you'll know it here," I said placing my hand over his heart. I was certain his connection with me would let him know if I was dead, but reminded me.

"Derrick, you can't come find me...even if you see me in

trouble," I ordered. "You have to stay here no matter what."

"All right," he answered, but didn't sound sincere.

"Delia's going to teach me some stuff...and then...," I just realized I'd be a shapeshifter if I made it to my birthday.

"Derrick, if I can make it to my birthday, I'll be like you," I said in shock. "Then people won't be able to hurt me, just the black and red blade in my human form, like what happened to you."

I pushed away the thought of shapeshifting, wondering what it would feel like. I'd save those thoughts until I was more certain that I would be able to shapeshift. I had too much on my plate already.

"*When* you make it to your birthday Erica, not *if*," Derrick said.

"I love you Derrick, but I have to do this."

"I don't want you to go. I can protect all of you...,"

"I don't want to risk it," I interrupted. "I feel that leaving is the right thing to do...that it will draw the danger away from here." I stood and reached for my bag but Derrick grabbed it for me and followed me up the stairs.

"Tell your mom thanks for everything," I said to Derrick on the front porch.

"She would have wanted to say goodbye."

"It would be too hard. Tell Miya bye for me too." My voice cracked a little.

Derrick dropped my bag and pulled me into his arms holding me tight. "I love you, Erica. Come back to me," he choked.

Tears fell from my eyes as I kissed him. The anguish we felt from being torn apart was hitting us both hard. We had to stop kissing. The pain was unbearable.

"I've got to go," I whispered against his lips, wiping a tear away from his cheek.

Derrick set me down and followed me to Delia's sedan. She popped the trunk when we were close enough. Derrick put my suitcase inside. I tossed in my cosmetic bag. Derrick gently closed the trunk and walked me to the passenger door.

Delia started the car. Knowing that I was leaving to protect Derrick, maybe not his life really, but protecting him from the pain of losing his mom and sister, or worse, watching them be tortured to death, was helping me stay focused. But my whole body hurt. I was leaving him on my own free will.

"I'll call my parents. I don't know what I'll say, but I'll think of something," I said quietly as I opened the door.

"You'd better take this," Derrick handed me the little wooden box holding the rainbow blades.

"Oh...thanks," I said taking the box from him. In the rush to leave, I'd forgotten about them. I opened the box and withdrew one blade. I closed the box and gave it back to Derrick. "You keep the rest," I said. "I have a feeling these can kill them. Serena had said something about them being poisonous. Maybe they will help protect your family."

He thought about it, then agreed after I insisted again.

"I will see you on your birthday, and then we'll go after them together," Derrick said cupping the side of my face with one of his large warm hands.

"It's a date," I confirmed sadly.

I stepped closer and gave him one last embrace, deeply inhaling his scent and taking comfort in his arms one last time. I let go and quickly got into the car. Derrick shut the door and our eyes stayed locked as Delia drove down his driveway, until the trees blocked our view from one another.

The pain was suffocating.

17011294R00196

Made in the USA
Charleston, SC
22 January 2013